David Quantick writes for television (*Veep, The Thick Of It, Brass Eye*) and radio (*One, The Blagger's Guide*). He is also the author of the comic novel *Sparks*, the comic book *That's Because You're A Robot*, and several short films, including the award-winning *Welcome to Oxmouth*. A script-writer, broadcaster, and comedy writer, David once appeared on *Celebrity Come Dine With Me*, where he came fifth out of five.

The Mule

David Quantick

This edition first published in 2016

Unbound
6th Floor, Mutual House, 70 Conduit Street, London w1s 2gf
www.unbound.co.uk

Typeset by PDQ

Art direction by Mecob

Jacket Illustration by Moose Allain

A CIP record for this book
is available from the British Library

ISBN 978-1-78352-100-5 (trade hbk)
ISBN 978-1-78352-144-9 (ebook)
ISBN 978-1-78352-143-2 (limited edition)

Printed in Great Britain by Clays Ltd, St Ives plc

9 8 7 6 5 4 3 2 1

For Jenna, Alexander and Laurence

Dear Reader,

The book you are holding came about in a rather different way to most others. It was funded directly by readers through a new website: Unbound.

Unbound is the creation of three writers. We started the company because we believed there had to be a better deal for both writers and readers. On the Unbound website, authors share the ideas for the books they want to write directly with readers. If enough of you support the book by pledging for it in advance, we produce a beautifully bound special subscribers' edition and distribute a regular edition and e-book wherever books are sold, in shops and online.

This new way of publishing is actually a very old idea (Samuel Johnson funded his dictionary this way). We're just using the internet to build each writer a network of patrons. Here, at the back of this book, you'll find the names of all the people who made it happen.

Publishing in this way means readers are no longer just passive consumers of the books they buy, and authors are free to write the books they really want. They get a much fairer return too – half the profits their books generate, rather than a tiny percentage of the cover price.

If you're not yet a subscriber, we hope that you'll want to join our publishing revolution and have your name listed in one of our books in the future. To get you started, here is a £5 discount on your first pledge. Just visit unbound.com, make your pledge and type Mule in the promo code box when you check out.

Thank you for your support,

Dan, Justin and John
Founders, Unbound

The Mule

The Mule

by David Quantick

PART ONE

It does not seem to me a common thing
for a mere 'text' to challenge, still less
convert, anyone.

J.B. Phillips, *Ring of Truth: A
Translator's Testimony*

CHAPTER ONE

I was in a bar. It doesn't matter where. It's not relevant to the story. (If there's one thing I've learned in my job, it's that things that aren't relevant to the story have to go.) The bar was pretty quiet, which suited me because I don't like to go to bars that play loud music, where everyone's shouting to get a drink and it's so dark you can't see the prices of drinks. Funny – loud and dark always go together with bars. You never see a loud, brightly lit bar, do you? It's like not content with numbing our senses with booze, the bars want us deaf and blind as well.

Anyway, this bar was pretty much perfect so far as I was concerned. There was no music at all, the lights were OK – I could see the drinks were a reasonable price for the middle of town – and there were no hen parties or big groups of people making their own racket.

I signalled to the barman, who had his name on a badge on his shirt. 'Good evening, Don,' I said, smiling, 'I'd like a martini, please. Vodka, and—' But he'd already turned away to make it. I think he didn't like me saying his name. If I had a job where I had to wear my name on a badge and people said my name, I wouldn't have a problem. If people said, 'Excuse me, Jacky, could you look at these pages before the weekend?'

or 'Hey, Jacky, this is more of a technical pamphlet but we figure you can handle it', I wouldn't mind at all. Of course I'd have to pick a version of my name that I felt comfortable with, which I admit would probably not be Jacky. Jacky is what my mother called me and I have never liked it. I would much rather be a Jack or even a J – 'Hey J!' – but there we go. Whenever I say to people, 'My name's Jack', they always look at me as if to say, 'Really?' and before you know it they're calling me Jacky. If they call me anything at all, that is. I have never had any luck with getting people to call me J.

All these thoughts were going through my mind as I waited for my martini. The barman didn't seem to be in any hurry to make it and I was wondering if I should call him over using his name – 'Hey, Don! Where's that martini?' – or just do what I always do, which is sort of mumble 'Excuse me ...' and hope he hears me, when a girl sat down next to me at the bar. Dressed in black, with smoky grey-blue eyes and dark hair cut in a fringe that gathered around her cheekbones, she stood out from the bar's other patrons like – well, I'm not one for fancy similes, but like a pearl in an ashtray. She looked at me, in that way where you're not sure whether someone is looking at you with some kind of interest in their eyes, or maybe you just caught their eye because of an unusual or deformed thing about you. I'm not saying I'm deformed or even unusual, by the way, I look pretty ordinary. My eyes are kind of big, though. At school, some kids called me 'Bug Eyes', until my mother went in and told the teachers that her Jacky was sensitive about his eyes. All this did was make the teachers start calling me Jacky. I was on the verge of persuading people that I was really called 'Jay', but after my mother went into the school one parents' evening, it was goodbye J, hello Jacky.

I averted my eyes – not so bug-like nowadays – from the girl, just in case I was staring back at her, and lifted my hand to wave at the barman. But I could still see the girl out the corner of my eye and I felt self-conscious – who would she think I was, waving at barmen like a rock star or something? – and tried to turn the wave into a different gesture, as if I were just about to scratch my nose. But as my arm was about eight inches above my head, I had to turn the wave into a stretch.

It must have looked odd, because the girl said, 'Are you having some sort of cramp?' She had a nice voice.

I'm sorry if that's not very evocative and I should have said, 'She had a voice like hot cream,' or something but I don't care for over-cooked phrases (they're the bane of my professional life), and besides, she did have a nice voice. I put my arm down slowly in a deliberate way as if I did have a cramp, and said, 'Yes.'

'Do you often suffer from cramp in your arm?' said the girl. She was lighting a cigarette, which I didn't think was legal in bars. 'Because if you do maybe it's your circulation.'

'No, my circulation is fine,' I said, wondering if perhaps she was a nurse. 'I jog sometimes and,' I added, but not in a pointed manner, so she wouldn't dislike me, 'I don't smoke.'

'Oh, does this bother you?' said the girl, as the barman appeared and, to my amazement, placed an ashtray on the bar in front of her. 'I'm sorry. They let me smoke in here when it's quiet.'

I was about to say that it wasn't quiet when she put the cigarette out in the ashtray. 'I'm being inconsiderate,' she said. 'I'm sorry. And you don't have a drink.'

I didn't know what to say to this. She seemed to be awfully popular in this bar, was my first thought. My second was perhaps she was a hooker. I know that's a word you tend to see more in print than in real life, but it's the word that came to my mind first. But she seemed too pleasant to be a hooker, and anyway I could hardly ask her outright, 'Are you a hooker?' in case she picked up her bag and walked out. Or worse, picked up her bag and said, 'Let's go, stud.'

It didn't matter that I had no reply, anyway, because she sat up and shouted, 'Hey you! Dan! This man doesn't have a drink!'

The barman came straight over and – glaring at me like I'd done a bad thing by actually coming into his bar and actually ordering a drink – said, 'I forgot what he asked for. I was coming back anyway.'

'Of course you were,' said the girl. 'You wanted another look down my blouse. What do you want?' she was asking me now. I repeated my original order, this time in full, and she said, 'The same for me, only with gin. And hurry up, Dan, we've been waiting.'

I said thanks to her, although I knew I could never come into this bar again. Dan would blank me for ever, or spit in my drink. Or maybe he'd just bar me. But when the drinks came (I checked mine for flecks of anything) I just clinked glasses and said, 'Bottoms up.'

Which she seemed to find very funny. '"Bottoms up",' she repeated. 'I haven't heard anyone say that for years.' She smiled.

She had a really beautiful smile, classy and a little bit melancholy as if she were a photo model advertising something sophisticated, like a perfume called Regrets. Excuse me. I should have just said, 'She had a nice smile.'

'Bottoms up,' she said, and toasted me.

By now, I was a little confused. I'm not an unattractive man – that is to say, I'm not ugly – but I was unused to this kind of attention from a woman, especially one with a smile like this girl's. I didn't think she was a hooker, partly because she looked so nice, and partly because I thought I'd read that hookers don't buy their own drinks, let alone those of their tricks, and I couldn't for the life of me work out why she was talking to me. Maybe she was drunk, or high on drugs. Then again, she wasn't slurring and her attractive grey-blue eyes weren't dilating.

Maybe, I concluded, she just likes you. Not enough for sex, or to get married, but she likes you. So I smiled back and said, 'Might I ask your name, if that's not being too rude?' This was perhaps a little formal, I realise, but I was being rational as well as polite. I knew nobody could be offended by being asked their own name, because everyone has a name and they should be used to being asked it. And the 'might I' and the 'not being too rude' were there giving her the option of saying, 'Actually, I have a kind of stupid name so please call me by my second name which is Perkiss,' or – as I was hoping – 'Don't be silly! My name is Tammy. Here's my card, look, with my number on it. In fact, forget the card – just come home with me now.' And she would leave money for the drinks, and we'd go, me shrugging at Dan as if to say, 'Well, the best man won.'

'What's your name first?' she said, a little coolly. I thought about this and decided it wasn't rude because after all I was a strange man in a bar and I could be anyone. And she had bought me a drink, so who was I to assume she was being rude?

'Jack—' I began, and stopped right there. 'Jack,' I said again, more confidently.

'Hello, Jack,' she said. 'Nice to meet you.' She gave me a slightly cock-eyed look, as if she didn't believe me.

'It really is,' I said. 'I guess some people just don't look like their own names.'

She gave me the look again and I thought that perhaps she had been drinking earlier, or maybe her martini had hit her harder than she'd expected. I sipped my drink. It certainly was strong.

'So ...' I began, and stopped before I could ask my next question. I thought quickly and realised that if she didn't want to tell me her name, she probably wouldn't want to talk about her job, or her life or her romantic status or anything personal. This left me with zero questions to ask her, so I decided to talk about myself instead. I know this is a no-no in books of dating and the like, but she wasn't saying anything so I thought maybe I could draw her out a little.

'What is it you do for a living, Jack?' said the girl.

I was amazed. This was exactly the thing I was about to reveal next. 'Are you a magician?' I said, making my voice sound jokey. 'That was exactly what I was about to tell you.'

'I'm not a magician,' she said. 'I have not been granted that particular skill. More's the pity.' Now she sounded a little sad, as though she would have really wanted to have been a magician.

I remember as a child reading that only men can become magicians and thinking that this was unfair, although I believe times have changed, perhaps because of those hugely popular books that feature both girl and boy wizards. I said none of this, because it might have made her angry, or bored, or both.

'Would you care to guess?' I said.

'Not particularly,' she said. 'I mean, I want to know and you can tell me. There's no need to introduce a vein of uncertainty, I think.'

I didn't understand what she meant, and now I think she was trying to say something about a 'Venn diagram of uncertainty', but had abandoned the thought as too complicated. Plus she had a good point. Why should I conceal the information I had when all she wanted was to know it?

'I'm a translator,' I said.

She just looked at me.

'A translator is a guy who—' I began.

'I know what a translator is,' she said. 'Do you think I'm an idiot?'

You see? People just think I'm obnoxious when I'm trying to be nice. I guess if I'd thought faster, I'd have realised that of course a girl like this would know what a translator was. But instead, because she didn't say anything, I assumed she didn't know, and now here she was, thinking that I thought she was stupid.

'I don't think you're an idiot,' I said, 'I just ...' And I tailed off, which probably to her meant I was silently adding, 'Actually, I do think you're an idiot.' But she looked angry now. I was kind of angry too. I mean, I was just trying to be helpful.

'I'm sorry,' she said. 'I was just taken aback.'

I didn't know what to say. But what I was thinking was, All right, you snap at me and then apologise and that's fine, but how would you like it if I called you a great big horse and then said sorry? Not that she was a great big horse, and that's not an expression I would ever use, but you see my point. So I said, 'Why would you be taken aback?'

'Because – no, this is crazy.'

When she said that, she did something that only attractive women do, where she turned her head away as she was talking, as if she were addressing her words to someone on the next bar stool. You never see men do that, or old ladies, or anyone who doesn't look good in profile. Also it's a good way of making sure people are listening. Try it. Turn away from someone when you're talking and nine times out of ten they'll lean in to hear what you're saying.

'What's wrong?' I said.

'Nothing's wrong,' she said, but this time even as she said it I knew she was going to apologise again. It's called 'emotional turmoil'. That's an expression I come across a lot in my work. The girl was thinking. She was doing it with her eyes, looking

11

at me, and at the bottles behind the bar, and at the counter, as though she were taking tiny photographs with her eyes. She finally stopped scanning the bar and said, 'Can you keep a secret?'

'Of course,' I said. In actual fact, I had no idea if I could keep a secret. Nobody tells me any secrets. Maybe they just figure I can't keep secrets. Sometimes I try to imagine a secret and work out how long I could keep it. But it's like pretending you're underwater and you have to hold your breath; after a while your brain realises you're not underwater and it tells you to stop being a dummy and breathe in. My brain says, you have no secrets, and anyway who are you going to tell? Your mother?

While I was thinking this – and it takes a lot longer to write it down than to think it – the girl was fishing through her bag. I don't know if you've ever noticed with girls and bags but there seems to be a rule that the smaller the girl, the bigger the bag. And vice versa. You see big ladies in fancy restaurants wearing fur coats and they have bags that you could just about squeeze a wasp into. And you see girls in taxis and when they have to find some money for the driver, they're rooting through bags that would be suitable for a large family's laundry. This girl was no exception. Whatever she was looking for wasn't coming out any time soon. If she had been looking for a vole, for example, the vole could have run around in the bag for minutes before she grabbed it. Not that she was looking for a vole.

Finally she found what she was after. She pulled it out. It was a tatty-looking hardback book, the kind you find on a stall with other tatty-looking hardback books. It had no dust-jacket, and it had obviously been on a shelf next to a smaller book because the front was faded by the sun down one side, from a deep red to a kind of weak pink. There was some writing in gold on the pink cloth, but I couldn't make it out.

'Translator, right?' she said.

I nodded agreement, in case actually saying the words 'I'm a translator' would get her angry again.

'OK,' she said, sounding tired, 'see if you can translate this.'

She held out the book to me and I reached for it. Then she pulled it back again.

'I'm just going to lay it on the bar and open it,' she said. 'Is your eyesight good?'

'My eyesight's fine with these,' I said, taking out my reading glasses and wondering what the hell was going on. Did she think I was a book thief? That I was going to steal her old red hardback and run out, laughing my face off? I put on the glasses in silence and she opened the book at random and slid it across the bar.

'Don't pick it up or touch it,' she said. 'Can you see it all right from there?'

'I'm going to have to get off this stool to look more closely,' I said. 'Otherwise I may topple.'

'Don't topple,' she said.

I got up and leaned over the book as if it were a rare antique I was valuing. I put my hands behind my back so I wouldn't accidentally reach out and touch it (for a moment I wondered if she thought the pages were poisoned) and I looked at the open pages. After a few seconds, I said, 'Is it all like this?'

In answer, she picked it up and opened it at random about sixty pages further in. Then, when I had looked at those pages, she went back to an earlier section and I looked at that.

I sat down again. 'What language is that?' I said.

'You're the translator,' she said. 'You tell me.'

I was feeling better now. The girl was obviously acting weirdly because she had this book in a language she couldn't understand. Maybe it was an inheritance or a gift from a friend, or something to do with a college course or a newspaper competition. Anyway, she had a book that she couldn't translate and then, hey presto, she goes to a bar and who does she run into but a translator? That would shake anybody up. Not me, obviously; it's amazing when you have an unusual job how often you run into people who have need of your skills. I imagine it's like being a doctor at a party: everybody's always telling you about their supposed illnesses and showing you their bumps and lumps. With me, it's almost the same. People ask me to translate the names of foreign foods on a menu, or the name of some classical piece they like. One time this couple asked me to translate a phrase they'd heard on holiday. 'Everybody kept saying it to us!' they said. 'We wondered does it mean "good luck" or "thank you" or something?' I told them it meant 'best of health'. It didn't, it meant 'screw off' but I didn't want to upset them. Later it occurred to me that they might have gone back to the same place next year and walked around smiling and saying, 'Screw off!' to everyone they met. It's hard to judge these things.

So I wasn't too surprised that she had shown me the book, but I could see why she might be. Things were fine, and we were getting on. There was no need to be upset at her earlier anger.

'Could we get another drink, please?' I asked Dan, who by some error of judgement was standing next to us, who were now his only customers. Dan looked at the girl as if he needed her permission and she nodded, a little impatiently. Come on, Dan, I thought, get to it.

The girl looked at me. 'Can you translate it? I'm guessing no by the way you're just standing there and looking into space.'

I decided to ignore the last part of her remark. 'I can't,' I said.

'Is it in a weird language or are you just a bad translator?' she said.

I was actually about to walk away this time when I saw she was smiling. I was pleased; it was an impolite joke but at least it was a joke. I feigned affront. (That's a phrase I came across in a book I worked on once. I'm glad I finally found an opportunity to use it. In fact, I'm pretty sure that even as I was doing it, part of my brain was thinking, Excellent, I just feigned affront.)

'I'm a good translator,' I said, looking hurt but also smiling so she'd know I wasn't really hurt. 'I speak most major European languages and, as I'm also a student of linguistics, I'd say that I would at least recognise 99 per cent of all world tongues.'

'All world tongues?' she said, making it sound sort of dirty. 'That's impressive. What about dead languages? Like Etruscan and so on.'

Now it was my turn to be impressed. Not everybody you meet in a bar knows Etruscan. Well, nobody knows it, it's a dead language as she said. But not many people even know there was a language called Etruscan, let alone that nobody speaks it. I raised an eyebrow to show that I was impressed and said, 'It's not Etruscan. It's not Mangue or Koro. It's not anything.'

She looked annoyed at this. 'What do you mean, it's not anything? It's a book, it's got to be something. Oh wait, is it like that stupid Latin you get on cushions? The one printers use?'

I had to think about that for a moment. Not much of my job involved cushions. Then I got what she meant.

'You're confusing two separate things,' I told her. 'The text sometimes used on fabrics is the Loqueris poem. It begins with the words *Si vis me flere*, which means, "If you want me to cry". But the printers' text, the one they use when they need random text to fill the page when they're doing a layout, is called *lorem ipsum*, which is short for *dolorem ipsum*, which means "pain in itself". It used to be done with hot metal but nowadays it's a computer program, I think. They're two different things.'

I was impressed with myself, having made the two connections just from her mistaken assertion. She didn't look impressed, though, possibly because she hadn't made the connection herself. In fact, she looked annoyed, so I made a mental note not to show off my knowledge of dead languages to girls and added, 'But you're on the right lines. I mean, it's not Latin, this text, but it could be that the whole book is written in random text. Like filler.'

'But it's got to be words, right? It's got to have meaning.' She seemed almost desperate now.

'I don't know that it does have meaning,' I went on. 'Here, look at this line of text ...' and I moved to show her the page.

She grabbed the book off the counter. 'Sorry,' she said. 'I know how I'm acting but this book is important to me and I can't let it out of my sight. Tell me where the line is.'

I told her and she read it out loud.

'You see?' I said, then realised I was talking to a layman. 'It's got the word *sunt* at the end, which is a common Latin verb. You would expect to see *sunt* in each and every Latin text. But next to it are these two words – *la furcheuxne* – which sounds like French to me. Except it isn't French. It's not *langue d'oc* or *langue d'oil* or ancient or modern French or anything. It's just French-sounding.'

'It could be a place name,' she said.

'It could be,' I agreed, 'although it's spelled irregularly even for a place name. Anyway, that doesn't explain *sunt*, and it doesn't explain the next word.'

'Which next word?' she said, peering at the text.

'The one beginning with "I",' I said.

'Oh,' she said, trying to read it out loud. '*Iiiiiiiiii-i-i.*'

16

'Yes,' I said drily, 'that one.' I can be dry when I want to, but sometimes people mistake dryness for sarcasm so I keep it in check. 'I mean, it could be some Papuan word or an exclamation in some obscure language, but put it next to *la furcheuxne*—'

'And *sunt*,' she said.

'And *sunt*,' I agreed, 'and you've just got nonsense. And the whole book seems to be like that. At least with the cushion texts they make sense in small doses, but—'

Our drinks arrived. I lifted mine and sipped it. Still no spit.

'It's just nonsense,' I concluded.

She looked disappointed, and a bit angry. I sympathised. Here was this random encounter that had promised so much – a translator when one was sorely needed! – and he had failed. Then she brightened a little.

'But what if it's not in a real language,' she said, and I stiffened, mentally, because I think I was able to guess what was coming. 'I mean, a real language, but not one like French or Latin? There're those books, aren't there? I don't know the names.'

I knew what she meant, unfortunately, and when I looked again at the book, which had a fancy binding and if you ask me a bit too much gold writing on it, I wondered maybe if some bookseller had done a number on her, telling her the book was in a mystical tongue or some hippy thing like that. There are lots of books like that. I shan't list them here, because I think they're silly. I have enough trouble extracting meaning from books in my own life without some smart alec coming along and writing a lot of gibberish that a muggins like me might one day have to translate. You know who I feel sorry for? Those poor people who have to render Lewis Carroll poems and Dr Seuss into different languages. I hate books like that.

I didn't say any of this to the girl. In fact, I'd kind of forgotten what she just said so I asked her to repeat it. By now she looked exasperated, which I don't blame her for being, so I apologised and said, 'I know what you mean, but it's not my field. I'm a workaday person. A meat and potatoes translator. If it's real, I can get my teeth into it, but if it's not real, if it's in Klingon or Elvish or something like that ...'

She looked suspicious and downcast at the same time, which was a thing to see, like somebody who was sad because she had just been told by a lawyer that there was no money in the will for her, but also wary because the lawyer might be crooked, too. It was a weird look, and it worked on me.

'Maybe,' I said, 'I could get someone at the publishing house to take a—'

'No,' she said. 'Thank you, but I can't. The contents of this book stay with me at all times.'

'Well, how about you scan some pages and print them off?' I suggested. 'That way you keep the book and ...' My words tailed off. I knew there was no way she would do that.

She looked up at me. There were tears in her eyes. 'Thank you for trying to help,' she said. 'You've at least cleared up one thing for me. Now I know the words have no meaning, I can stop wasting my time.'

'I didn't say they had no meaning,' I said, 'just that they're not in any known language. The text as a text is incoherent. Even if you Googled the individual words, it wouldn't help any. But, as you say, it could be in a fictional language. It could be in some code. I don't know. There could be all kinds of meaning here.'

At that, she laughed. She actually threw her head back and made a kind of bitter, self-mocking sound. 'Oh,' she said, and pushed the book across the bar at me, 'there's meaning.'

The book was open at a page of photographs, what they

call 'plates'. There were five black and white photographs. Each photo was of a girl, and in each photo the girl had been killed in a different way – knifed, shot, strangled, drowned, the last one I forget. The girl was the same girl in all the pictures. She was the girl in the bar.

'There's plenty of meaning, all right,' said the girl.

After that, I don't remember very much until we were at my apartment. ('Flat' seems too grand a word for where I live, whereas 'bedsit' is inappropriate, as I have more than one room.) She was pretty shaken up now and I'd had a couple of drinks more than I might usually have. I remember asking her in the bar if she was OK and she said she was, but clearly she wasn't. She said she didn't want to stay in the bar, though, and she didn't want to go home. And she looked at me as if I had to fill in some puzzle, and finally I got it. So we were at my apartment and she was looking for wine in a cupboard.

She found some and I opened it. I gave her a glass and she raised it.

'To you,' she said, and clinked her glass against mine.

'I've never had anybody drink a toast to me before,' I said.

'That's sweet,' she said. 'Sad, but sweet. But I can't say "to us", because we just met.'

'How about "to you"?' I said. It wasn't the wittiest thing I'd ever said, but it was at least inoffensive. Or so I thought.

'No, let's not do that. There's no point,' she said, and looked sad again.

I didn't know what to say to that, so I moved over on the settee. She leaned her head on my shoulder.

'I'm going to bed,' she said, and got up.

I didn't know how to tell her there was only one bedroom but I reckoned she looked more in need of the bed than me, so I said, 'I'll see you.'

'Oh,' she said, 'aren't you coming?'

I stared at her, letting the words sink in.

'Sure,' I said, trying to sound like women invited me into their beds – into my bed – whatever – all the time.

'Is this your bathroom?' she said, and walked off, leaving me in a highly confused state.

Women, I have observed, take a long time in the bathroom. I understand this is to do with make-up, and personal hygiene, and so on, but that only applies to getting ready. It's a start of the day thing, surely. I don't really get why it doesn't take a woman a shorter length of time to get, as it were, unready. I mean, if a woman had a false leg, obviously, but at this time of night a woman is only washing her face and cleaning her teeth. I don't really know. I have limited experience in this area.

Anyway, she was a long time in the bathroom and that's why I did it. Or at least that's the excuse I made for myself afterwards. I was sitting there on the settee, with nothing to do. I couldn't go to the bathroom because it was occupied (I'm sure married couples use the facilities jointly all the time, but we were scarcely at that stage of our relationship, or any stage). I couldn't undress because it would seem forward, and anyway, I'd still need to get up again and clean my teeth and wash. And I didn't want to drink any more. So I put the glasses in the sink and found a stopper for the wine bottle and then I saw it.

The book was next to her bag. If it had been in the bag, I wouldn't have done it. I would never open a lady's bag, or anybody else's bag come to that. But the book wasn't in the bag. It was just lying there. She had said only that I couldn't take the book away. Well, it was in my apartment already. There was nowhere for me to take the book to. I had already looked in it.

I listened for the sounds of hot water, and opened the book. There again on the page was the jumble of words. It was immensely frustrating. Just when they seemed to make sense, any possible meaning evaporated. It was like language but not, like a fly that disguises itself as a wasp (I mean through heredity, not deliberately. Flies can't deliberately disguise themselves, to my knowledge). I could make no sense from this brief look. I needed more time. Just a page would do, a page with a good deal of text on it. But I couldn't exactly rip out a page. That would count as 'taking the book' to a more than debatable extent. But there was one solution. It was morally on a knife-edge, but I didn't care. I just couldn't stand the temptation. Here was I, a translator, with a book that could not be translated. And I might never see it again!

So I made my way over to my computer station, and turned on the printer, which contains a scanner. I clicked at the keyboard until the computer woke up, and looked for the scanner icon. I clicked on it and waited for it to acknowledge my request. And then I picked up the book and, opening it at the page I'd first seen in the bar, placed it on the scanner. The icon flashed at me that it was ready to go. I closed the scanner lid carefully on the book.

'Bastard!'

The girl was screaming at me and striding towards me too. She smelled of steam and soap and she was really angry. I couldn't speak. What had seemed like a rational argument for making a copy of the pages now looked in her eyes, I could see as surely as if I were looking through them, like a gross invasion of her privacy. She pulled the book out of the scanner and looked at me with eyes full of rage and hurt.

'I'm really sorry,' I said.

She didn't reply. She just clutched the book to her chest and went back into the bathroom.

I could hear her dressing, and speaking to someone on her mobile phone. I just stood there, feeling awful.

I don't know about you, but I've never been a huge fan of dreams. They're confusing and too many things happen and none of them makes sense and when you try to remember them, half the time you just remember the odd detail, like there was a talking cat or you were drowning. I don't like dreams and I don't hold with the Freudian idea that a big tower means something erotic and all that. I don't see how you can analyse something that makes no sense at all.

Take that night, for instance. What with the girl and my foolishness with the book, a logical person would say that any dream I might have would be about the events of that evening. But the dream I had that night was nothing to do with the girl, or the book she showed me, or anything at all that I could see.

I was in some sort of large open space. It was a bright sunny day. Far off I could see some trees, and the silhouettes of people. There was nothing else there. I had the feeling that I was in the middle of a big city. I sat on the bench for quite a while. I looked around me a few times, but nothing happened. I was about to walk away when I woke up. I defy any psychiatrist in the world to analyse that dream and make the least particle of sense from it.

I certainly wasn't going to be spending any time looking up dreams that day, because I had woken up with a pretty nasty hangover. I don't drink a lot, even though I do go to bars. And I'd had two martinis, and some of a glass of wine. Outside, delivery men were swearing at each other as they emptied a lorry. There was a loud banging coming from somewhere. And I could hear rap music coming from a car parked down below.

But more than the hangover, I woke up because all through the grey waking hours I had been subconsciously needled by something just under my mental radar. I'm sure you get the same feeling. You know there's something 'on the tip of your mind', as one of my writers put it. (Actually, if I can be allowed some immodesty, what she wrote was less interesting in her own native tongue. I put some spin on it, which can be risky for a translator. Authors don't like the fruit of their creation to fall far from the tree, as it were.)

I lay there in bed, trying to remember what it was that was needling me. It wasn't meeting the girl, or her showing me the book, or even those photographs. It wasn't her being angry, although that was pretty upsetting. Then I had it. It was what she said when I was walking her to the ground floor after she had gone into the bathroom to call a cab. I know that sounds weird, after what had just happened, but when she came out, she just said, 'I don't want to be mugged on top of all this', and asked me to walk her down to the street. She didn't say anything else, so I picked up my keys in case I locked myself out and we went.

It was cold outside, I remember, and she was wearing a coat that looked like two black sheets of rumpled cloth crossed over each other. It was such a big coat that when I opened the taxi door for her to get in, it took her a while to get herself all into the cab, as though the coat were the wings of a bat. It also muffled her words so I had to strain to hear what she was saying.

'Don't look for me,' she said, 'but don't forget me.'

And before I could say anything to that, the cab drove off. I stood for a moment as it disappeared into the late-night traffic, hoping it might stop and she'd get out and walk back towards me in the big black bat coat, but she didn't even turn her head.

CHAPTER TWO

I work from home, which has its plus side and its minuses. On the plus side, you're your own time-keeper. You can work for an hour, take a break, and then go out for lunch – although I generally stay at home and have something from the fridge. You can surf the net and you can even watch TV if you want to, although again I find that's not something I like to do. People say to me, 'Jacky, if I had your job, I'd just be watching TV all day.' Yes, and you'd starve to death because you'd get no work done, I always reply in my head. The minus side is you tend not to see people. Although I know from when I have worked in offices that they're claustrophobic places, where you're forced to interact with people you might not otherwise even want to look at, let alone chat to in a friendly manner.

Another thing I've noticed about offices is that the people are all the same. I don't mean that they're clones of one another, just that there are always the same four or five recognisable 'types'. There's the ambitious type who's cold to you if you can't help them ascend the career ladder. There's the gossipy type (who can be a man or a woman) who seems friendly but really just wants to leech juicy titbits from you. There's the innocent kid, and there's the old-timer serving out their tenure until they can cash in their pension. It's like being in a soap opera where the faces change but the personalities are the same. I mentioned this to my mother once, after I'd worked in a couple of different offices and all she said was, 'So which one are you, Jacky?' My mother isn't always very sympathetic.

So today I welcomed my home-working status, because, hangover aside, I was feeling unsettled after the meeting of the night before, and if I'd been in an office with other people, they might have noticed my distracted state and joshed with me about it. Or they might have read something into it and said, 'What's her name, then?' and kept up some running banter that would have got annoying pretty quickly. So being alone was much better. It also enabled me to sit at the computer and do some searching, which of course you could be penalised for in an office. Here, though, in my own home, I was able to go online to do some research of my own. I have a pretty good memory for words, perhaps because I encounter so many, so I was able to remember the three weird ones that had come up in our conversation last night. I closed the window so the banging was a little quieter and started typing in the words.

The word *sunt* was so common as to be almost meaningless. There were over 250 million entries on Google for it, everything from proper names and trademarks to made-up obscenities and random web host names. Most of the uses of *sunt* were, as I said to the girl, in its normal Latin sense, which is of course the third person plural of the verb 'to be'. In layman's terms, it means 'are'. I tried Eureka and Babelfish, which at least stripped out the proper names, but still ended up with pretty much the same thing.

I should tell you a little about my job, I guess. When I say 'translator' to people, all kinds of images come into their heads. Sometimes they picture me at the United Nations with headphones over my ears, rapidly conveying the words of an important Iranian diplomat into English, just one verbal slip away from plunging the world into a nuclear conflagration. Sometimes they imagine me at a legal aid office, helping new immigrants with application forms. And every so often, someone will know a little bit about the real world of translation, and they'll assume that by 'translator', they mean someone who spends their time rendering technical documents and practical handbooks into English, things like manuals for driving Russian tractors or schematics for wiring up satellite dishes. The bread and butter of translating, you might say if you were feeling poetic about it.

Nobody ever gets it right. I mean I have done some of those manuals, but they require a technical knowledge of the specific fields of relevance of those manuals. Say I was asked to translate one of those hypothetical tractor manuals – well, I know that the Russian word for tractor is *traktor* but that's about it. The rest of the technical vocabulary would be as new to me as it is to you. And that's just tractors. I'm someone who, probably just like you, doesn't know anything about tractors. Yet people often assume that I'm Mr Manuals. Which should really annoy me. I don't look at a man in glasses and tie with a bald spot and think, Aha! Accountant! or see a blonde in a tight leather skirt and think that she's a call girl. But people hear me say that I'm a translator and suddenly I'm an expert on Eastern European agricultural vehicles.

Iiiiiiiii-i-i was slightly better, in that it only cropped up on Google about seventeen times but mostly in the names of websites or webmasters, basically as a way of naming something quickly and meaninglessly. And that was without the hyphenated spacing. With the hyphens, it just took me to sites composed apparently of nothing but the letter i. This might be interesting to an algebraist, but it didn't help me. Of course, *Iiiiiiiii-i-i* could be the phonetic transcription of a cry of pain or a war whoop or something similar, but that would only make its meaning decipherable in context. And context was what I did not have.

What I actually do, as a translator, is this: I translate novels and poems. I'm not one of the big boys, as I call them: I'm no Jay Rubin or Gilbert Adair or even Norman Thomas di Giovanni. Publishers don't send me the classics. I've never translated Goethe or Schiller or Dostoevsky (which, concerning the last, is probably a good thing, especially if he writes about tractors much). But that doesn't bother me. In fact, it's actually a good thing. The big boys can keep the giants of literature – you can buy a thousand translations of any of those writers at any charity shop or second-hand store in the world and their fields are, with all due respect to these talented people, somewhat overploughed. A translator gets to Dickens or Balzac and the cupboard is pretty much empty. There's not much you can do when everybody's had a crack at 'To be or not to be' or '*Où sont les neiges d'antan?*'

But the writers I translate – my 'stable' as I like to think of them – are entirely mine. You want to read an English rendering of *Soldiers of War* by Max Hemnitz? That was me. Fancy casting an eye over *Ecstasy's Dagger: The Complete Poems of Padre Alessandro*? I did that. That much-thumbed copy of *She Walked Among Men* by A.J.L. Ferber? Check out the credit on the title page, just below the author bio. Me again.

True, I don't make a lot of money. I do stuff like office temping and helping out on the phones at my publishers to make ends meet, but I'm a frugal sort. My apartment is as clean as a rich man's castle but that's the only thing it has in common with a gilded palace. But I do have a computer, and a cooker and a washing machine and a TV, and I don't really need anything else.

Next I keyed in *la furcheuxne*. This at least led to a reduction in the number of possibilities, as the search engine told me that there were 'no results found for *la furcheuxne*'. The same held for *furcheuxne* without the *la*, and possible variant spellings like *furcheusne*, *furcheune* and *furchene*. It was a nonsense word. A made-up collection of French-sounding letters whose meaning, if any, was 'red herring'. A total waste of time. But I'm a diligent person and I expanded the search to include *vercheusne*, *fercheuxne* and other possibilities. That was also a complete waste of time. Finally, almost stabbing at the keys, I Googled '*la furcheuxne sunt iiiii-i-i*'. Suddenly the screen filled with results and the mystery was solved. I'm kidding. Once again, there was nothing. I had wasted almost an hour on a search I knew would be useless right from the get-go. Now I became overwhelmed with a sense of futility and disgust. Futility on fairly obvious grounds, but disgust for reasons that were both personal and professional.

A couple of years ago, I went into the offices of R.J. Walker-Hebborn Publishing, the company for whom I do freelance translating. It's not a big firm by any stretch of the imagination, but the owners had cannily snapped up some writers who were biggish names in their own countries but unknown in the English-speaking world and, by swiftly bringing out decent translations of their books, made a tidy profit. Nowadays that kind of thing is a lot harder, I'd imagine. A kid puts a short story on a blog in Budapest and within hours the whole world's heard about it. But this company still had a reputation for being sympathetic to 'foreign' writers, and so their European and Asian counterparts continued to use them.

Anyway, this one day I was coming in to use the phones, on legitimate translator's business. I needed to speak to an author, which is not as common as you might think. Authors can be very hands-on in the writing process, consulting with editors and publishers, but once the book is out, they usually like to move on to the next project. (I imagine this is why the famous J.D. Salinger had such a reputation for uncommunicativeness: he just wanted to get on to the next project.) And with translators, authors find they have even less to say.

Which was the case that day. I was translating from French, funnily enough, one of the books I mentioned before, *She Walked Among Men* by A.J.L. Ferber. I don't know if you're one of Ferber's fans, but she has quite a following, I'm told, although personally I find her work quite dense and challenging. Which is probably why, if I'm honest, I wasn't looking forward to telephoning her. Madame Ferber, as she liked to be called, was the kind of person who didn't suffer fools gladly. And as she was also the kind of person who thinks most of the human race are fools, there was always a strong chance when talking to A.J.L. Ferber that you would receive the sharp edge of her tongue. (I have since been told that she left behind a string of ex-husbands and angry girlfriends. I can see why, believe me.)

I dialled Madame Ferber's number and listened as the telephone shrilled its unfamiliar, exotic continental ring. Then, just as I was sure she must be out, someone picked up and Madame Ferber's distinctive voice said, '*Oui?*' in a tone that suggested that somebody had better be in mortal danger at the other end because otherwise they were wasting a famous author's valuable time.

'Hello, Madame Ferber,' I said, 'this is Jacky, your English translator.'

'Oh,' she said, making the word sound like a piece of lead.

I once read about a lighthouse keeper who was standing at the bottom of the stairs in his lighthouse when it was struck by lightning and caught fire. A piece of molten lead from the lamp flew out and leapt straight into the poor man's mouth, killing him outright. They put that lump of lead on the lighthouse keeper's gravestone, and whenever I think of it, I think of Madame Ferber saying, 'Oh.'

'I thought the translation was complete,' she said.

'It is,' I replied, 'but I'm just clarifying a few minor ambiguities in the text.'

'I see,' said Madame Ferber, perhaps a little coldly.

I don't understand this about authors; they spend all their lives telling people that their books are layered with meaning, and nothing is ever black and white, but the moment you suggest to them that maybe some of their book is confusing, they get all huffy.

'It's just a small thing,' I said soothingly. 'On page 583—'

'Young man,' said Madame Ferber, 'I cannot be expected to memorise the pagination of my own books.'

I ignored that, because I was sure at least one wall of her apartment was probably insulated with copies of her own books. 'Let me read you the line in question,' I said, and hurried on in case she had an objection to someone reading her prose out loud to her. '"In that moment of plangency, Odile reflected on Corale for the first time, yet it was only in the calmness of her later years that she realised that Corale had somehow reflected on her."'

There was a silence at the other end of the line. Even though it was just a silence, it sounded annoyed to me.

'That's the line,' I said.

'I am aware that that was "the line",' said Madame Ferber. 'I did not think that you had somehow acquired the ability spontaneously to generate prose.'

'I was wondering about the use of the word "reflected",' I said. 'Do you mean that Odile was thinking about Corale for the first time, or do you mean that Odile was having some kind of effect on her, like reflected light?'

There was another silence on the end of the line. This time, it sounded puzzled. For the first time, I could hear hesitancy in the silence. It was as if – and I knew that my imagination was running away with me, to say the least – it was as if Madame Ferber didn't know the answer to my question.

'Or is it,' I said, as the silence lengthened, 'meant to be ambiguous?'

There was a crash at the other end as the phone was slammed down. I made a mental note to put this query in an email to Madame Ferber, put her file back in the 'Authors' cabinet, and was just about to leave when the door opened and R.J. Walker-Hebborn came in. With him was a short man with terrible hair and a pair of eyebrows that seemed somehow impossible.

'This is Euros Frant,' said R.J. Walker-Hebborn. 'He's a very exciting author.'

I was surprised to hear this, not because Mr Frant didn't look exciting – authors are like their books, I say, in that they can't be judged by their covers – but because Walker-Hebborn didn't deal in exciting authors, or if he did, at any rate he wasn't sending them my way. To my certain knowledge, neither Padre Alessandro nor Max Hemnitz had ever penned an exciting word in their life. (And nor, I was prepared to bet my life's savings, had A.J.L. Ferber. In fact, sometimes, on long nights stranded in one of her sentences, I pictured Madame Ferber writing an exciting word and hurriedly scratching it out lest the infection spread to the other words.)

Euros Frant nodded with such violence that he nearly dropped the large package he was holding. As it was, several sheets of paper fluttered out from it, and both Walker-Hebborn and I lurched to grab them from the air.

'Well,' Mr Walker-Hebborn said, 'I'll leave you two to get better acquainted.' And he wafted out of the room.

I motioned Frant to a chair with a sinking feeling in my stomach. The papers floating from his parcel could only be part of a manuscript – and if that parcel was composed entirely of manuscript, it was going to be a hefty piece of work. Combine that fact with Walker-Hebborn's keenness for me to meet Euros Frant and his rapid exit from the room and that could mean only one thing. Euros Frant had written a very big book and it was going to be my job to translate it.

'Shall we go for coffee?' I said to Frant, wishing I hadn't as he started nodding and the sheets of paper began to shake out again.

In the coffee shop, Frant turned out to be an agitated kind of man. His eyebrows worked as he talked, and he talked like he moved, in short jerky bursts, and he looked around every time he spoke, as though one wrong word would bring hidden assassins running from the shadows. He had ordered an enormous cup of coffee – to be fair, he'd had no choice, as the coffee house only sold coffee in enormous cups – and he sat behind it like a tail-gunner, occasionally reaching out to it and finding it either too hot to drink or too heavy to lift.

'This book,' he said in an accent that was both thick and staccato at the same time, 'is my life's work.'

I must admit that isn't a sentence a translator wants to hear. It sounds fine on the radio in an interview or at a fancy awards ceremony, but when you're the poor fool tasked with rendering someone's 'life's work' into readable English, it has to be bad news. The life's-work brigade are very fussy about anybody tampering with their precious prose and tend to take every alteration or improvement personally. Should we say that your first memory involving a red toy fire engine was 'heavy with emotive force' or 'pregnant'? It's a minefield. Opt for 'heavy' and you risk being accused of making something beautiful into a workaday cliché. Use the word 'pregnant' and you're somehow pre-empting the next six chapters dealing with the birth, and subsequent jealousy, of your younger sibling. I'm not kidding. I have had a writer say that my vocabulary suggestions 'disembowelled' his narrative.

Frant didn't look as if he might be a future narrative disembowelment accuser, but he had a light in his eye that I had learned to distrust. Say what you like about 'boring' technical manuals, but the men and women who come up with those rarely accuse you of stealing their souls when you ask if a word means 'spanner' or 'wrench'.

I was about to ask Frant what his life's work was about when he slammed it down on the table between us and pulled out a few pages.

'Here,' he said, 'tell me what you think.' And he sat back in his chair, cradling his coffee cup in both hands like a huge dormouse.

I looked at the pages. They were typed, manually, and they were in Italian. I mean, sort of. They were in Italian the way that *Ivanhoe* and that kind of stuff is in English, all *thee* and *verily* and *forsooth* and so on. It wasn't medieval Italian in any real way (which I was relieved about, because I'm no scholastic translator) but it wasn't 'real' Italian either. It was all, as I say, knights in armour stuff.

I scanned a few paragraphs. 'There are a lot of words in here that are new to me,' I said. 'And some unfamiliar place names.' I flicked back to the title page, and my heart sank. *La Chronac De' Mondinos Imaginarios.*

'I don't quite understand,' I said. Frant smiled in a way that even I could tell was meant to be indulgent and knowing. It just made his face look crazier. 'This isn't—'

'Oh, I know', he said, his eyebrows dipping condescendingly. 'I know. It's not conventional medieval Italian, at all. It's a dialect of my own invention – a parallel dialect, if you know what I mean.'

I did know what he meant but I was damned if I was going to say it.

'This book – whose name I'm sure you've discerned – is called *The Chronicle of Imaginary Worldlets*.'

'Worldlets', I was finally able to say.

'Yes', he said. 'It's a palimpsest, an anachronistic samizdat, a found text – a bulletin from a place that has never existed. Cities, rivers, people – stories ... all from these imaginary worldlets.'

'You wrote this?' I said.

'Every word', he said, 'and straight into the dialecta of the *Chronac*. I didn't want to obscure the purity of the text, you see.'

'No, I can see that', I said. 'I expect that's my job.'

'I would like to work very closely with the translator on this', said Frant. 'I want to be sure that the translation is as accurate as possible.'

The translation of your half-made-up language? I wanted to say. Instead I said, 'But you speak English yourself. Why not just write it out in English?'

As I spoke, Frant began shaking his head. 'No no no no', he said. 'The text has to be translated, just as if it were a real medieval text only recently discovered.'

I decided not to point out that if it were a real medieval text it would be in Latin, not some half-assed *Lord of the Rings*-fan pretend Italian. It's not my job to point things out in that way. So I simply said, 'Well, it will be both a challenge and a privilege to work with you.'

Frant just sat there smiling like a booby. I picked up

the manuscript and pretended to gaze at its awesome magnificence. In reality, I was weighing it.

I don't know if you have ever read *The Chronicle of Imaginary Worldlets*. I'm guessing by its frequent appearance in discount bookshops and 2 For 1 bins that you're one of the thousands of people who haven't. If so, I'd like to take the opportunity to tell you how fortunate you are. Because it is an awful book. I don't generally like to tell tales out of class regarding the books I work on, for obvious reasons (like nobody would ever hire me again, for example), but in this case I think I'm safe. After the sales figures came in, Walker-Hebborn made darned sure that Euros Frant's name was never mentioned in the office again. The book did not go on to become the new '*Harry Potter* for adults' that Walker-Hebborn and no doubt Frant had hoped for. Instead it went on to become lavishly bound landfill.

None of this would have mattered if it hadn't taken up six months of my life. I was paid (to some extent) for my work, but I'd give back every penny just to regain the brain cells and ounces of sanity that I sacrificed to that horrible project. Let me just recall a couple of examples. The whole idea of the book was that it was meant to be some kind of lost encyclopedia from another world. Or our own world only different, or from the old days only everyone had forgotten about it. I have to say that Frant was pretty vague about the whole thing.

I once read, when I was going out with someone who used to subscribe to the music press, an interview with a rock musician about something he called a 'concept album' and the interviewer called a 'rock opera'. The rock star kept trying to explain the story of his concept or opera but every time he delved into the details he got confused and it soon became apparent – to me at least, if not to his adoring fans – that there was no coherent story, just a bunch of music with roughly similar themes. Euros Frant's book was like that. He said it was from another world, but one where for some reason they spoke bad medieval Italian. So to justify that, sometimes he said it was from the real Middle Ages, but it was about some places that we'd all forgotten about. And those places weren't in this world.

And that was just the backdrop to this drivel. The *Chronicle* was supposed to be a magical repository of stories and new legends. It wasn't: it was a lot of half-digested bits of mythology and other people's books. One bit was *Tristan and Isolde* with the names changed, one bit was like *The Hobbit* only instead of a hobbit, the hero was a carpenter. And one bit was like the phone book. I mean it: it was just a list of names that Frant had made up, with stupid made-up medieval jobs. *Lla dirretori estradale di Monto Royale*, he called it. I won't tell you what I called it when I realised I had to make up – sorry, 'translate' – all these job names into English.

Frant wasn't too upset when the book did so badly, largely because he hated the finished product. He said it didn't look authentic (he wanted it to be printed on that raggedy yellow paper American publishers use to make their hardbacks look 'classy'), he said the illustrations hadn't caught the spirit of the book at all (Walker-Hebborn used some Dungeons and Dragons person, Leonardo Da Vinci being unavailable), and the publisher's refusal to print the opening 500-stanza poem, *Intradozza In Chronaca*, rendered the whole thing meaningless (the book was already meaningless and the poem – which wasn't included because Frant forgot to write it until the week of publication – was the kind of doggerel that makes that one about going placidly among the noise and haste look like Tennyson).

Every so often, Walker-Hebborn would receive letters from Frant, demanding that he reprint the *Chronac*, and each letter was stuffed with press cuttings about 'similar' books that had done well. I imagine Walker-Hebborn loathed the television show *Game of Thrones* because every time a new series came on, Frant would write him another long letter that usually began with the words, 'NOW MORE THAN EVER IS THE TIME ...' in big wobbly capital letters.

All of which goes to explain in a roundabout way why I did not wish to go anywhere near the world of fictional languages and made-up words. It's just gobbledygook to me and I really try to avoid it if I can. (If I'm honest, my favourite of the writers whom I translate has to be Moîre Herone. When I tell you that her three bestselling novels are called *Too Many Murders Spoil the Broth*, *A Rolling Stone Gathers No Murder* and *Red Sky at Night Murderer's Delight*, you can probably guess what kind of book she writes. The kind that's pleasant to translate is what.) I just don't want to run into any terrible *Chronacs* of stupid *Mondinos Imaginarios*, that's all. And the book the girl had brought to me looked to be set firmly in this kind of world, so I was now almost glad to be rid of it. Besides, I'd hit a brick wall and there was nothing I could do without the actual book in front of me, so I just decided to forget about the whole thing. It was an annoying puzzle, and I don't like puzzles. When my father left, my mother became obsessed with puzzles, but she was terrible at them, and so the house was always littered with half-completed puzzle books, word ladders and crosswords that she'd just abandoned. I was a lot younger then, in fact I was still at school, so my brain was more attuned to IQ examinations and aptitude tests and so forth, and I would gather up the puzzle books and sit in my room and complete the unfinished puzzles. I almost always managed to finish them, but I never got any real pleasure from it. It was just the idea of leaving them undone that drove me to it. Call me OCD (I'm not, though) but the thought of the bin being full of incomplete puzzle books just distressed me on some level.

But this puzzle looked to be one I could do nothing about. I had a feeling I wouldn't be seeing the girl again, even if I were to hang out in that same bar every night, or go to all the bars in the area. It's true that she had expressly forbidden me to look for her, but I was concerned. Then again, what would I do if I found her? She would almost certainly just tell me to get lost. So no girl. And no girl meant no book. Without the book, the puzzle was insoluble. Even with the book, the puzzle might be insoluble, but that was something I clearly had no chance of discovering for myself. So I did what I always do when I find I can go no further down the road I had hoped to travel.

I went back to the start.

Bars are a lot different at lunchtime to the way they are at night. A bar at night is a place where artificial light seems to sparkle off glasses and mirrors and everyone looks a little bit more glamorous and even the lonely guy in the corner looks like he's stepped out of a New York photograph in black and white. If there's music it sinks down into the crowd and whispers its way through the night. And everyone's laughing and talking and you just know that if you could hear what they were saying, it would be clever and funny or just sad and wise.

A bar in the daytime, on the other hand, is a horrible place. Everything seems to be made of tin and the walls, the floor and all the surfaces clatter and jar with every sound. If there's music, it echoes around in an irritating fashion, and it's always a song you hate. Everyone's in a foul mood, from the bar staff to the customers, and there are only two types of customer: alcoholics who need their late morning fix, and people who don't know the area and think the best place to get an early lunch is a bar that only serves cold French fries and damp sandwiches.

I suppose I would fit mostly into the latter category, except I was having some kind of baguette with frilly salad and bits of bacon and whatnot. I was the only person eating, too, which would indicate that the place wasn't exactly renowned for its cuisine. The other customers were either drinking as heavily as they could considering the hour – there was a fellow with his glass of Scotch at the bar – or pretending they weren't in a bar at all. In the corner a small group of men and women in jackets were crowded around a laptop computer with big cups of coffee, having some kind of meeting or presentation and trying to ignore the crash of metal barrels being delivered from a truck parked right outside, as if this was their office and they were always trying to work while a lot of beer was being delivered.

There were only two things that connected this place to the way it had been last night. One was the slightest odour of cigarette smoke, which was so faint that I might have been imagining it, and the other was the barman, Don. I don't know what kind of shifts he was pulling, but from the look of his eyes, he hadn't been home to sleep yet. Maybe he'd caught a nap out the back, or perhaps he was relying on stimulants to get him through the day. Either way he looked even more morose than he had the previous evening and I wasn't looking forward to engaging him in conversation.

This, you see, was my somewhat simplistic plan. Don the barman was my only connection to the girl, and might even know her outside the bar. Although she had told me not to find her, I didn't see what harm there would be in learning more about her. That was to me a small but significant difference, and meant that I could keep my interest in her at arm's length, without coming over as some kind of stalker or something.

As it turned out, I didn't have to worry about engaging him in conversation. When he brought over the bill for my baguette and coffee, he recognised me and said, 'You were in here last night.' I was about to confirm this, even though I was aware that it was unnecessary because he had already correctly identified me, when without waiting for me to speak or even nod, he went on, 'That girl you were with? She left something behind.'

I could have been candid, I suppose. I could have said that I didn't know her whereabouts, or even her name. I should have told him that I wasn't the one to speak to, that he probably knew her better than I did and maybe he should just hand in whatever she left to the police. Instead I said, as casually as I could, 'Really? What is it?'

'Oh,' he said, his concentration falling away for a moment from tiredness, 'some sort of book. Wait there, I'll get it.'

They say that time can change speed, that it's entirely subjective. I know that when I'm working on a really tricky passage in a translation I can look up at the clock and see that I've spent two hours on a paragraph and it feels like a minute has passed. Conversely, five minutes in the dentist's waiting room can feel like a lifetime.

The time I spent waiting for Don to come back was nothing like that at all. Time seemed to expand and contract in all directions at the same time. The people at the laptop were talking nineteen to the dozen while a drunk sipped his drink as if it were his very first. A bus went past outside at its usual lumbering rate while my heart hammered at my ribs like a monkey panicking in its cage. In the centre of it all, my mind seemed still and calm but also freaked out as time stretched and flew around. I was experiencing time in the way, I imagine, a drug addict or a hibernating animal might.

And then Don reappeared and time went back to normal again. 'Maybe you can give it to her next time you see her,' he said.

Even in my nervous excitement to see the book, I could hear the slight mix of resentment and envy in his voice. He thinks I'm her boyfriend! I didn't correct him. I just reached out my hand for the book and thanked him. He nodded and handed it over.

It wasn't the book. It was a book, sure, but it was completely different. It was a medium-sized bound notebook, not one of those with fake Victorian bindings, all marbled end-pages and creamy paper, but a modern one, with a bright green vinyl cover and ring-bound pages. It seemed to be pretty full but there was no name or address or even a contact telephone number. I must admit, I was so disappointed I was about to toss the notebook but something made me hesitate, not least the fact that this wasn't my book to dispose of, and also that if it belonged to the girl it might be important to her. Maybe not as important as the other book, but then it wouldn't be. After all, that book contained photographs that appeared to be of her dead or unconscious body, whereas this was just a notebook.

I opened it again and looked at the first page.

CARRIE AND THE LEGIONS

The Future/ Night Life

MINIMAX

In my long career I don't think I've ever seen a more promising debut than this single. Released on retro-leaning blood-red vinyl, Carrie and the Legions' first release showcases two wildly differing styles in a musical schizophrenia that's far from displeasing. A-side 'The Future' is excitingly optimistic, full of promises that both voice and melody seem likely to keep, and has an entirely apt chorus – 'Here comes the future/ I need it/ I want it/ I like it.' Flipside 'Night Life' is an entirely different kettle of mystery, a smoky jazz creep through the small hours. 'When it's dark,' sings Carrie huskily, 'I wonder who I am/ And where I'm going.' On the strength of these two songs? Far. I don't know about the rest of the world, but in these offices we cannot wait for that debut album. ***

I'm not what you'd call a 'rock fan', or really much of a music fan at all. I sometimes have the radio on when I'm driving, but at the moment I don't have a car and anyway most pop music strikes me as pretty inane, classical music just makes me feel stupid, and jazz goes right over my head. I have a few old CDs a girlfriend burned for me when I was at college when she felt I could do with a bit of a musical education, but I don't have a CD player any more. I suppose I could play the CDs in my computer but truth to tell I never liked the music on the CDs very much even at the time. However, this girlfriend I'm speaking of used to buy the weekly music papers, English and American, and from time to time I would glance inside one of them to see exactly what it was I was missing. And to be honest, the writers were worse than jazz.

I mean, I'm a translator but these writers were beyond anyone's comprehension and they were writing in English. They would refer to everyone by their first name, and if they were writing about a band they'd shorten the band's name, or use a whimsical or aggressive nickname, so that half the time even if you had heard of a singer or a group you still had to work to find out who they were talking about. They wrote in a peculiar mixture of sneering and enthusiasm, like a teenager who wants to be excited about something but doesn't want to sound too happy about it, so he puts it down more than he praises it. And they didn't seem to know if they were newspaper writers with snappy and concise prose or real writers using poetic similes and metaphors or just angry kids. The whole thing was entirely baffling and I was sorry when my girlfriend and I split up but also relieved that I didn't have to pretend to know who the Rolling Stones were any more.

But when I skimmed that first clipping, it all came flooding back. It was a review of a single, what they used to call a 45rpm record. I had thought that these things were no longer made, but my then girlfriend assured me that they had become fashionable and cultish again. Anyway, this was a review of a single by a band called Carrie and the Legions and it was a sort of gush, I suppose you could say, very frothy and verbose.

The next piece was a live review, where the writer had been to see a band play a concert and written about it, and once again the band was Carrie and the Legions. The review was favourable and ended, predictably enough, with a line about the future belonging to Carrie and her band. After that, there were some more live reviews in the same vein, a review of a second single ('Not Your Girl'), and a couple of letters from the magazine's mailbag page, both expressing contradictory viewpoints about – you guessed it – Carrie and the Legions.

I was disappointed, I have to say. Not that it's my place to comment on anyone's personal possessions, especially those of someone I could scarcely claim to know at all, but I had spent some time with the owner of the notebook and maybe I'd expected her to be a little more – I don't know – sophisticated. This was the kind of thing a teenager would keep, a fan's scrapbook of some untouchable fantasy star. I don't know, maybe I was being harsh, but somehow I thought that the girl who'd come to my apartment last night would be above such adolescent obsessions. But then I suppose that goes to show that often first impressions aren't correct, and someone you think is one kind of person might be an entirely different kind of person. Not of course that that makes them a bad person, or one deserving opprobrium, just a little bit of a disappointment.

That was how I felt then. Here in the present moment as I recall the feelings I had as I looked at the little book of cuttings, I have two sensations. One is a slight sense of shame at how unsympathetic I was to this actually touching indication of humanity, which was really a sign of endearing human frailty that I should have been sympathetic to. And the other was just how dense I can be. Because it didn't occur to me until I had put the notebook in my pocket and returned to my apartment that this might not have been a teenage girl's scrapbook of adulation, but a collection of pieces from the subject's career made by the subject herself. How obvious did it have to be for you to realise, I almost want to scream at myself, that this was not a notebook belonging to an overgrown follower of Carrie and the Legions, but the property of Carrie herself?

I should make it clear that when I say things weren't going to plan that I didn't actually have a plan but even if I had had one, well, things weren't going to plan. For a start, now there were two books. The book I didn't have but wanted, and the book I didn't want but turned out I might need after all. I was none the wiser, the way you sometimes are when at least the tiny amount of information you have kind of balances things out. Before, I knew where I was. I was looking for a book and, if I found it, maybe I could help Carrie, or whatever this girl's name might be. Instead I had found a notebook which, to be honest, only made things more complicated. I hadn't planned on tracking down a singer, in fact I hadn't planned on tracking anyone down at all. I didn't want to approach the girl until I had some good news for her. I suppose it was a kind of a fantasy, me as the knight in a white suit of armour saving the fair damsel from a mysterious I didn't know what, and winning, if not her heart or her praise, then at least her forgiveness for going through her stuff. OK, so the last part wasn't very medieval but you get the idea. I was embarrassed that I'd acted out of character and I wanted to make amends.

But here I was now with no way of making amends and a lead I didn't necessarily want. I could track her down now but what would I say? 'Hi, I know you didn't want me to get in contact with you again, but I did. And I'm no nearer to solving your problem than before.' I could present her with the notebook, sure, but it was just a notebook full of rock articles. And whichever way I looked at it, her parting words had been very clear.

The whole situation was in every way the polar opposite of what I actually wanted to achieve. On the other hand I had no alternative plan, so I might as well just look for Carrie and the Legions and maybe along the way something might turn up.

This was as it turned out the nearest to what I could call a plan, anyway. It wasn't very good when it started and three hours later, as I ploughed my way through Google and the websites of five or six rock magazines, it seemed that it had got even worse. There was nothing on the internet about Carrie and the Legions. Once again, I'd hit a dead end. This struck me as bizarre. My girlfriend and her pals at college were constantly marvelling at the fact that the internet was always throwing up more and more obscure rock groups, and they even used to vie with one another to find bands or singers that nobody had heard of. It was almost as if they valued the obscurity of the artist more than their actual music. Well, they would have been shocked and stunned to learn that of all their acquaintances, I would be the one to find an act that didn't appear anywhere on the internet. In terms of obscurity points, I was the clear winner. Not that this was any consolation. There was no way I could go back in time and impress these students with my find. And, more pertinently, I was yet again stymied.

Even the individual words in the name 'Carrie and the Legions' were so common that it wasn't so much like looking for a needle in a haystack, as it was like finding a needle that scattered into its various component atoms as soon as you picked it up. Clearly Carrie and the Legions – with or without the records they had made – were not a successful or popular act. I stood up and got a glass of water, and I thought hard. Why was this more difficult than looking for *la furcheuxne* and the other words? They were made-up fragments of nonsense from a fantasy world, whereas Carrie and the Legions were surely as mundane and real as any other wannabe rock band.

And then it dawned on me. With the whole *la furcheuxne* conundrum, I at least had an inkling that I was dealing with a fantasy language. And why? Because language is my business. I'm a translator! I speak several major European languages. I know the beat, as it were. But with groups and bands (and I don't even know the difference between a 'group' and a 'band'), I'm completely at a loss. I haven't a clue, you might say. I don't go to concerts, I don't buy T-shirts with the names of bands (or groups) on. I'm just not in that world.

But I did know someone who was.

It had been a long time since I left college, but not so long that I'd seen fit to throw away my old student address book. We students, of course, all lived in temporary accommodation in those days, but most people had mobile phones and even if those numbers had changed, well, I had their parents' details from those long vacations when we would visit each other at 'home'. I'm sure they had mine, too, but years had passed and people make new friendships or fall in love or just die, so I wasn't too upset that none of my old college acquaintances had been in touch. Besides, if I wanted to contact any of them, or just see how they were doing, there was always my trusty old friend the internet. A lot of people had posted photographs from their university days on various social network sites and I could often see myself in those photographs, crowding in to get nearer to the centre, or caught unawares in the background of some group shot.

I don't want to give the impression that I was not one of the gang as a student. I'd say it was one of the happiest times of my life. I joined various societies, ones whose activities didn't clash with my courses, and it was there that I met my girlfriend. We went out for a couple of years until she met the guy she married, who was on one of my courses. In fact, I sort of introduced them to each other, which goes to show that sometimes when you think you're being the main actor in your own life, you're in fact a supporting character in someone else's. But they got married, so at least I can take some credit for bringing happiness to two people there. Also, the fact that they stayed together makes her dropping me less bad, somehow. It wasn't as though I had planned to marry her, after all.

All these thoughts and some more besides were in my head when I tried the first number I had for my old girlfriend in my address book. The phone rang and rang but didn't go to answerphone. I was just about to put the receiver back in the cradle when a man said, 'Hello?'

'This is Jacky,' I said, recognising the voice at once. He was the guy who I had introduced to my girlfriend. Once again I was pleased they were still together. It validated me introducing them even more.

There was silence at the other end of the phone.

'From college,' I said, adding the names of the courses we had taken.

'Oh my God,' he said. 'Jacky, of course. How are you?' And before I could reply, he shouted something muffled. I was confused until I realised he was probably calling out to my ex-girlfriend. I couldn't catch what he said, though, but it must have done the trick because seconds later her voice was in my ear.

'Hello?' she said. 'Is that you ... Jacky?'

I could hear her saying my name like it was rusty, or like something in a drawer she was unwrapping cautiously for the first time in years. She sounded wary, which I suppose is reasonable when somebody calls up the way I was doing, with no introduction. For one crazy moment I wished I had written to her first, warning her that I was going to telephone, but that would have been a worse plan, now I come to think about it.

'Hi,' I said, 'I'm very sorry to call out of the blue like this.'

'Not at all,' she said, and her voice seemed more relaxed now. 'You were never one for the social niceties, after all.'

I set this comment aside, because it patently wasn't true, and went on in fact to disprove it by saying, 'So how are you?' Then I added, 'How are you both?' because that would disprove her claim regarding me and social niceties.

'We're well,' she said. 'We have a baby now, a boy. In fact I think I can hear him crying.'

I couldn't hear a thing, and I wondered why her husband didn't go and attend to the baby. Perhaps she was breast-feeding and didn't want him to use a bottle. Nevertheless to be polite – and also because it was possible she was using the baby as an excuse to keep the call short – I decided to take the hint, if hint it was, and get straight to the point.

'Congratulations,' I said. 'But I won't keep you. I just wanted to ask you something.'

'Oh?' she said.

'Yes,' I said. 'You know about rock music and pop and that kind of thing, don't you?'

She had to ask me to repeat the question, so I guess it must have thrown her slightly.

'Rock music,' I said again. 'I remember at college you were always reading music papers and going to concerts.'

'Yes,' she said. 'Of course, it was a long time ago. You certainly have a good memory.'

'Thank you,' I replied politely. 'So I'm calling to ask you if you've ever heard of a group or a band called Carrie and the Legions.'

There was quite a long pause on the line. I listened for the sound of a baby crying, but could hear nothing.

After a while she spoke again. 'That's it? That's what you want to know?'

'Yes,' I said. 'I realise it's an unusual request but I couldn't think of anybody else to ask. And before you say anything, I have tried the internet.'

'I see,' she said, slightly heavily. 'It's been, what, ten years? Since we last spoke.'

'Maybe more,' I agreed. 'Perhaps I shouldn't have called like this.'

'No, it's fine. Really. I think I'd just forgotten what you were like. Um, let me think.'

But instead of thinking, I heard her shout to her husband. It sounded like 'Lemuel wants to know ...' and then the rest was muffled, because now I actually could hear a baby crying. Then the husband was shouting, and there was really a lot of noise at the other end of the line. In fact, I could hear something drop and smash. After some time the noise quietened down again, but, to be sure, I said, 'Hello?' into the telephone.

'No,' she said tersely. 'I don't know of any band called Carrie and the Legions and neither does he. Sorry.'

I could tell she was about to hang up but I had another question, this one motivated purely by personal curiosity.

'Before you go,' I said quickly, 'what did you say to your husband then? It sounded like you called me "Lemuel" or "Emu" or something like that.'

'No,' she said, amusement surfacing for a moment. 'It was our nickname for you at college.'

I was surprised, and almost a little flattered. I hadn't known I'd had a nickname. This made me see some of my old college acquaintances in a different light, I must say.

'And it wasn't Lemuel or Emu,' she said. 'It was "the Mule".'

I could hear the baby crying again.

'Why did you call me the Mule?' I said.

'Why do you think?' she said and put the phone down.

CHAPTER THREE

Of all the meals of the day, I think lunch has to be the least interesting. With breakfast, no matter how simple it is, even if it's just an apple and a cup of tea, there's the anticipation of the first meal of the day. You're hungry and you crave instant satisfaction and there it is. Dinner is in many ways the opposite. It can crown the day, as a big celebration or just a well-deserved blow-out. It says, well done for working so hard, here are the fruits of your labours. With dinner you can perhaps have a glass of wine and indulge yourself.

But lunch, in my experience, is neither of these things. Lunch is a necessity, a mid-point in your working day when you have to take a break and refuel yourself. Unless you're a rich aristocrat or a fat-cat businessman, for whom lunch is just one more pig-out in your gluttonous day, of course, but I'm not. Lunch for me is at best a bowl of soup and a toasted bagel, and at worst, something stale from a cafeteria.

Today's lunch was no exception, except that it was particularly poor. I had somehow forgotten to go to the shops and buy any provisions, so my midday meal was a rye cracker with margarine and half a banana that I'd found in the fridge, carelessly wrapped in its own blackening skin. I had no milk either, something that made the cup of instant decaf coffee I prepared myself even less pleasant. All in all, I would say it was one of the worst lunches I had ever had.

I could have gone out and bought myself some lunch, but to be honest I didn't feel like it. I suppose the telephone call to my old girlfriend had upset me a little, as had the information that I had apparently been known to all and sundry at college as the Mule. However you look at it, the Mule isn't a flattering nickname. Nobody's face ever brightened up at a shout of, 'Hey, Mule, get over here!' or 'Great! Here comes the Mule!' Nobody ever heard of a cool Mule, that's for sure.

I abandoned my lunch and went over to the mirror. I studied my face for several minutes. Maybe the large eyes were like those of a mule? I couldn't see it myself. I certainly didn't have long ears or a prominent jaw. Admittedly, my expression could sometimes tend towards the mournful (as it certainly was doing at the present moment) but all in all, I could see nothing in my physical appearance to justify someone calling me the Mule.

I took down my *Children's Encyclopaedia*, which contained several facts about mules concerning their use as beasts of burden and their unusual parentage. None of this seemed to apply to me. I am, as far as I know, the product of normal breeding and while it's possible I cannot reproduce, there's no cause to suppose that this would be the reason for my nickname. Mules in fiction are few and far between; there's a character of that name in a science fiction novel but as he travels the galaxies having thrilling adventures, I saw no connection there either.

I spent the rest of the afternoon and some of the evening researching the word 'mule' and its possible applications to myself before I noticed that it was dark outside and therefore time for dinner, a much more exciting meal.

*

I don't know if you've ever woken up at three or four in the morning, plagued by doubts. Apparently it's by no means uncommon. A man can hit the hay in the best of moods yet suddenly sit bolt upright in bed as if bombarded by every awful thought possible. I've read that it's caused by a lack of endorphins or the like, which are the natural drugs the body produces to keep us feeling OK during the day as we go about our formerly primitive tasks, so we would feel happy about being hunted down by mastodons or not having invented fire and so forth. And it seems that at about three o'clock in the morning these endorphins shut down, the body being asleep and therefore able to cope with its natural, untranquillised state. That's what I heard, anyway.

Unfortunately, if like me you're prone to waking up during this unendorphinated time, all bets are off, mentally speaking. Every bad thing you can think of just walks into your mind without so much as a by your leave and blows away any plans for the future you might have, pleasant notions or optimism. And that's exactly how I was feeling at this moment, depressed and doubtful and worried, with the most terrible ideas running through my mind.

For a start, there was the issue of my nickname and the nagging feeling that perhaps all those years ago the people I had thought were my friends might have been mocking me. But that was something I could cope with. After all, it had been a long time ago, even if it was fresh to me. No, what was worrying me now was the business with Carrie, as I had now started calling her. The more I thought about it, the more disturbing her situation seemed to me. The mysterious book, which so intrigued me as a text to be translated, was surely more upsetting for her because of the photographs it contained, rather than any peculiar quirks of linguistics. How had she come by this book? I realised with a shock that

I had no idea if she had picked the book up randomly in a shop or been sent it. Either way the effect on her must have been distressing. And I had been of no help at all. Quite the opposite: just when she wanted some kind of comfort, I had instead decided to go through her stuff. I'm aware that I was driven by curiosity rather than malice, but the result was the same: I had made a girl who was already quite upset even more upset. It was no wonder she had no desire to see me again. And my efforts to help her since she had gone were no better. I had no idea what the book was or what it might mean, and my visit to the bar where we had met was almost as fruitless; in fact it raised more questions than it answered.

The more I lay there, the more my mind was disturbed by these thoughts. Sleep was clearly not going to be easy to recover. I opened my eyes and decided, reluctantly, that I might as well get up and make myself a cup of tea. The room was still dark, so there were clearly some hours to go before dawn. The darkness was illuminated by a green blinking light, which might well have been what woke me up. I'm a light sleeper and any small thing can bring me out of my slumber. I got up and went over to the source of the illumination. It was the scanner on my printer, which I had obviously left on since shamefully attempting to copy some of the book. It hadn't woken me last night, but then I had been exhausted.

I was about to turn it off when I noticed an edge of paper peeping out from the printer tray. I removed it. Partly smeared but largely legible were two pages scanned and printed from the book. Somehow the machine must have been copying when the girl snatched it from the scanner. I took the paper from the scanner, scarcely believing it. There was a big smudge across the top of the paper, but it only took up about as much room as perhaps a lid on a jar of sauce takes up on the jar. And while the type on the page was small, it was still entirely legible – three cheers for digital imaging – and anyway I could blow up the scan for clarity. But best of all there were two drawings on the page – drawings with captions. This may not seem like particularly exciting news to you but believe me as a translator thrown into the position of becoming a comparative linguist, this was a real bonus.

Most translation work is based on the simple assumption that the person doing the translation is fluent in both or all of the languages required. They speak and write the language the document is written in and also the language the document is required to be rendered into. That's surely a given. You would find it pretty odd if a book claimed to be translated from French by a person who admitted they didn't speak a word of French. Almost certainly, they'd have to make it up. You may laugh, but this used to happen all the time: English translators who didn't speak, say, Spanish, would get a copy of the book that had already been translated into German, for example, and translate from the German into English. The results would be, as you can imagine, pretty mangled.

People think translation is easy. They think all you do is take a word in one language and trade it for a different word in another language. Like you're sitting there and you take *oiseau* and exchange it for *bird*. Actually, that's a bad example, but when you deal with authors and poets like I do, there's a whole world of nuance involved. It's very hard to translate expressions, for instance. You may have heard the old translator's joke about the language computer that translated the English phrase *out of sight, out of mind* into Russian and then back into English, and it came back as *invisible maniac*. That's an extreme example, and an inaccurate one too, as modern translation software would acknowledge *out of sight, out of mind* as a pretty common colloquialism and render it more accurately. Also when I ran the phrase through the Babelfish site, it was translated into Russian as *из визирования, из рассмотрения* and back into English not as *invisible maniac* at all, but *from the sighting, from the examination*. Which, I have to admit, makes even less sense, but that's not the point. Translation is not as simple as it looks.

And that's just if you're dealing with languages that everyone is familiar with. When it comes to mystery languages, you need a key. No doubt you're familiar with the Rosetta Stone, the big carved piece of rock that enabled Jean-François Champollion to translate Egyptian hieroglyphs by comparing them to the texts underneath. Will all due respect to Jean-François Champollion, the stone has to be the number one luckiest discovery of all time. Armed with a copy of the Rosetta Stone, the average baby could probably translate Ancient Egyptian texts. It must have been Christmas come early for anyone with a standard nineteenth-century knowledge of classical tongues. I might be sounding a little envious here but, to be honest, as I stood in my apartment holding that piece of paper in my hand, I could have done with a Rosetta Stone of my own. But instead I had those two drawings, with their captions, and that might just be enough of a visual and verbal cross-reference to get me going. It was all I could do to put the paper down on the table and go into the kitchen and make myself a cup of coffee. It was an important moment, and one that could arguably lead to a breakthrough, but I for one was not going to be hasty in this instance. I went back to bed, and lay there until sleep finally came.

I made my morning coffee and ate a bagel – toasted, to ease digestion – and then I sat down at my desk. Normally at this time of day I would have begun by checking my emails, and I must admit, I was torn – should I answer duty's call or just throw caution to the winds? In the end, I reasoned that if one of the emails I received that morning was something I couldn't ignore – an urgent work request, perhaps, or a message from my mother, asking me to come and deal with one of her increasingly bizarre problems – I'd become distracted and have to put off the task of looking at the text in my scanner.

So I clicked 'log out' on my email account and sat down with the two pages. There they were, smudged at the top and densely packed with text elsewhere, the mass of words broken up by the two drawings. I would have guessed that there were just over 300 words on each page. It was clearly the same nonsense as before, a mishmash of hybrid words from Latin, French, German and God knows what else. One thing was for sure: it might be in a made-up language or it might be complete random drivel, but it was no historical document or mysterious missive from the past. As to what kind of idiot had the time, the resources or the desire to sit down and churn out page after page of this drivel I really couldn't say; it seemed to me totally pointless, like most obsessions. I was guessing it was an obsession because to be frank I couldn't see someone sitting down and casually turning out this stuff after a hard day at the office. I was reminded, suddenly and kind of bizarrely, of a poem. I don't read poetry, as a rule, because I dislike the ambiguity, but sometimes in my job I have to translate the stuff, and it's hard graft which is probably why it sticks in the brain. Anyway, there was this one poem by Padre Alessandro Marchese, whose *Ecstasy's Dagger* I had recently had the mixed good fortune to translate, which suddenly just walked into my mind with its big boots on. You may know the verse from the more well-known Edwardian translation:

Made with care in commerce's fury –
None deny endeavour

Let me set this before God's jury –
Made for love be made for ever.

Pardon me if I blow my own trumpet for a moment but I found, with all due modesty, that my own translation seemed to express the padre's sentiments just as well:

Made for money or for need
Fine for the begetter
But I prefer the amateur deed:
Made for love is better

Although, if I am completely honest, it now strikes me that neither of them is particularly good, and I'm wondering if the fault lies with the original poem. And, thinking about it further, it's not even a sentiment I agree with in the present case, as the pages in front of me continued to just plain annoy me. I mean, what is the point of writing an entire book in some made-up language? Even Tolkien, who was a bit too fond if you ask me of his Elvish and his Gnomespeak and whatnot, drew the line at writing a whole damn book in the stuff. No, my point of view for what it's worth is simple: there are enough languages in the world without some fool coming along and adding a few more to the mix. And that includes Esperanto and all the other languages invented to bring about world unity and the like. I'm sure it's all very noble and high-minded of people to think of these things, but if people wanted to go round saying, '*Mi voli kelka fromagxo*' or whatever, surely there'd be no stopping them. Instead, everyone would rather bomb the hell out of each other while issuing commands in their own familiar languages.

I agree that I've strayed from the point slightly here, but you can see how strongly I feel about this topic. It's one that's close to my heart, after all, and I can say with confidence that on this, at least, I know what I'm talking about. So you can imagine that, even though these pages were the lead I'd been hoping for, I still wasn't exactly jumping for joy at the thought of having to plough through them. Be careful what you wish for, I guess. But I put aside all negative thoughts concerning the topic of made-up drivel and decided instead to concentrate on the two diagrams, in which I had invested most of my hopes.

You see, because this pair were captioned, they were as near to a Rosetta Stone as I was likely to get. Not that I was looking at a mass of different texts that could be co-related and rendered into English. All I had was a couple of pictures and what I was hoping would be descriptions of the pictures. It wasn't much, but if one of the pictures was of, say, a man walking his dog, then the caption would probably be the words 'Here is a man walking his dog' in the fictional tongue. Of course, it's entirely possible that the caption might be something not directly connected, like 'Everyone enjoys the outdoor life', or even completely irrelevant – 'Buy Sudso soap!' – but I was hopeful, and besides, it was all I had.

The first picture wasn't a man walking his dog. Nor was the second one. I didn't really expect them to be. But they were clear depictions of real, or at least fairly real, things. One was a small girl looking at two grotesquely fat people, and the other was a chessboard. They were not very good drawings but I had no difficulty recognising the subjects. In fact, these were images I was already familiar with. I even knew that the drawings I was looking at were inferior copies, or perhaps pastiches, of better-known drawings. Because the two grotesquely fat people were called Tweedledum and Tweedledee, the small girl was called Alice, and the chessboard was a reference to the framing device of a book I was familiar with from my own childhood, *Alice Through the Looking-Glass* by Lewis Carroll.

I sat back in my chair, mixed emotions running through me like several rivers. My dream of finding my own personal Rosetta Stone had come true. In a sense, this was the most extraordinary piece of luck. Despite the lack of textual information I had at my disposal – two partly blurred pages in a scanner – I now knew that, with the smallest amount of cross-referencing, I would be able to translate the bizarre language of the mysterious book into English, although there would be some linguistic irrelevancies in the form of some of the author's invented 'portmanteau' words. On the other hand, the text itself, now about to be revealed, was not what I had hoped it would be. I have to admit I had know idea what was going on, especially regarding the macabre photographs. I hadn't really thought about that, but I suppose I was hoping it would be something that would explain everything. Instead it seemed pretty doubtful to me that a copy of *Alice's Adventures Through the Looking-Glass* would contain any useful information whatsoever. Engaging and timeless though the adventures of Alice and the Tweedle brothers – here renamed in the caption in a way that set my teeth on edge, Alassa and Tradelidon é Tradelido – might be, they would surely bring me no closer to finding out what was going on.

There were more questions than answers. Some didn't puzzle me. As a children's classic, and a favourite of fans of puzzles, *Alice Through the Looking-Glass* (as it's generally known) has been translated into hundreds of languages, including Latin and Ancient Greek for the benefit of academically inclined idiots with too much time on their hands. It didn't surprise me that somebody would render it into an imaginary tongue. That sort of thing, pointless though it is, goes on all the time. It would probably be a vanity pressing, privately paid for (which would also explain the poor quality of the illustrations, almost certainly drawn by the person who had put the book together).

As to the book being something the girl – Carrie – would pick up, seemingly at random, I wasn't surprised about that. Very few of us would resist the temptation to look at a book we are familiar with, only to abandon it when we discover it's written in a language we don't understand. I can only imagine her reaction when she opened the book. I can see her now, in my mind, flicking through the pages, maybe a little amused at this peculiar labour of love, perhaps picking out a scene here, a name there, that she recognises. Then, getting a bit bored with a book she can't really read, about to put it down when she notices something you wouldn't expect to find in an edition of *Alice* – a series of photographs. Turning to those photographs and seeing not Victorian daguerreotypes of Charles Lutwidge Dodgson and Alice Liddell, but contemporary images. A dead girl with her face.

Thinking about this, I felt more strongly than ever that I had to help her. But my one hope – that the book would turn out to be the key to everything – had led me into a cul-de-sac. All these pages could do for me was help me translate *Alice Through the Looking-Glass* into English, which, given that it was already available in English and had been for over a hundred years, wasn't especially helpful. There was nothing I could do and nowhere I could go. I was a failure. Once again, Jacky shot for the hoop and missed. Only it wasn't Jacky, was it? It was the Mule. A dumb animal fit only for carrying other people's baggage up hills and through deserts.

I was feeling sorry for myself, I knew, but why not? Every so often a person is entitled to feel sorry for themselves, and God knows I had enough to feel sorry about. All this day needed was a phone call from, say, my mother, asking me to come over and spend the afternoon with her at the hospital and my day would be just perfect. That sounds bitter, but sometimes I wish she knew some people other than me who would always be at the end of the phone for her. When my father was around, they were always entertaining. I know, I was upstairs in bed at 6pm listening to the sound of laughter and music from below. And then my father went and my mother just kind of gave up. Her health sank like a stone – one minute tennis club, the next wheelchair – and all her friends floated away, leaving me as the one who was Always There for her.

As I thought this, I realised how bitter and ungrateful I sounded to myself, and reminded myself of the love and affection that existed between us. So, when the phone did ring, a few seconds later, I found myself picking it up and sounding pleased to hear her voice when I said, 'Hello, Mother, how are you?'

'I am well, thank you,' said A.J.L. Ferber, 'but I very much doubt that I am your mother.' I stammered an apology, but she had already moved on.

'I have been thinking about your query concerning the line on page 583,' she said.

I had no idea what she was talking about. Then I dimly realised she was referring to a translation in progress. I reached out in the direction of a heap of manuscript papers – Madame Ferber never sends attachments or PDFs, just couriers her materials over from Paris – and pulled out the dog-eared pages of *She Walked Among Men*. This was some task, as the script was the size of a young television. Riffling through the thick wad with one hand, trying to find page 583, I tried to tell Madame Ferber what I was doing, but she was in the middle of an uninterruptible stream of thought.

'At first I was quite angry at your suggestion,' she said as I dropped half the manuscript and struggled to pile it all back together with my one free hand. 'After all, the opacity or otherwise of an author's work is surely in the lap of the author, not their translator. But the more I considered the point, the more I began to see that perhaps you may have accidentally stumbled on a point not without relevance.'

So you're telling me I was right, you old boot, I thought to myself, although to be honest I had no idea if she was an old boot or not. There had been no public sightings of A.J.L. Ferber since the 1980s and for all I knew she could be a stunning woman of a certain age. I doubted it, though; anybody who talked the way she did, which was more like a mahogany cabinet than an actual person, probably wore fox furs round their neck and a black hat with a dead bird on the brim.

'In short,' said A.J.L. Ferber, 'I have decided that the answer to your query is yes.'

'Oh,' I said. 'Oh! That's ... that's good to know, Madame Ferber.'

There was a pause. I realised I was the one making it.

'Could you – it's been a while, you'll have to excuse me – could you refresh my memory as to what my query was?'

Another pause. This time longer, and clearly coming from the continental mainland.

'Really, I'd have hoped that you might keep better notes ...' she sighed. 'The query to which I refer is the one concerning page 583 ...'

'Yes, you did say.'

'Specifically the use of the word "reflected" in the sentence, "In that moment of plangency, Odile reflected on Corale for the first time, yet it was only in the calmness of her later years that she realised that Corale had somehow reflected on her." You recall now?'

'Oh yes,' I said. 'It's quite a memorable sentence.'

'You had suggested that there was some perhaps unnecessary or even unintended ambiguity about the use of the word "reflected".'

I did, and you slammed the phone down on me, you probable old boot. 'I remember that, yes ...'

'At first I thought your question came from ignorance, or possibly a deeper misunderstanding of my work, but I gave you another chance, and I considered the sentence and I think I was wrong. The word "reflected" is too ambiguous. It might even be that I simply failed to notice that I had used the word "reflected" in the first part of the sentence and then used it again to mean something else entirely. Please replace "reflected on" in the second part of the sentence with "influenced".'

I scrabbled for a pen and made the correction. 'Thank you for clarifying—' I began, but she butted in once more.

'No, it is I who should thank you, young man.'

And before I could fully register my astonishment, A.J.L. Ferber rang off.

I sat for some minutes in stunned silence. As a translator I've noticed that there are quite a few different kinds of silence. 'Stunned silence' is pretty big among the writers I translate. There's 'awkward silence', too, which you get a lot with the more modern writers. But my favourite kind of silence has to be 'companionable silence', as in 'they sat together in companionable silence, reading their books.' I don't know why I like 'companionable silence' the best, because if I'm honest it seems to be something you never come across in real life. You see a husband and a wife in a coffee shop and they're never sitting in companionable silence: they're either bluntly ignoring each other because they no longer have anything in common, or they're bickering about who has the ticket for the car parking or who's going to cook dinner tonight.

For some reason, these thoughts were in my mind as I took a taxi to visit my mother in hospital. After I'd mistakenly thought A.J.L. Ferber was my mother on the telephone, I took that as a sign, or at least a prompt, that I should go and see her. Also I had reached a brick wall with the whole book thing, so maybe some pleasant conversation with a family member would return me to the real world. I knew that my mother hadn't actually invited me to visit her, and I hadn't even called in advance to check that it would be OK to go and see her, but she was probably well enough to receive visitors. It had been more than a week since she'd had her fall and while the telephone call from her neighbour, Mrs Dreyfuss, saying that my mother didn't want visitors, had been clear enough, I still felt I should stop by and see her. (Besides, Mrs Dreyfuss was eighty-four and had a habit of getting things wrong; she'd once told me that my mother wanted me to bring her sandwiches and milk at work and when I'd got there, my mother told me that she was not allowed anything with yeast in it or any dairy. So I drank the milk and ate the sandwiches in the park before I went home.)

My mother is the independent type, I guess. She's had to be ever since my father went, raising me and running her store as well (she has a small shop selling kitchenware in town), and while the experience hasn't made her bitter or cynical in any way, I think any softness in her went out of the window the day my father left us. But she's quite capable of love and affection in her own way, as is amply demonstrated by the way she is with her dog, Duke. Duke is almost fourteen years old now and as blind and deaf as it's possible for an animal to be; he's still continent, most of the time, but whatever it is that my mother feeds him makes him so windy that his entire tiny body shakes every time he breaks wind. As I stepped into the lobby of the hospital and bought some flowers (an unscented variety, in case my mother's allergies had now expanded to include perfumes), I was looking forward to seeing her, and maybe passing an hour or so in conversation, or even companionable silence.

My mother was in a good mood. I could tell when the nurse cautiously opened the door to let me in and my mother looked over the top of her rimless bifocals and smiled at me. She didn't put her book down, in fact she went straight back to reading it, but I was just glad she was feeling OK. I gave her the flowers and immediately she said to the nurse – as I knew she would – 'Put these in water, please.' My mother, you see, has always wanted to live her life in movies and books, and in a movie or a book, when someone in a hospital bed is given flowers, she always says to the nurse, 'Put these in water, please.' It was, if I'm honest with myself, the main reason I had brought her flowers, just so she could ask the nurse to put them in water. And now my mother laid her book down and sighed.

'This really is the most marvellous book,' she said. 'I had hoped to finish it before lunch.'

There was, I couldn't help noticing, a substantial number of pages remaining to be read in the book, so unless lunch was being served at four o'clock in the morning, I doubted my mother would be finishing it before then. It was just her way of saying that perhaps I could have called to let her know that I was coming to see her. But if I'd done that, she would have said – as indeed Mrs Dreyfuss had – that she wanted no visitors as she didn't like to be seen in a vulnerable state. I was simply glad that she was so pleased to see me. My mother proffered her cheek to be kissed and then, as she always did, pulled her head away just before my lips touched her skin.

'How lovely to see you, Jacky,' she said, and I could swear I felt the nurse pause in her search for a flower vase, as if thinking, Jacky? That's no name for a grown man! Although I may have imagined it. 'And thank you for the flowers – no, put them over there, please.'

This time my mother's fondness for living in a movie confused the nurse, who had found a vase and intended to put it on my mother's bedside cabinet, which was the only flat surface in the room except for the floor. She settled for placing the vase on the floor and left us.

'How are you, Mother?' I said. 'You look well.'

'I am well,' she said. 'I just have this swollen ankle but when that goes down, I'll be going home.'

She raised her leg under the sheet, in an impressive display of muscle control for a woman in her early seventies.

'How did it happen?' I asked. 'Mrs Dreyfuss wasn't entirely clear on the phone.'

'Mrs Dreyfuss is never entirely clear on the phone,' my mother said. Then she looked slightly shamefaced. 'It was Duke.'

'Duke did this?' I imagined Duke suddenly lunging from his basket to savage my mother and found it hard to picture.

'I did it to myself, really,' she said, Barbara Stanwyck about to go to the chair. 'I was going into the breakfast room when I tripped over Duke in the hall. He never usually goes in the hall, do you, Duke?'

For a moment I thought my mother had begun to lose her mind and was talking to a dog that wasn't there. Then I became aware of a familiar odour in the room, something between old wet cardboard and the smell of a takeaway meal that should have been thrown away some days ago.

'You brought Duke in here?' I said, astonished. 'How many hospital rules is that breaking?'

As if on cue, the dog stuck his head out from under the bed.

'I told them Duke would die if he was left on his own. I told them he had nobody else and I had nobody else. That's why,' my mother added hurriedly, 'that's why I didn't want you to come in. If they knew I had a son they'd ask me why you couldn't look after Duke.'

'I can't look after Duke,' I said. 'The terms of my lease expressly forbid animals.'

'That's not the point, dear,' she said. 'And please stop doing your face.'

'What do you mean, doing my face? I can't stop doing my face, because it's my face.'

'You've been doing your face ever since you were a little boy. That expression you make. Every time we told you that you were wrong and you thought you were right, you would make that face. It's the cowboy trousers all over again.'

I had no idea what she was talking about, so I ignored her peculiar remark and looked in the mirror. I couldn't see anything out of the ordinary and said so.

'Really?' She sighed like Katharine Hepburn at a boring soirée. 'I expect that's because you're doing it all the time now. Is everything all right at home?'

I was taken aback. My mother rarely expressed concern about other people, in case it encouraged them to talk about themselves excessively. I could see the fairness in this, as she also disliked talking about herself, and to be honest, I don't really like to talk about myself anyway, so it worked well on both sides. But now she was asking me a direct question about my life, and I didn't really know how to answer it.

'Oh dear,' said my mother after several seconds, perhaps a minute, had passed. 'Is it a girl?'

'In a manner of speaking,' I said.

'Who is she this time?' said my mother. 'Another unattainable siren? You really must start dating women who you have a chance with. Of course, that would mean you might actually have a relationship with a real woman ...'

We had had this conversation before and I knew where it was heading. So, perhaps, did Duke, as at that moment he elected to live up to his name and let out a world-class guff.

'Then again, when you did go out with a girl, I was entirely baffled. And so, I suspect, was she. Didn't she marry your best friend at college?'

'That was years ago,' I said, moving away from Duke's mordant cloud, 'which reminds me. Did you ever hear anyone call me the Mule?'

'The Mule?' said my mother, Celia Johnson recalling a time long gone. 'I can't say that I did. Now that you mention it, you can look somewhat mule-like. I think it's that expression of yours. Anyway, please go now, I'm very tired.'

I was used to my mother dismissing me abruptly, and frankly I was glad to go. I didn't know what she was talking about and she was beginning to annoy me. In fact, everything was beginning to annoy me.

'Goodbye, Mother,' I said, kissing the air near her cheek. 'I'll call Mrs Dreyfuss every day to see how you are.'

'Call her in the mornings,' said my mother, 'that way you'll have more chance of getting some sense out of her.'

I got to my feet. I wanted to ask her about cowboy trousers but she was either falling asleep or feigning it.

'Aren't you going to kiss Duke goodbye?' she said drowsily.

'No, thank you,' I said, and left. There are limits to filial devotion.

Stress isn't a large part of my life, in fact it's something I've tried hard to minimise. My reasoning is this: other men, with families and large social circles, cannot hope to avoid stress. It's there all the time, from crying babies to work colleagues with a beef. But they'd say, I expect, that the bad times go with the good times, and they enjoy being in the bosom of their families or going bowling with their buddies, and so on. I don't have a family and I don't have any reason to go bowling, so as compensation for that I feel I should enjoy the benefits of a quiet life. I am, as I say, my own boss, I keep my own hours by and large, and the deadlines for translation aren't too strenuous (because when all is said and done, you're working on a book that's already been written, proof-read, edited and published in at least one country). Thus I'm free to live a calm life as a matter of course. I can listen to the radio (not that I listen to the radio very much), I can read (which obviously is something of a busman's holiday for me) and I can go for long walks or take holidays (I find walking dull, I have to admit, and whenever I go on holiday I wish I was home). At the end of the day, I'm my own man. My stress levels are pared to the bone.

But not lately. Lately everything seems to be conspiring against me. Even the out-of-the-blue compliment from A.J.L. Ferber was unnerving. In all the years I had worked on her books, she had never praised anybody. Mr Walker-Hebborn himself, who'd signed Madame Ferber to the company, was no stranger to the rough end of her tongue and had never received even the briefest word of thanks when he'd shown his faith in her work by continually bringing out her early, unsuccessful books until finally the public caught on and she became the profitable authoress she is today. And he's the boss. Everyone else was even more of a target. The woman who designed the cover of *There Is No Mountain* was woken at four o'clock in the morning by a furious call from Madame Ferber asking why there wasn't a mountain on the jacket of the book. When she explained that as the book was called *There Is No Mountain* she felt the image of a mountain was not appropriate, Madame Ferber apparently told her she had missed the whole point of the book and had her sacked. Distributors, publishers, magazine editors had all been the unwitting victims of Madame Ferber's ire, and woe betide the typesetter who, perhaps growing drowsy in the denser thickets of Madame Ferber's prose, allowed a typo to slip in or lost a semi-colon (as a writer, A.J.L. Ferber is to the semi-colon what Enid Blyton was to the exclamation mark).

And yet here was I being singled out for praise by the woman. It made no sense, and in my stressed state I could only imagine that she had some deeper, ulterior motive. Perhaps she was piling up examples of my cupidity (a word she was very fond of, incidentally) in order to present them to Mr Walker-Hebborn and thereby ensure a case for the prosecution so strong that I would never work in publishing again and would end my days teaching useful English phrases to Danish businessmen. Except I don't speak Danish. Clearly I was becoming too stressed to think clearly. I stopped walking down the street – I was too burned up by my visit to my mother's bedside to sit on a slow hot bus – and looked at my surroundings. There were two restaurants, a shoe shop and a bar. The day was passing and I had no work to do.

Three minutes later I was sitting in the bar, a large martini in front of me, and feeling very slightly better. I don't want you to get the impression that I'm some kind of heavy drinker. I'm not. I don't keep alcohol in my apartment and I very rarely go out drinking. But on this occasion I felt that a small amount of booze would erase some of the frustrations and irritations of the last couple of days. I drank half the martini and immediately I started to feel better. Who the hell did A.J.L. Ferber think she was anyway? She was just some writer who got lucky because she wrote big, thick books that take up a lot of space on the shelf and people like that kind of thing because they think they're getting value for money. Walker-Hebborn might as well sell her books by weight: 'Hi, I'd like some A.J.L. Ferber, please.' 'Certainly, sir, would you like two or three kilos?' 'Hmm, cut me off six chapters and let's see how we get on.'

The more I thought about it, the more I wondered why she was so popular. Because, don't get me wrong, A.J.L. Ferber was very popular. Not like the crazes you have nowadays where the charts are stuffed with some thick yarn designed to last throughout your foreign holiday, but in a more solid, long-term way. Madame Ferber had been turning out a book every couple of years since for ever was a kid, and she knew how to fill a shelf. All the books had important-sounding titles like *Earth Thou Sluggard* or *A Heavy Woman* or *Society's Elephant* and they were all pretty much the same book. There was always a woman working for some corporation who nobody appreciated, and she was in a relationship with some man who also didn't appreciate her. Sometimes she was in love with the man and sometimes she wasn't, and sometimes it wasn't a corporation, it was a university or a school or even a church. But it always ended with the woman rising to the top of her profession and dumping the man (who now realised how much he loved her). I had no objection to any of this. I've always found feminism rather sensible and I agree that men can be pretty dim. What I did find hard to stomach – and as a translator you have to remember that for me there was no avoiding this, no skipping the pages until the words THE END appeared – was A.J.L. Ferber's unique brand of philosophy.

I won't attempt to explain it here, because I can't. Suffice it to say that the books are a mixture of mysticism, communism, capitalism, feminism and even anti-feminism. A.J.L. Ferber's heroines believe in the power of the mind, the triumph of the will, the freedom of the masses and the superiority of the individual. They believe that women are equal to men, that masculinity is a superior trait to femininity, that love will triumph and that love is for sissies. In her long career, Madame Ferber has been accused of being a Nazi, a Red, a lesbian and a raving lunatic. Somebody once said of her that she made Ayn Rand look like A.A. Milne. None of these accusations, however, has prevented her from winning several prestigious literary awards or selling substantial numbers of books.

She has also, like most successful writers whose books make no sense, a large following of crazy people. You know the type, I guess. They can read meaning into anything, from a reference to early Iron Age religious practices to the fact that the author likes to use semi-colons (and, as I said, A.J.L. Ferber likes to use a lot of semi-colons). If the author's books also have a vague world philosophy and are filled with phrases like 'victory of the Power Inside' and 'overcoming the Soul Demon', then it's Christmas on Riverside Drive so far as these nutjobs are concerned. Which I imagine is also the reason Madame Ferber shuns publicity. She rarely gives interviews, there have been no public sightings since the 1980s and all her money is paid into a special bank account. When she calls me, the number's withheld, her manuscripts come to me via her agent, and that's it. Even Mr Walker-Hebborn has hardly met her (I asked him what she was like. 'Tall,' he said, 'tall and rude.') And now here she was telephoning my apartment to praise me. I wished I could have felt flattered but the whole thing unnerved me. I felt like someone who has a hunch he's going to be the victim of a prank but doesn't know what it's going to be, only that people are being extra-nice to him and therefore it's going to end badly.

Maybe I was being stupid. Maybe she liked me – but she had never shown any signs of liking me before. And the way things were going, she'd be swimming against the tide of popular opinion if she did. These last few hours had just been a wash of criticism and failure for me. A stunningly beautiful woman had run out on me thanks to my own stupidity, I'd failed to help her when I was arguably ideally placed to do so and I'd been roundly abused by my own mother just for having a romantic streak. Oh, and I'd learned that everybody calls me a stupid nickname. All in all, things were just hunky-dory and tickety-boo.

'Excuse me?' said the girl behind the bar, and I realised that I'd just said, 'Hunky-dory and tickety-boo,' out loud. If I was a character in a sitcom, I would have made the phrase into an amusing euphonym, so she would think I'd said something normal. But I wasn't. I was the Mule and I was feeling sorry for myself, so I shook my head, got off my stool, and was about to leave the bar when I saw something on the seat next to me. It was that morning's newspaper. I don't read newspapers very often, I find they contain pretty much the same news that's on the radio and TV, but today I hadn't listened to the radio or turned on the television. Besides, this wasn't headline news, just an inside page of the paper someone had folded to a middle page and carelessly left behind. But it was important enough to me. Under the headline MISSING GIRL – POLICE APPEAL was a photograph I recognised. It was Carrie, the girl I had last seen in a different bar.

I picked up the paper and left, folding it and placing in my pocket until I could get back to my apartment. Once inside, I took it out and put in on my breakfast table. The photograph was not one I'd seen – that is, it wasn't one of the images Carrie had shown me. It was a passport shot, in fact, and not a new one. Her hair was different and she seemed a few years younger. But it was definitely her. The text below the photo was frustratingly brief. It said that police had released the photograph in an attempt to get anyone who remembered seeing her to come forward. It also added that the girl – whom they didn't name, which I thought was odd – had been missing for a couple of days and 'concerned parties' were anxious to trace her. All in all, it was one of the vaguest missing person appeals I had ever seen.

I admit, my knowledge of the whole missing persons process is a bit slender. In fact, my only experience of it comes from the time my father left my mother. He had been supposed to come home that evening and when he wasn't home by midnight, my mother steeled herself to call the police who, while not exactly mocking her, did manage to suggest that it was perfectly natural for a husband to stay out late and not call the little lady to tell her what he was doing. In fact, the officer on duty, according to my mother, even went so far as to imply that if he were in my father's place, he too would come home as late as possible. But the shoe was on the other foot when, twenty-four hours later, my mother called the police again, this time entirely distraught, and they were forced to put out an alert.

My father, of course, turned out not to be a missing person in the strict sense of the phrase, in that he had simply decided to move out and was now staying with a friend (he said) in the next town. He claimed he had written a note 'which would explain everything' but we were never able to find this note. In fact, on the day that my mother and I moved out of the house, when it was empty of furniture and effects, I made my own search (waiting until my mother had gone on to the new flat) and turned up nothing. I now suspect any 'note' my father had composed never left the confines of his own active imagination.

So the situation with Carrie was slightly different, but it was still quite odd. Why didn't the report give her name? Whether she was called Carrie or not, the people who had reported her missing would surely know what she called herself. And who were the 'concerned parties'? The whole thing seemed to have escalated from a simple case of a girl going AWOL for a few hours into a concerted and urgent effort to trace someone who was apparently in some sort of danger.

And then I realised that I myself would be an object of interest to the police. I was, quite possibly, the last person she had seen, with the exception of the driver of the cab that took her from my apartment (and, if they were a different person, her abductor, if indeed she had been abducted. It was a very vague newspaper report). But apart from the matter of the book, which was still embarrassing to me as a breach of manners and good faith, I had literally no information of use to anyone, let alone the police. Admittedly, I had the notebook, but what use could rock group reviews be in a missing persons enquiry? There could be no earthly way that I could help find her. All that aside, I reasoned, I was a witness of sorts and the police are trained in discovering information that a witness may not even realise they possess. And, to be cynical, if the barman or anyone else in the bar that night were to come forward and say, 'Yes, I saw her, she went home with this man,' and described me, I would be more than a witness. I would be a suspect. Suspected of what, I had no idea, but a suspect nevertheless.

Finally, however, it was something else that roused me. Not my own possible involvement, or worries for my own self-preservation, but the photographs in the book. I didn't know what these images of the murdered girl were or how they had come into existence but I did know one thing: I didn't want them to be predictions of what might actually happen.

Finding a police station is harder than you might think. For a start, they don't look like police stations any more, but instead resemble offices of the most anonymous kind. There are no blue lamps, precinct signs or revolving orange light outside, just a small sign which the unobservant might easily miss. I didn't know if I should go to my local police station, or even if I had a local police station. The numbers on the police website were useful only if you wanted to talk to someone about noise-related issues (which were apparently not a police matter), community relations (which sounded rather broad-based) or to make comments about the website itself. I was loath to dial the emergency police number, because I wasn't sure if this was an emergency.

So instead I traipsed the streets for an hour or two until eventually I found a small, grey-faced building which looked like it might have been happier as a public records office or a library. One or two squad cars were parked outside as I pushed open the door, but inside there was very little evidence of anything police-like. The reception area was drab and there were perhaps a few more metal grilles and security doors than you'd find in a normal office, but this effect was offset by several garish posters that wouldn't have been out of place in a kindergarten or a community centre. There was nobody behind the somewhat battered front desk, so I pressed a small recessed switch in the wall, which immediately sank into its own rim and refused to resurface.

After a while, a desk sergeant appeared, as if by coincidence, and when I caught his eye I said, 'Excuse me, I have some information concerning a missing person.'

The sergeant looked mildly vexed, as if I'd accused him of not completing his tax return, and said, 'Stay there.' He disappeared, and returned what could not have been but felt like half an hour later with a woman police officer.

'Yes?' she said and I repeated what I had said to the sergeant. She looked at me with the same annoyed expression as the sergeant's, but instead of walking away, pressed a switch that caused a security door to open with a loud clunk, and said, 'Come through.' After a brief walk through some unpleasant corridors, she showed me into an interview room similar to the kind I had seen on television. 'Wait here,' she said, and left the room.

I took a seat and imagined myself a criminal lawyer. 'Say nothing,' I would advise my client. 'You can't touch him!' I sneered at a tough detective. 'My client has nothing more to add – good day!'

I passed several pleasant minutes this way until the door opened again and this time two extremely sour-looking people came in and sat opposite me. They were a male detective and a female detective and they stared at me for several seconds until the female detective said, 'How can we help you?' She had a name badge that said she was called Detective Sergeant Lisa Chick.

'I think I have some information regarding a missing person,' I said.

'What kind of information?' said Detective Sergeant Chick.

Her colleague corrected her. 'What missing person?' Chick looked annoyed, as if he did this a lot.

I showed them the newspaper. 'I met this girl,' I said. 'We had a drink together the other night.'

They said nothing.

'In a bar,' I added fatuously.

'This girl?' said the male detective, whose name badge I now saw said DC CHRIS QUIGLEY, which was also no help.

'It says in the newspaper report that anyone with any information should contact the police,' I said.

'And that's it?' said DS Chick. 'That's your information?'

'Yes,' I said.

'Nothing else?' she said. 'You had a drink with her.'

I don't know why but instead of going on, I said nothing.

'You see, we know she had a drink with some guy,' said Quigley. 'There were several witnesses. She was a pretty girl and people notice pretty girls.'

'The thing is, those witnesses said you left together,' said Chick. 'But here you are, and you don't mention that. So who do we believe, you or witnesses?'

'She did leave with me,' I said, looking at the table. 'She came back to my apartment but it didn't work out.'

'What didn't work out?' said Quigley. DS Chick looked at him, and he laughed.

'Oh!' he said. 'Oh, right. Well, I can understand that. You'll pardon me for saying, but you do look like the kind of man that things don't work out for.'

And they both laughed.

'So she left your place when?' said DS Chick.

'About one,' I said. 'I went with her to the taxi rank, to be sure she got a cab.'

'And did she?' Quigley said.

'Yes,' I said.

'Can you describe the driver?' said Quigley.

'I didn't see him,' I said, 'it was dark.'

'Often is, at night,' DS Chick said. 'Convenient.'

People saying that something is 'convenient' when it clearly isn't is one of my bugbears. I know it's meant sarcastically but it doesn't make sense to me. For example, in this case surely it would have been convenient if I had been able to see the cab driver, rather than not. The fact I couldn't see him was actually inconvenient, as I was unable to prove my story. I didn't point this out, of course. I wasn't going to draw attention to any flaws in my story.

Then Quigley said, 'So, do you have the book?'

I froze. 'What book?' I said.

'We spoke to the barman,' said Quigley. 'Jesus, who do you think we are? The barman said you came in the next day and he gave you a notebook.'

My hand went to my pocket and at once Quigley's and Chick's eyes were drawn to the movement. I had scanned in most of the notebook's pages and I could quote large chunks of the reviews of Carrie and the Legions, but I was reluctant to hand it over. It was a direct connection to her, something she had made, and I didn't like the idea of it just going into an evidence bag and then into a metal drawer.

'It's just copies of reviews of records and concerts,' I said. 'Some group called Carrie and the Legions.'

'It's evidence,' said DS Chick. 'We can jail you for withholding it.'

'It's hers,' Quigley said. 'How could it not be evidence? It's not yours to keep.' Suddenly he sprang from his seat and jammed his hand into my pocket.

'Shouldn't you be wearing gloves?' I said, but he ignored me and dragged out the contents of my pockets. There was a handkerchief and some coins, but no notebook. I had, sensibly, left it at home, along with the scanned pages from the copy of *Alice Through the Looking-Glass*.

'Very funny,' said Quigley.

'Carrie,' I said. 'Is that her name? Carrie?'

'You should know, stud,' said DS Chick, and she snickered. Then her face changed. 'You've got twenty-four hours to bring the notebook in or we'll arrest you for wilful obstruction. And we'll need your telephone number.'

Quigley jotted it down as I dictated, one eyebrow raised as if to suggest that even the digits in my phone number were ridiculous.

'Goodbye,' DS Chick said as she opened the door. 'I hope things work out for you.'

They left the room, laughing.

CHAPTER FOUR

A few minutes later, I found my way out into the street again, angry and none the wiser about what was going on. One thing was for sure: the police had as much idea as I did. While I doubted that the notebook would get them anywhere and they clearly didn't have any other leads, I had now made enemies. It was cold so I stuffed my hands into my overcoat pockets and began to walk home.

As I crossed the road at the traffic lights, it suddenly occurred to me that I hadn't mentioned the other book at all. While I doubted that police officers of the low calibre of those two clowns would have the ability to do what I, a trained translator and linguist, had failed to do, and make some link between the disappearance of the girl and a copy of a Victorian children's book rendered into an imaginary language, the translated *Alice* was as much evidence as the notebook, possibly even more so. By rights, I should not only have mentioned it but also brought the two scanned pages down to the station, where better qualified experts might have made head or tail of it. But I didn't, and I was glad. I was starting to understand that I had a personal link to this case – I felt odd using that word but 'case' was the correct description so far as I could see – and, while I was happy that the police would attempt to make inroads using their conventional methods, I had my own ideas, which certainly didn't involve a pair of flatfoots trampling all over my hard-won insights. Not that my insights amounted to much, that was certain. All I had discovered was that the missing girl collected reviews of a band called Carrie and the Legions, whose singer she may or may not have been, and that she had come into possession of a translation of *Alice Through the Looking-Glass* which somehow contained photographs of her apparent death.

On the minus side, it looked like I had nothing to go on. On the plus side, it was time for some food. I hadn't eaten since breakfast, I realised, and a hot meal might revive my exhausted brain cells.

'Are you OK?' asked the waitress. She was a pretty red-haired girl who I hadn't seen in this particular restaurant before. Like most solitary diners who regularly patronise the same establishment, I knew and was known to most of the staff. I don't know if they liked me or not – I wasn't a particularly big tipper because I'm not a millionaire – but they were all friendly enough and once, when I'd mentioned to a waiter that it was my birthday, they brought out a small bun with a candle in it and sang 'Happy birthday' to me. But tonight none of the usual staff seemed to be on duty.

'I'm fine,' I said to the waitress, although I wasn't. I couldn't decide what to order and the whole business of the day was weighing heavily on me. I'd never been humiliated by police officers before and I was beginning to resent my treatment – after all, I had been the one who had come to them, quite voluntarily.

'If you're sure you're OK,' said the waitress, and she seemed slightly offended, as if she knew I wasn't really telling the truth.

'I'm not fine, actually,' I said, which made her tense up, as though I were about to complain about the service or maybe come on to her (although how a sentence like 'I'm not fine, actually,' could be the precursor to a come-on, I wasn't sure). 'To be frank, I've had a bad day, and on top of that I have a problem that I can't solve.'

'Oh,' she said. 'I'm sorry to hear that. May I take your order?'

Clearly I had gone too far in my confidences. Maybe my voice had sounded harsh and bitter ('Modulate your voice,' my mother often used to say to me, 'you're very loud'). I gave her my order and she went away. I concentrated on the breadsticks and drank some iced water. A few minutes later the waitress returned with my soup.

'You know,' she said, when she had set the bowl down in front of me, 'sometimes when I have a problem and I cannot see a way out, I go and tell it to someone else and nine times out of eight, they totally see what to do.'

She stood over me expectantly and I smiled. 'So is that all I have to do?' I said ruefully. 'Just tell my problem to someone?'

'Yes,' she said. 'But it has to be the right person.'

I stared at her. Of course!

'Thank you,' I said. 'Thank you very much.'

'Not a problem,' she said. 'Enjoy your soup.'

I didn't enjoy my soup, because I gulped it down so quickly I burned my tongue and the back of my mouth. But now I knew what to do. I also knew why I hadn't done it before. A mixture of my own vanity – I can do this! – and a certain reluctance to register what should have been staring me in the face had combined to create a stumbling-block out of what should have been a logical step forward. You see, from my point of view, the translated *Alice* was, as I've indicated, a dead end.

True, it was possible that this version might contain crucial textual variants and reveal itself as an encoded cipher that would answer all my questions, but when I sat down and looked at the text, already recognising whole lines from the book even in this absurd fictional tongue –"*Contrazze!*" *dixizt Tradelidon*' and so forth – this seemed unlikely.

And even if it did – even if these two pages did somehow hold an encrypted key that would magically reveal all – how would I know? I was a translator of real languages. Real languages have real rules and, even if they do veer off into irregular verbs or grammatical variants that make no sense to a tyro, they're rules that work because they have grown out of the daily application of that language. So what if, for example, 'girl' in German is neuter (*Das Mädchen*)? It works. Who cares if the past tense of 'strive' is not 'strived' but 'strove'? Hundreds of years of linguistic evolution is on the side of 'strove'. Here's the bad news, Klingon speakers: your language isn't real and will never be real until real people use it in their daily discourse. Boo hoo, Esperanto – nice try, fellows, but nobody cares. When a language is fictional, its rules are nothing more than a big book of 'if you say so'. And with this text I had no way of knowing which parts were deliberate errors or clues. If, indeed, any.

And now you can see what had blinded me. My own arrogance. My own prejudices, which in my work were perfectly valid and even practical. But, in the present circumstance, my background as a translator had caused me to have a closed mind concerning anything of this sort. A book translated into an imaginary language is, to a man like me, a red rag to a bull rather than an intellectual challenge.

I was, in short, not the man for the job. But now a thought occurred to me. A thought I had put as far in the back of my mind as I possibly could. Because I might not have been the man for the job but I knew a man who would be. A man who, in any other circumstances, I would cross the road to avoid. A man whose self-belief was matched only by a corresponding pompousness. And yet he was the only person I knew who might be of any use in this extraordinary situation.

There was nothing else for it. I was going to have to call Euros Frant.

You may have gathered from remarks I made earlier that this was not a decision I was making lightly. Not only was Frant a person in whose company I was reluctant to spend much time – his table manners alone were bad enough in themselves, while even his eyebrows had repellent personalities of their own – but also he represented everything I disliked. I mean, not literally everything, just the things that I suppose I held most dear. I was someone who spent his life trying to bring clarity to books, making texts easier to understand and – sorry to blow my own trumpet – helping people who didn't speak each others' languages to communicate with one another. Frant was devoted to spreading confusion and nonsense, making things up that weren't necessary, and generally practising the science of moving the goalposts. If something didn't fit his world, he just made up his own explanation for it.

I'll give you an example. One time I met Frant in a café to discuss a particularly knotty section of his atrocious paper-filling exercise (I refuse to call it a 'book'). I had coffee and he had some peculiar purple fruit tea, and I wanted to talk about a passage whose details I won't anger myself by recounting in any depth, but it contained the words *yna Roisa*. By now I was enough used to Frant's garbled car-crash fake medieval gibberish to take a guess that *yna Roisa* meant 'a rose'. And when I put this to Frant, he confirmed it. Or rather, he dipped his head and smiled as if he were a great chevalier conceding a fine point to a vulgar peasant.

'But if this word means "a rose", then the rest of the sentence isn't entirely clear,' I said, as Frant removed his herbal teabag from his cup, squeezed it out between thumb and forefinger and raised it, unbelievably, to his nose. His nostrils flared copiously as he sniffed it and then let it fall onto the café table top.

'How so, "not clear"?' said Frant.

'Well, you've said that the rose, in this context, grows upon the waves of the ocean,' I said.

'Ah, that passage,' Frant said, and I was sure that in his mind he was being accompanied by a lute as he went on to quote himself. '*Yna Roisa sor lis ellas ondas della marri*, to be precise.'

'So if it's a rose,' I pressed on, 'how can it be growing on the waves of the ocean? Is it a sea rose?'

'No,' said Frant, his eyes narrowing as if in self-defence, 'it's not a sea rose, it's a metaphor.'

'Oh,' I said, 'please excuse me. What is it a metaphor for?'

'I should have thought that that would be obvious,' Frant said, but I noticed he didn't offer an explanation.

'I'm sorry, I'm not especially poetic,' I said, and thought for a moment. 'No, I don't get it. Can you tell me?'

'My work is not a riddle to be deciphered,' said Frant haughtily. 'It stands and falls on its own.'

He made his work sound like it was a drunk trying to get home from a bar. I decided not to press the point, but I did notice when I received the next draft of the *Chronac* that the words *yna Roisa* had been changed to *yna lilia di agqua*. Which I would have said made a mockery of the metaphor. Such as it was.

I recount that little gem not just to reveal the depth of my feelings concerning Euros Frant as a person, but also because I believe it indicates what to me is the root problem with Frant and his kind. They are frauds. I admit that Madame Ferber has her moments of shall we say obfuscation and I don't buy into her whole Inner Power of Triumphant Spirit hoo-hah, but compared to the idiocy and charlatanry of Euros Frant she is a fount of clarity and common sense. Also she at least believes in the stuff she pumps out, which to my mind is key in a writer. I very much doubt that Euros Frant used to sit down at the end of a hard day's *ellas* and *frondurondls* and goodness knows what else and say to himself as he lit a cheroot, 'Well done, Euros Frant. Today you have contributed to the sum of human happiness.'

Then again, maybe he did. The man was awful enough.

Either way, you can appreciate that I wasn't looking forward to calling him. In fact, when I got home, I discovered that I had actually made my views on this clear to myself by deleting all his contact details from my computer and mobile phone, as I soon found. If I'm honest, my actual address book is not what you'd call bulging. Sometimes I'm not sure why I have one, except that I have to write down the small number of essential contacts I do have somewhere. It's always a tricky one, isn't it? You don't really need a full-scale contacts book – there are always, let's say, going to be several letters of the alphabet with no names under them (and I don't just mean X and Z; I worked out the other day I didn't really need L, R, Q or T either) – and yet you can't fit everyone you know on the back of an envelope (I did try once, but as it was a used envelope, some of the names went over the flap. I guess I could have got some under the flap too but that's not the point here).

Anyway, it didn't take me long to flick through my address book, although I did do so, I must admit, with more than usual thoroughness because – well, what if the girl had written her number in there? We'd both had quite a bit to drink and while most of the evening is etched firmly into my brain, there was always the chance I'd forgotten or she'd done it on a whim while I was in the bathroom. But she hadn't. There weren't even any of those annoying numbers without any names attached, or penned next to a pair of mysterious initials, let alone a set of digits standing guard by the words 'CALL ME! CARRIE X'. If indeed Carrie was her name.

It was pretty clear, too, by the time I'd got as far as Y, that I'd never written Euros Frant's details in the address book. This wasn't too surprising; as I said, I didn't like the man and maybe I was hoping that by keeping him out of my address book I was also putting some distance between him and my life. I tended not to put important clients in a book I might easily lose – there were no details for A.J.L. Ferber, for example (I had memorised those, though) – but I hardly counted Frant as important, unless he was an important idiot.

I would have to go into the office to get the information I needed. I could look it up without anyone wondering why I wanted to get in touch with a man everyone wanted to avoid. I wouldn't necessarily be detained in chat or get embroiled in some minor but vexing administrative conversation, I could just pop in, get the email address and telephone numbers I needed, and pop out again. It was a simple plan, which was fine by me; I had no intention of letting Euros Frant take up any more of my time than necessary.

The bus into town was extremely slow. It crawled towards the next set of traffic lights and slowed down, as if the driver were peering at them in the hope that they might turn red and absolve him of any responsibility for getting his passengers into town in time for their appointments. He was almost always right, partly because by the time he'd reached the junction, they'd gone from green to amber to red. I balled my fists in frustration as the same cyclist overtook us time and time again, and several times considered forcing the doors open and jumping out. Eventually the bus found its reluctant way into the city centre and now, even though I was several stops away from my destination, I did alight, shooting the driver an angry glance that I hoped he would see in his rear-view mirror. As I walked away, the bus seemed suddenly to lurch into life and accelerated down the high street with alarming speed.

A few minutes later, I found myself in the reception area of Walker-Hebborn Publishing. I gave my name to the receptionist and to my surprise he said, 'Go right up, please, Mr Walker-Hebborn is expecting you.'

I was so surprised, I asked him to repeat what he had just said, and he did. I said, 'I didn't know I was expected,' and the receptionist looked at me as if I'd tried to say something funny and slightly failed. He buzzed me in and I took the lift to the fifth floor. Once there, I didn't entirely know what to do. Apparently I was supposed to be seeing Walker-Hebborn, although I had no idea why. Then again, I had come in for an entirely different purpose, and perhaps it was this that I should address first. It would only take a moment and besides I could go and see Walker-Hebborn afterwards.

In the end, the problem was solved for me when, as I headed for the room in which Walker-Hebborn Publishing kept all their filing cabinets, Walker-Hebborn himself came out of the men's room and headed towards me.

'Good day!' he said. 'I'm glad you got my message.'

As he turned and walked towards his office, obviously intending that I should follow him, I sneaked my mobile phone out of my pocket. I had turned it off after looking for Frant's details, but now, as it lit up, I saw that there was a message from Walker-Hebborn, asking me to come into the office as soon as possible. Reflecting that I was unlikely to be popping in or out of anywhere today the way things were going, I followed him into his office and closed the door.

Walker-Hebborn sat behind his desk, without inviting me to sit down.

'What in the name of God did you say to A.J.L. Ferber?' he said.

'Excuse me?' I said. I didn't like it when people sprang things on me.

'She's been on the phone to me three times this week,' Walker-Hebborn said. 'And every time she called, your name came up.'

'I hope I haven't caused any trouble,' I said, but I knew that the pompous old authoress had almost certainly decided to take umbrage at my earlier queries, and I was certain now that the call in which she had thanked me was either a smokescreen or an example of her possible derangement. Either way, my goose was cooked. I was clearly about to be frog-marched from the building with the contents of my desk in a box. Not that I had a desk, it was more of an image in my head.

'For a long time now, Madame Ferber has been a troublesome author,' said Walker-Hebborn. 'The prestige and sales her work brings to our imprint have always been balanced out by her difficult nature, which for some reason she seems to feel are part and parcel of the creative urge.'

'I have never deliberately tried to upset Madame Ferber,' I said.

'Oh, you don't have to,' said Walker-Hebborn. 'The slightest misunderstanding and the crazy old trout will be on the phone to me for hours. My God, a deliberate attempt to offend her would probably result in some form of world war.'

Walker-Hebborn, while he was joking, wasn't joking. Leaving aside the appearance or otherwise of a mountain on the cover of *There Is No Mountain*, there had also been an occasion when Madame Ferber had turned down a major literary prize on the grounds that it was only open to writers and she found that elitist. When it was pointed out to her that the only people who write books are, by definition, writers, and a writer is anyone who writes a book, she issued a statement defending what she called 'those who write without knowing that they are writing'. The next year, when her new novel was perhaps understandably omitted from the shortlist for the same literary prize, she told the press that she was glad as the judges of the prize were clearly 'against writing'. 'One either writes,' she announced to the world, 'or one does not write. There is rarely a middle ground.'

None of this was any fun for her publishers, who were constantly being asked to defend not just the indefensible but also the incomprehensible. Despite this, Madame Ferber was always threatening to leave Walker-Hebborn and sign up with a more globally noteworthy publisher; and from time to time, when her contract had expired, she had been seen with the representatives of some glossy multinational. Yet whenever crunch time came, the lawyers of A.J.L. Ferber were once again crowded into Walker-Hebborn's office, thrashing out contracts that half resembled the whims of pop singers and half the demands of fairy-tale witches.

'You realise,' said Walker-Hebborn, as if reading my thoughts, 'that A.J.L. Ferber's contract is once again up for renewal. With this in mind, we are very keen not to offend her. We have been sweet-talking the old maniac for months now with gifts and assurances. And the end of this week is the deadline for signature.'

I knew what he was driving at. Unlike writers who base their self-image on what they have read about writers in books (possibly their own books), A.J.L. Ferber was a stickler for deadlines. She would be silent for months and then, at the very last minute, deliver a novel the size of a surgical boot. It was as if she were able to vomit up millions of words in a single session (and some of her critics suggested that this might indeed be her preferred method of working). The same applied to any business deals. As a deadline for signing loomed, there would be silence from Madame Ferber until the very last minute, when she would appear in a cloud of lawyers and sign on the dotted line. But until then, not a peep.

Until now. 'She's been calling you,' I said, 'about me.'

'Yes,' said Walker-Hebborn. 'It's very clear that the present situation is entirely down to you.'

I didn't know what to say. With everything else going haywire in my life, the last thing I needed was to lose my work with Walker-Hebborn.

'I'm extremely sorry,' I said. 'I just wanted to clear up a couple of minor issues in the translation.'

'I understand,' said Walker-Hebborn. 'But I don't care. I'm a publisher, and the odd garbled sentence in a book means nothing to me.'

This was true. In one of Walker-Hebborn's early purchases, a novel by an Italian detective writer had been translated (by my predecessor, who drank) so hastily that the last chapter – the murderer's confession – actually made no sense at all. Fortunately, the murderer was an escaped lunatic and most reviewers praised the author for his insight into the mind of a psychopath.

'What I do care about is the contentment of my authors. And in this case, you have made Madame Ferber very happy.'

'I can only apologise again,' I said and then found myself doing a double-take, like a hunter in a cartoon when his prey taps him on the shoulder and asks him what he is hunting. 'Excuse me, I think I misheard you.'

'You have made Madame Ferber very happy,' said Walker-Hebborn. 'She told me she admired your work and your attitude. She said that although you were only a satellite of her planet, your contributions and your effort were all to the greater good of her work and her work alone. And for that reason alone, she would be signing with Walker-Hebborn again.'

There were people in Walker-Hebborn's office and there was cava in plastic cups. There was a toast involving my name and a couple of jokes about 'translating success' and 'talking our language'. I hadn't been the centre of so much fuss since I came off my bicycle as a boy, and even then nobody signed my cast apart from my mother. Today if I'd been wearing a cast, it would have been covered with more signatures than an important treaty. Instead Walker-Hebborn explained again and again to the people in his office how I had kept the wolf from the door by somehow luring Madame Ferber back into the fold. There were hints of a sexual nature and much winking until finally Walker-Hebborn signalled that everyone should return to work and then, as the room emptied, said to me: 'I hope that when Madame Ferber comes to sign her new contract, you'll be there to hold her hand, as it were.'

'Of course,' I said, although this was not a hope of my own. Leaving aside the fact that I was a translator and not a chaperone, looking after Madame Ferber wasn't something I felt I would enjoy at all. If anything, I would be more worried that some chance remark on my part might undo all the good work I had apparently and accidentally done so far. I must have said as much to Walker-Hebborn because he made a remark about me being too modest and not to worry and managed to suggest, without actually naming a specific sum, that there might be some kind of remuneration for me. 'A finder's fee' was the exact phrase he used, as though Madame Ferber was a rare document that I had unearthed in the course of my researches.

Which reminded me. I made my excuses to Walker-Hebborn and left. The key to the filing cabinet was on the shelf above it (there are some advantages to working in a small publishing house) and within seconds I was able to extract Euros Frant's personal details and copy them into a notepad. I replaced Frant's details and was about to lock up when I saw, filed neatly and predictably in front of his, a sheaf of papers marked MADAME FERBER.

I don't know if you are familiar with the story of Pandora and her box, a cautionary tale that has always seemed rather unfair to me, as poor Pandora was tempted beyond endurance to investigate its contents, and in fact I've always suspected was set up for a fall by her creator who did everything he could bar handing her the keys to ensure she would open it. I didn't feel quite such a temptation on this occasion but the coincidence of the news I'd just received concerning A.J.L. Ferber, combined with the appearance of her name right under my nose, was too striking to ignore. There was something I'd always wanted to know and now, unless Madame Ferber and I became intimates, was possibly my only chance to find out. *Carpe diem* as the Romans said, a motto with which Pandora would have agreed heartily as she was chased about the room by various emotionally coded demons.

There was nobody about, the office having decided to continue its drinking in nearby bars. Quickly I removed the sheaf of papers and riffled through them. There were letters from Madame Ferber to Mr Walker-Hebborn, some vexed emails and one or two angry telegrams to his lawyers. There was in short a wealth of correspondence, most of it headed with Madame Ferber's personalised letterhead – the address of her apartment in Paris and a fat-headed lion crest which she had claimed in some interviews to be the 'Ferber arms'. A crest is not the same as a coat of arms, but Madame Ferber could hardly be expected to be an expert on heraldry as well as politics, theology and philosophy. The address, I was interested to note, was that of an apartment on a well-known street in Paris, as well known as, say, Whitehall in London or Unter Den Linden in Berlin.

I riffled on through the correspondence, the fat-headed lion and the letterhead a ridiculous static flick book. Soon, though, not every item of correspondence was headed with the crest but every single one was signed the same way: 'Cordial regards, A.J.L. Ferber'. Several contracts nestled at the back of the cabinet and, while I avoided looking at their details, once again I flicked through to see the signature, which in each case was A.J.L. Ferber (Mme). The woman appeared to have no first name whatsoever. By now my curiosity had turned to slight guilt. Admittedly, all I wanted to do was find out what Madame Ferber's name was, but clearly this was something she wished to conceal and I had not done the right thing by snooping. What if I had found it out anyway? Would I have had said casually, 'Oh by the way ... Annette ...' as we sipped cocktails on a balcony? I very much doubted it.

Once again my curiosity had shamed me. At least in this instance nobody had come in and demanded to know what I was doing and this time my punishment was just knowledge of my own wrongdoing. I put the papers back, silently apologised to Madame Ferber, whatever her first name was, locked the cabinet, replaced the key, and left the building.

Sometimes I wish there was a kind of menu or screen you could use to plan or at least direct your dreams. Mine are always ridiculous and so far as I can tell would never be any use to a psychiatrist. Tonight's was no exception. I woke up in the early hours of the morning from a dream in which a fat-headed lion kept tugging at my shoulder and announcing that its name was Lizzy. The significance of this dream would not have taxed Sigmund Freud, to be frank. I looked at the watch by my bedside cabinet. It was 9am. I had slept in. I got up and toasted a bagel and sat down at my desk. The notebook with Frant's details in it sat by my computer, next to the absurd translation of *Alice Through the Looking-Glass* and the second notebook of Carrie's reviews that I had been told to give to the police. I was if nothing else amassing a small and peculiar library. I imagined myself vanishing and my landlady telling the detectives investigating my case that I was a man with few possessions and fewer friends, while they scratched their heads over the three disparate items on my desk.

This brief flight of fantasy reminded me that I had in fact a serious task in front of me. I was clearly starting to lose it as far as focus went, looking up people's first names in filing cabinets and imagining myself as a one-man *Mary Celeste* (I know that was a ship, and not a person, but you get the idea). I had work to do. I picked up the phone and dialled the number I had copied into the notebook the day before.

A familiar voice answered.

'Hello, Mr Frant,' I said reluctantly.

'Who is this?' said Frant. 'I'm very busy.'

I doubted this was true. 'It's Jacky,' I said, 'from Walker-Hebborn Publishing.'

'Oh,' he said, 'the *translator*.'

'Yes, that's right,' I said, ignoring the way he'd said 'translator'. 'I'm glad you remember me, Mr Frant.'

'How could I forget?' he said. 'That entire episode was one of the most humiliating in my entire life. Since then I have been entirely unable to write.'

At least something good came out of it then, I thought. 'I'm very sorry to hear that,' I said. 'Since we last met, I've strongly come to see just how good the *Chronac* is.'

'Really?' said Frant. 'That's surprising. At the time I seem to recall you had some difficulty with the *Chronac*.'

'I think,' I said, swallowing all my pride at once, 'I think that a work of the magnitude of the *Chronac* can only be appreciated by a select few, and even then not immediately.'

'Of course,' said Frant. 'I'm glad you finally noticed. Now, unless you've been asked by that moron Walker-Hebborn to tell me that his tinpot company is going to republish my book and promote it properly, I really must get on with my day.'

'I'm sorry to interrupt your schedule,' I said, picturing Frant five minutes ago staring at his telephone in disbelief as it made an unfamiliar ringing noise, 'but I'd very much like to meet up with you.'

'Why would you want to do that?' said Frant, and I thought I could detect genuine surprise in his voice.

'I have a problem,' I said, 'a linguistic problem, and I think – no, I know – that you are the only person who can solve it.'

'I see,' he said. 'Your alleged skills as a translator have deserted you, then.'

I wished for a second that I could reach my arm down the telephone wire and punch him in the face.

'Yes,' I said, clenching my fist around the receiver, 'this is a task for a genuine expert. Also the text appears to be written in a tongue I am not familiar with at all.'

'The text? You intrigue me,' Frant said. 'Very well, I am prepared to forgive you for what's done and buried. I will assist you for a fee.'

'A fee?' I said. 'I'm afraid I'm not—'

'You might have untapped reserves of wealth,' said Frant, 'but I do not. I am an impoverished scholar, and I do not farm out my talents for no recompense.'

'All right then,' I said. 'We can discuss terms when we meet.'

'Now is fine,' said Frant and put the phone down.

I had to go and make myself a very strong cup of coffee after my conversation with Frant. The man rubbed me up the wrong way in a manner that made Madame Ferber seem like charm itself. In fact, after a chat with Frant, I began to appreciate just how jolly Madame Ferber could seem. Her minor rudenesses and idiosyncrasies were at least based in a genuinely artistic temperament, whereas Frant was almost completely talentless. A.J.L. Ferber was an internationally successful writer subject to the pressures of fame, but Euros Frant was a dolt who nobody liked.

And in a short moment I would be spending time with the dolt. I almost considered adding a shot of whisky to my coffee, but decided against it. It might be more tolerable to be in Frant's presence completely hammered on booze, but I had a serious task to perform. I finished my coffee, got up and found the pages from the translated *Alice* that I would take round to Frant's. Just as I was looking up Frant's address in my *Streetfinder* – I know people like to print maps off the internet nowadays but it seems silly when you can just buy a pocket atlas and carry that around – there was a barrage of knocking on my front door.

I wasn't expecting anyone, so I slowly raised the sash window and looked outside to see who it was. Downstairs were Quigley and Chick, the two cops I'd met yesterday. Obviously they didn't trust me to bring in the notebook, and frankly I didn't blame them. I had no intention of handing over a direct link to the girl who might be called Carrie. But I had no idea how I was going to avoid giving them the notebook. I was clearly not cut out to be a master criminal.

Quigley and Chick hung around for a minute or two, pressing some bells and smoking cigarettes. Finally they ground out their stubs on the doorstep and left. I waited a few minutes to make sure that they had actually gone, and weren't lurking around the corner smoking even more cigarettes, put the notebook in a shoulder bag with the pages of *Alice*, and went downstairs quietly. Once in the street, I consulted my *Streetfinder* and headed off for Frant's apartment, which luckily was in the opposite direction from the way the police had gone.

I was a few hundred metres away from Frant's front door when my mobile phone began to ring. The caller's number was unfamiliar to me but I had a pretty good idea who it was, so waited until it had gone to voicemail and then played back the message. It was Quigley.

'Hello,' said his voice, 'we met yesterday at the police station. You have something that we'd like, a notebook. You told us you were going to bring it in today and yet here we are, it's today, and we haven't seen you. This is just a reminder to say that you've got twenty-four hours until we come back with a warrant. In other words, bring in our evidence or you will be a suspect in a murder investigation.'

The message ended and I deleted it. I didn't like this at all. It's one thing to avoid helping some police officers who you think aren't up to the job, but it's another to be accused of a crime you didn't commit. I made a mental note to visit the police station after I'd seen Frant – assuming I still possessed the will to live – and continued down the road.

I know it's an absurd thing to say, but the moment I saw the apartment block where Euros Frant lived, I disliked it. It was a turn-of-the-last-century building with art nouveau touches, all curlicues and curved arches. Normally I might have admired its design but on this occasion all I could think as I stood there looking at the front door was how typical of a man like Frant to live somewhere as fussy and overblown as this. I half expected to see a penny-farthing leaning on the railings, and when I rang his doorbell I was surprised to hear it buzz rather than chime.

Frant's voice came from a tiny speaker on the doorframe. 'Yes?' he said, as though he were constantly being bothered by people beating a path to his door.

'It's me,' I said, 'the translator.'

After slightly too long, he buzzed me in. I climbed the stairs, which smelled, to Frant's flat, passing several doors in a variety of conditions, from freshly painted to thoroughly kicked. Frant's door was covered in white wrought-iron work, like a trellis, and there was a fake Victorian coach lamp to one side, which had clearly been put there by someone who loathed continuity. I waited a few seconds for Frant to open the door, reasoning that as he had spoken to me and buzzed me in, he would be expecting me. When the door didn't open, I began to thump it softly.

After a while's thumping, Euros Frant opened the door. 'Don't bang my door,' he said.

'I thought you'd forgotten me,' I said.

'How could I forget you?' he said. 'We had a conversation only a few seconds ago. Come in.'

He opened the door just wide enough to admit a broomstick and I sidled into his apartment. Once again, Frant did not fail to annoy me. The apartment was decorated with what Frant would probably have called bric-a-brac (or, more likely, *bruc-o-brec*) but what you and I would identify as junk. There were reproductions of engravings of fishing-boats and vintage motorcars. There were paintings of vases and earls and spaniels. There were miniature soldiers and miniature cats. And over everything was the depressing must of charity shops. In fact, the place so much resembled a charity shop that I found myself picking up a particularly unpleasant porcelain cow and looking to see how much it was. All Frant's apartment lacked was a box of stained easy listening LPs. Perhaps he kept those in his bedroom.

Frant ushered me into a small back room which I assumed was his study, as it contained a chair and a desk with an old computer on it and a blotter covered in ink stains and the impressions of signatures. There were no fountain pens or quills in the room so he had clearly bought the blotter from – where else? – a junk shop, purely for the visual effect. Under the desk were several boxes, each containing, I could see, copies of the *Chronac*.

Frant saw me looking. 'When that thief Walker-Hebborn turned me down,' he said, 'I was forced to buy back the overstocks so I could sell them myself.'

'I thought they went for landfill,' I said.

Frant just stared at me.

'So, how is it going?' I said, sounding quite interested in the circumstances.

Frant cast a glance down at the boxes. 'There are issues with distribution,' he said.

I bet there are, I thought. I looked at an ormolu clock on top of a dresser. Unless it was wrong, I had only been here for two minutes. I decided to move things on.

'I've brought you something,' I said.

'Ah, the mystery text,' said Frant. Then he stopped. 'I've forgotten to offer you a hot drink,' he said, and looked concerned. 'Never mind,' he continued. 'Have you brought the item?'

'Yes,' I said, and took it out of the bag.

Frant removed it cautiously from the brown paper bag I'd brought it in and sat down at his desk. 'This is very unusual,' he said and took out a magnifying glass. I realised that instead of getting to the point, Frant had decided to play the part of a television antiques expert and was going to milk his moment in the imaginary spotlight. I supposed I should be grateful he hadn't screwed a jeweller's eyepiece into his eye. But I had no choice but to let the awful fraud get on with it.

'Why, it's *Alice!*' said Frant, as if greeting an old friend. 'The second *Alice*, unless I'm much mistaken.'

Oh well done, I thought, you've identified one of the most famous books in the world. I'm glad I came.

'*Alice Through the Looking-Glass*, isn't it?' I said, trying not to sound completely ignorant. Clearly I had failed, as Frant immediately corrected me.

'*Through the Looking-Glass and What Alice Found There*,' he said. 'To give it its proper title.'

'Yes,' I said. 'I got as far as identifying the book, but beyond that ... well, I decided to contact you because you're the only person I know who is—'

'Who is expert in *las linguas fantasticas*, as Jorge Luis would have put it,' said Frant. 'Who is not only cognisant of imaginary tongues, but is a master composer in them. You came to me, quite rightly, because I am the sensei.'

'Yes,' I said again. 'That's right.'

'You did right,' Frant said. 'Although this is a fairly drab find.'

'Oh,' I said, 'in what way?'

'*Through the Looking-Glass and What Alice Found There* is probably one of the most translated books in the world, as you may know,' said Frant. 'Along with its precursor – *Alice's Adventures in Wonderland* – it has been rendered into most languages, including Latin, in which it is called *Aliciae Per Speculum Transitus*.'

This still seemed ridiculous to me. Translating a book into a language that nobody spoke was an extraordinary waste of time. But then I was in the presence of a man who had devoted his life to discovering new and more excruciating ways of wasting time. I stood there, waiting for Frant to tell me something I didn't know.

'More excitingly, there are also translations of *Alice* into languages outside the normal frame of reality,' said Frant. 'I myself attempted a rendition of "Jabberwocky" into Elvish when I was fourteen.'

He paused, and I realised I was supposed to say something.

'That's remarkable,' I said. 'You must have been incredibly – precocious.'

'I was,' said Frant, 'I was.'

'And is that what this is?' I said. 'Is this *Alice* in an imaginary language?'

Frant looked peeved. 'I was getting to that,' he said. 'But yes, this is *Through the Looking-Glass and What Alice Found There* in what you call an imaginary language.' He stared at me. 'Have you brought the money?'

'The money?' I said.

'From here on in, you will be paying for my time,' Frant said. 'I charge a hundred an hour.'

I tried not to look shocked, or pull Frant to his feet and

knock his teeth out. Instead, I took the money from my wallet. Frant counted it, carefully licking his finger between each note, and then put it into his pocket without a word of thanks. Then he picked up the scanned pages again and studied them closely. He looked at the text, then the illustrations. Then he read a few lines under his breath.

'My God,' he said. 'Do you realise what this is?'

For the first time since I'd met him, Frant seemed genuinely shaken up.

'Well,' I said, 'it's a translation of *Through the Looking-Glass* in an imaginary language. I know that much.'

'Yes, but what language, man?' said Frant, still looking agitated.

'I'd say a mixture of Romance languages,' I said, 'with some suffixes and verb endings mixed in from Nordic tongues. It shouldn't be too hard to work out with an original *Alice* as a gloss.'

'You don't understand, do you?' Frant said. 'This is more than a silly children's book made into a puzzle for scholars.'

'Scholars' was pushing it. A bright teenager could have worked it out given a day or two. 'Then what is it?' I said, finding new reserves of patience to run out of.

'This is the key,' said Frant.

'The key to what?' I said.

'The key,' said Frant, 'to the Von Fremdenplatz documents.'

Frant paused for dramatic effect. Unfortunately I still had no idea what he was talking about. The Von what? The man was an idiot wrapped in a moron and I was beginning to regret bringing him my best clue. But I had come this far and I had paid him money for his non-existent services so I humoured him some more.

'I'm afraid I've never heard of the Von Fremdenplatz documents,' I said.

'No, no, I suppose you wouldn't have. They are hardly in your dull remit,' said Frant.

There was another pause.

'What are they?' I said.

Without speaking, which was something at least, Frant got up and went over to a bookshelf. He pulled out a big thick book. Instantly I knew I was going to hate this book. It was covered in gold filigree writing with big purple flowers etched into it, like a mishmash of a medieval manuscript and an Edwardian book about fairies. Frant handed it to me carefully.

'I shall let you have the joy of discovering the Von Fremdenplatz documents yourself,' he said.

I looked at the book. It was large enough, and a fairly recent printing, by a reasonably reputable publisher. On the cover were the words 'A VON FREMDENPLATZ CATALOGUE: KNOWN PAGES OF THE MYSTERY 194?–1989'. I skipped the introduction, which looked to be very much School of Frant and discovered that I was looking at lavishly copied plates from an admittedly gorgeous book. The plates were extremely odd. There were medical and botanical diagrams of an old-fashioned nature next to paintings of unnamed twentieth-century cities. There were photographs of fairly modern-looking men and women next to engravings of clearly mythical beasts. Medieval banners and ancient flags sat next to black and white photographs of board meetings from the 1940s. Tanks and biplanes jostled for space with crumhorns and astrolabes. The whole thing was clearly the random fantasy of a maniac, but it was curiously compelling.

To my surprise I found myself saying, 'This is beautiful.'

'Isn't it?' said Frant. 'And this is just a tiny hint of the wonders of the Von Fremdenplatz documents. Only the first volume has ever been displayed, and that only by special appointment. The book in its entirety – all six volumes – has never been revealed to anyone.'

'How come I've never heard of it?' I said. 'You'd think nowadays with all these silly books about secret codes and mysteries this would be top of the bestseller lists.'

'Not everyone is as mercenary as you are,' said Frant, who had just demanded money to take a book down off a shelf. 'The guardians of the Von Fremdenplatz are concerned with higher things than profit.'

'But still you'd think it would be better known.'

'Really?' said Frant. 'Just as the Voynich Manuscript should be better known, I suppose. Or the Rohonc Codex. Or the Emerald Tablet of Hermes.'

'The Emerald Tablet of Hermes?' I said. 'You're pulling my leg.'

'I never pull people's legs,' Frant said. 'I find practical jokes distasteful.'

An image of Frant putting a bucket of water on top of a door and giggling came to mind. I dismissed it, and said, 'These things you mentioned – the Emerald Tablet and the Rohonc and the other thing. They're real?'

'They are,' said Frant. 'Naturally, for a "pragmatist" such as yourself, rooted in the mundane, they are perhaps absurd. But I can assure you that they are in fact some of the most remarkable documents in creation.'

Frant pulled out another book.

'Sit down,' he said, indicating a crippled settee. I perched on the edge and Frant sat next to me with the book on his lap.

'Look,' said Frant, and opened the book with something approaching affection. I swear he was like a proud grandmother showing off a family album.

For the next hour or so, Frant let me into his obsession. I won't say that I was won over to his view of the world exactly – I'm too much of a realist for that – but for the first time I began to see just why he was so keen on this stuff. There was a book written in a script that nobody could read, with extraordinary drawings of plants and constellations. There was a stone with inscriptions that looked like they ought to make sense, but just stayed slightly out of understandability. There were alphabets that looked like codes, and languages that looked like picture stories. I had no idea if any of these manuscripts and documents were real or not, but in a way it didn't matter. They were exotic and mysterious and – something I would never have found myself thinking a few days ago – it sort of didn't matter that nobody had been able to translate them and work them out.

My feelings must have shown on my face because Frant looked at me in an almost kindly way and said, 'Now you understand, I think, something of what inspires me.'

'But what has all this got to do with the text I brought you?' I said.

He shook his head. 'You are not an observant man, are you?' He opened the Von Fremdenplatz book again.

'See this word here?' he said, and I looked. In the middle of a caption apparently referring to an engraving of monoplanes were two words.

La Furcheuxne.

'It's the same,' I said. 'My text and the Von Fremdenplatz are in the same language.'

'Well done,' Frant said. 'Now you see what I mean. The *Alice* is the key to the Von Fremdenplatz.'

'It's a Rosetta Stone,' I said.

'Exactly,' said Frant. 'It should be the work of a day or two to put this *Alice* back into English, and use it as a rudimentary grammar-cum-vocabulary. Once I have achieved this, I should be able to commence rendering the Von Fremdenplatz into English. It will be a major breakthrough.'

'I'm glad,' I said, and in a way I was. Frant could have his major breakthrough in translating made-up books from made-up languages. But I also wasn't sure how much wiser I now was. True, this was a lead of sorts, but a lead in the direction of what? I didn't know anything about these Von Fremdenplatz documents, let alone what they had to do with anything. But they were now the nearest to a way forward I had, so I said to Frant, 'I'd really like to take a proper look at that Von Fremdenplatz book, if you don't mind.'

'Not so fast,' said Frant, moving the book away from me as though I were about to grab it and jump through the window. 'I've answered your questions. Now if you don't mind I have a few of my own for you.'

'OK,' I said, though I didn't recall this being part of the arrangement.

'Where did you come by this book?' Frant said.

I hesitated. Frant noticed my hesitation.

'Normally I would not ask the provenance of a text,' he said, 'but in this instance it may be very important.'

'I was shown it,' I said, 'by ... someone.'

'Well, that narrows it down,' Frant said. 'Was that "someone"' in the book trade? Were they trying to sell it to you? More relevantly, why do you only have this palimpsest?'

'Excuse me?' I said.

'I'm no detective,' Frant said, 'but from the blurred nature of the text it appears that you copied it in something of a hurry, to say the least. As though you were trying to get it done, perhaps, before the owner discovered what you were doing.'

I said nothing.

'Never mind,' said Frant. 'I myself am no stranger to the tiresome restrictions imposed by privacy issues. There have been times when I have been forced to circumvent the irrelevance of who owns what.'

I realised he was telling me that he stole things, and nodded. I imagined that Frant saw himself as a kind of archaeologist and explorer all in one, as entitled to take what he wanted like some modern-day Lord Elgin, or that Tutankhamun fellow. I nodded, to show Frant that yes, I was like him, even though we were in reality as different as water and earth.

'I can assume then that you were unable to acquire the original *Alice*,' said Frant. 'But equally it is clear that you had access to it.'

'I did,' I said. 'But only for a short time.' I tried to look like an important thief, rather than someone who'd messed up badly.

'A pity you failed to retain the original,' said Frant. He paused, as if giving me time to consider my folly. 'Still, we have enough text here to begin our task.'

'Our task?' I said.

'Yes,' said Frant. 'You and I are in this together, are we not? And now we must translate the Von Fremdenplatz.'

I looked at him. An hour ago he disliked me with a mouldy fervour, but all of a sudden Frant wanted me to work with him. I was keen to pursue all options, true, but I didn't see how becoming Euros Frant's new collaborator was going to help any.

'You want us to sit down with that bit of *Alice* and go through your Von Fremdenplatz book?' I said.

'Of course not,' said Frant. 'This book is only a series of extracts, a gift-shop chocolate box for dilettantes.'

I said nothing, wondering how much time Frant had spent poring over this particular gift-shop chocolate box.

'No,' Frant continued. 'If we're to truly unlock the secrets of the Von Fremdenplatz, the mountain must go to Mahomet. A filleted copy is not enough. We need to study the actual documents, the originals.'

'And where are they?' I said.

Frant's eyes gleamed.

'Paris!' he said.

One of the words that Madame Ferber's characters are fond of using, in their peculiarly inhuman way of talking, is 'epiphany'. It's also a word whose meaning I never knew until I became a translator, because people in real life tend not to have epiphanies. Ferber characters have them all the time, of course, and are always telling each other that they're having epiphanies, like some kind of minor surgery. In fact, my favourite moment in any A.J.L. Ferber novel would be the scene towards the end of *Society's Elephant* – which despite its heavy title is in fact the shortest of her books, a comparative novella at 580 pages – when the two main characters have what I think today's movie critics would call an epiphany face-off. It's meant to be a crucial illustration of the difference between the philosophies of the two main characters – the arms manufacturer Kelf Matternicht and the ballet dancer Søren O – but it hinges on them both having their epiphanies at exactly the same moment.

Matternicht goes first, and explains that he has seen the light and will renounce his arms trading, all because he realised not, as you might expect, the effects of his weaponry, but he has become so wealthy from arms dealing that he has somehow entered a financially enhanced karmic state. Conversely, O has had both her legs broken by her ex-lover, a jealous strongman, and this has enabled her to see that the true dance comes from within.

All this would be confusing enough were the twin epiphanies not laid out in overlapping dialogue, as Matternicht and O seemingly try to outdo each other in a battle of freshly minted spiritual awarenesses. In fact, the scene is so confusing that some readers maintain that it's Matternicht who believes dance comes from within, while O just expresses some conventional pacifist views. As a translator, I can say that this chapter cost me days of sleep, and it has never been a surprise to me that *Society's Elephant* is the worst-selling of all Madame Ferber's books. But at least it hammered home to me the meaning of the word 'epiphany' and its lack of application in my daily life.

Until now, that is. Because for the first time in my life, as far as I could see, I was having an epiphany. As Frant prattled on about taking the train to Paris and packing for a short journey, the events of the last few days seemed finally to sort themselves into a coherent order in my mind. That night in the bar, where I met the girl. The return to my apartment and the embarrassment thereafter. The discovery of her notebook, and its odd contents. The report of the girl's disappearance and the appearance of the police. And finally, the revelation of the meaning of the *Alice* text, and Frant's insistence that we needed to take a trip to Paris to see his beloved Von Fremdenplatz documents. All these events coursed through my mind, sifting and correlating themselves until a pattern seemed to emerge.

And what was that pattern? Simply put, it was a tracery of nothing. A random set of images. Blind alleys and culs-de-sac going nowhere. If there was any meaning or direction in these events, I couldn't see it. If any of the things that had happened to me lately were clues, then I was too dim to work them out. And now Euros Frant wanted me to go abroad to look at some weird book whose connection to the girl's disappearance seemed tenuous at best and coincidental at worst. This was the nature of my epiphany. It wasn't a very positive epiphany, but it was at least entirely clear. And so with a sense, finally, that I was following the straight path of reason and that for once I knew exactly what I had to do next, I found a weight lifting from my shoulders. I was, in short, relieved to know what I had to do.

I looked at Frant and I said, 'Thanks for your help, but I've had enough. I'm not going to Paris.'

I hadn't felt this good in a long time as I walked down the stairs and out of Frant's block. Until now I'd been unaware of it, but for the past few days I had been gripped by a strange sense that I was being spiralled down into a kind of mental whirlpool, or that I couldn't control what was happening to me. This was absurd, I realised, because nobody had asked me to take this course of action and I had always been free to just carry on with my life as normal. I'd met a girl and she had disappeared. I'd been shown one book and found another. And that was it. The oddest thing that had happened all week – the sudden announcement by A.J.L. Ferber that I was now her favourite boy – wasn't even connected to anything else, as far as I could see.

And it had taken Euros Frant and his ridiculous obsession with made-up books and silly languages to snap me out of it. I doubted I would ever be grateful to Frant for anything, but on this occasion I could almost have shaken his hand and thanked him for allowing me to extricate myself from this situation. Now I could go home and carry on with my work and my normal life. I would capitalise on the new situation with Madame Ferber and talk to Walker-Hebborn about getting some sort of hike in my freelance rate. And instead of hanging out in bars on the off-chance of meeting women, I would start answering lonely-hearts ads or join some sort of club. That sort of thing.

Frant had looked displeased, although it was hard to tell if my announcement had given him fresh displeasure or merely topped up his usual permanent well of displeasure. He had made a few remarks about fair-weather friends but this had only helped to confirm me in my decision, as I had no desire to be thought of as any kind of friend of his, fair-weather or otherwise. I stood firm as Frant's eyebrows waved their disapproval at me and headed out of the door with, for once, a sense of relief in my heart. Now I approached my own front door with these happy thoughts. The rest of the day was mine. I would throw away the notebook and the piece of paper – well, perhaps I would keep the notebook, but I would be well shot of the *Alice*. Perhaps I could telephone my mother to see how she was and ...

I suddenly stopped in my tracks. Outside my apartment block were the two cops, Quigley and Chick, and they weren't alone. There was a large police van idling nearby with its lights flashing, and in the back sat three or four uniformed officers. I couldn't see clearly in the increasing afternoon gloom but at least one of the officers appeared to be armed. Chick was ringing several doorbells, and then someone must have buzzed her in, because the door opened and she and Quigley went in. The uniformed officers followed and I saw that what I'd thought was a gun was in fact a kind of portable battering ram. The inference was clear. Clearly Quigley and Chick did not believe I would bring the notebook in. Jumping to conclusions, they had arrived at my apartment with back-up and were now going to break the door down, an action for which I presumed they had a warrant. I wasn't going to hang around to find out, though. Suddenly my epiphany seemed entirely irrelevant. I was, in the eyes of the police, apparently the last person to see the girl alive. It was clear that the police had failed to find the cab driver and I wasn't even sure if they had thought it was worth looking for someone they probably thought had never existed. Worse, when asked to produce a piece of evidence, I had lied and failed to co-operate.

I could, I suppose, have handed myself in but something held me back. I was now an official suspect and, on the basis of the facts as I saw them, there was little or no chance of convincing anyone of my innocence. Quigley and Chick looked the types to secure a conviction for the first likely person they met, and as they hadn't exactly taken to me, I wouldn't have been surprised to be that person. I also doubted they could have solved an open and shut case, let alone the nebulous situation they were currently investigating. Plus I had the notebook with me, which made me look like not just a suspect, but also a bit creepy.

All in all, I felt justified in turning around and retracing my steps down several back streets until I found myself some distance away from the police and my apartment and was able to take out my mobile phone and make a call in safety.

'Hello?' said a familiar voice.

'Mr Frant?' I said. 'I've changed my mind. I'd like to leave right away.'

I waited for, and was rewarded with, a long and deep sigh.

CHAPTER FIVE

'I see that,' Frant said. 'I, however, am a scholar and as such am encumbered with the various properties of my calling.'

He nodded as if in approval at the green paisley valise and six or seven other equally unpleasant-looking bags and cases that were strewn about the floor. Frant had spent the last few hours cramming his collection of luggage with all manner of dictionaries, grammars, pamphlets and sheaves of paper he'd clearly printed from the internet. He called these his 'essential texts', though I doubted that the world would be in any way deprived if a brief apartment fire took the lot.

Frant finished locking the cases, patted his pockets a few times to reassure himself that he had his passport, his front door keys and his gold-rimmed bifocals, and then suggested that I call a taxi. I wondered briefly if he thought he might get an electric shock if he picked up his own phone, and turned to dial a cab number on the wall behind his desk. As I did so, I heard the rattle of a belt buckle being loosened. I looked at Frant's reflection in the mirror above the desk and saw that he was undoing his trousers. He began to wrap something long around his middle, and I realised that, for the first time in my life, I was witnessing someone strap on a money belt. I wondered what dangerous brigands and murderous footpads Frant thought we might encounter on the streets of Paris. Then again, he might just be extremely cautious with his money. On reflection, this seemed the more likely of the two options.

Frant closed up his trousers and I was able to turn around.

'The taxi's on its way,' I said.

'Excellent,' said Frant. 'The game's afoot.'

In all my time with Euros Frant, I never came closer to braining him than when he said that. Which, given what happened later, seems slightly ironic now.

The train charged across the sunny landscape, and I tried to look at the scenery.

'You might also have been tempted to make merry of the similarity between my surname and the name of the country in which we now find ourselves,' said Frant. 'Again I must commend you on your restraint.'

I had never 'made merry' in my life or met anyone who had, but I guessed that in Frant's world people were making merry all the time, when they weren't ringing the wassail or singing ho for the life of a woodsman fair. I wanted very much for this journey to end.

My mobile phone made an unfamiliar pinging noise which turned out to be a notification that it was now operating via a French phone network. A second ping indicated that I had received a voicemail message. As Frant prattled on, I asked him to excuse me while I worked out how to play the message. Finally I succeeded.

'Quigley here,' said the man about to smash his way into my apartment. 'We're very concerned that you haven't been to see us. Please do make the effort to contact myself or my colleague. In fact, if you're smart, make the effort right now.'

'Important call?' said Frant, clearly miffed that I wasn't hanging on his every word.

'Not in the least,' I said, and turned off the phone. I was out on a limb now, and there was very little I could do about it. Frant made a vague noise in his throat, leaned back in his seat and closed his eyes. The silence was by no means unpleasant. The countryside became less and less rural, and was now dotted with all manner of prefabricated sheds, power lines and the odd clump of houses. We would be in Paris within the hour.

Frant was now riffling through his man-bag in search of peppermints or similar so I took the opportunity to remove the notebook from my pocket. I hadn't had a chance to look at it since I'd called my ex-girlfriend and learned that I was known to her and all her friends as the Mule. Perhaps that was why. Maybe I was associating the two things – the notebook and the nickname. Maybe not. I'm no psychologist. I shook my head to empty it of irrelevant thoughts and opened the notebook at the first page. This I had read before, it being the review of Carrie and the Legions' first record 'The Future' (backed with 'Night Life'). The anonymous reviewer was extremely enthusiastic and appeared to predict great things for the band or singer (I'm not, as I said, an expert on this sort of thing).

The second page of the notebook was written in the same hand, though, which suggested to me that Carrie – if she was the owner of the notebook as well as its subject – had decided to copy all these reviews out longhand rather than go through the process of cutting them out of magazines. It seemed to me a laborious process, but people have their own quirks. For example, when I'm translating a book, no matter what the author or the compositor has done, I always put the first three words of the first paragraph of a new section into capital letters. I believe it makes the text look more elegant and, as nobody has complained so far, it makes me feel more part of the process of writing the book. I'm aware, obviously, that I'm not the author, and don't have the creative talents of the writer or writers, but I like to think of those three capitalised words as my own personal signature.

So I could understand why she had gone to all this trouble. Copying something can make it more yours, as well, as the words turn from the harshness of machine print into the rounded figures of your own personal hand. And Carrie, or whoever, had excellent handwriting. It was very easy to read and even its more idiosyncratic features – a squiggly initial 'C', for example, or a slight similarity between initial 'Q' and the ampersand – were perfectly legible in context. And it made ploughing through the rather shrill rock-writer prose in the reviews a lot more pleasant.

I began to read the second piece in the notebook. It was, as I said, a lot longer, and while it was in the same handwriting, it was clearly the work of a different writer, a journalist who to my surprise was much less enamoured of Carrie and the Legions' work. It also, somewhat confusingly, seemed to be a retrospective piece, suggesting that the writer wasn't commenting on something new, but looking back in time, and, to my surprise, treating what was clearly a pop record with all the seriousness and consideration of an important historical artefact:

CARRIE AND THE LEGIONS

Showtime? **

MAYOR KIM FORWARD RECORDS

On this, her first album, Carrie Legion showed but little of the promise of her early singles, shows and – if we're going to alliterate – sessions. The pros are, there was everything to play for for the sophomore singer, a sense of real possibility and the idea that anything could happen in the next 47 minutes and 32 seconds, and throughout Legion's voice reverberates with that sense of freedom – almost literally at times, as it ranges from the Gothy tremor of a slightly nervous Nico to the confident girlie trill of a Kate Bush or a Tori Amos. It's a lot to unpack, to be sure.

And that's almost it for the pros. There are a few echoes of what made people love the Legions – the unusual use of retro synthesisers, the reluctance to utilise any form of percussion other than BIG WEIRD DRUMS, and right from the off, that oh so Carrie Legion habit (it used to be an oh so New Order habit) of never putting the title of the damn song in the chorus. The first clue that something was amiss was in the album's writing credits. Where once all tracks were band-credited with lyrics all by Carrie, here was a new voice – producer and 'sound guru' (whatever that may be) Henry J. The enigmatic but heavy-handed J is all over these songs like a cheap suit, adding unnecessary keyboards, guitars, backing vocals and everything bar the fabled kitchen sink. And where once Legions' songs were both original and immediate, like hits you'd never heard before but wanted to hear again and again, now everything sounded – to quote one reviewer – 'awfully familiar and at times familiarly awful'.

That was, admittedly, a harsher view than most. *Showtime?* is and was a serious disappointment. Fans rarely discuss it on the forums and it's never found on even the crummiest budget reissues. Its only redeeming track is, perhaps significantly, a reworking of early Legions' B-side 'Night Life', which not only remains free of the drab bombast of Henry J's other work on this record, but contains a significant new lyric: 'The night is nearly over now / But still the dark is growing / I don't like where I've been somehow / And I'm scared of where I'm going.'

It's almost like she knew what was coming.

The review puzzled me, to say the least. Here was a writer saying that Carrie was possessed of a great talent – even I had heard of some of the big names she was being compared to – and yet somehow she had apparently lost her way before she had even begun, as it were. I also assumed that the two stars at the top of the review were not two stars out of three, but some larger number. Clearly Carrie and the Legions had incurred some important critical disapproval. To be frank, I wasn't at all sure what it was Carrie had done wrong. Surely the variety of sounds would be exciting to a listener, while the ability to create catchy songs that sound instantly 'familiar' is the hallmark of a professional songwriter, not an amateur?

Then I remembered the conversations my ex-girlfriend would have with our friends. They liked to sit up late in our apartment, drinking coffee and playing the newest CDs over and over again and discussing them as if they were important works of art or missives from the front line of culture (which to them I suppose they were). I have to admit I found these conversations a bit hard to follow, as I've never really been what you might call a rock'n'roller. In fact, I once said those exact words to my ex-girlfriend – 'I've never really been what you might call a rock'n'roller' – and she had to leave the room to go and laugh behind a door. I can see, or rather hear, the appeal of, for example, the Beatles or Beethoven, but not much else.

And that's at the quality end of the spectrum. Some of the music that my student acquaintances enjoyed seemed to me to be almost deliberately unpleasant or designed to be annoying. Men who sang ridiculous disjointed lists of words in the voice of an angry dog were particularly popular, as were women who keened abominably over acoustic guitars about their awful boyfriends, who often turned out, according to my ex-girlfriend, a fan of the music press and its gossipy pieces dressed up as serious analysis, to be the self-same dog-voiced men, who all seemed to possess the enormous beards of lumberjacks but were only nineteen years old. I didn't enjoy any of this music and so, when the latest CD by some hairy fellow had been taken out of the player and flung unceremoniously into a corner of the room (respect for the artist did not seem to extend to their actual product) I'd usually just say goodnight and slip away unnoticed as the debate got more heated and people began to raise their voices to one another.

Despite this unwillingness to engage with the world of pop, I still managed to pick up a basic knowledge of the central ideas and prejudices of our group. They had a very hard and fast set of rules about what was and what wasn't acceptable. There were some variants – the feminist students, obviously, disliked lyrics and imagery that were offensive to women (although they were always prepared to make an exception for any song that, no matter how spectacularly unpleasant its content, was 'just brilliant') but as a rule there were certain simple criteria for acceptability in music. Being 'real' was very important and while it seemed to me that every act was as real as the next one, I was told that some people were 'fake' and others weren't. Again, having a beard was a good indicator of being a real person, while wearing bright clothes and smiling was a sign of moral fraud.

'Not doing it for the money' was very important, too. In most jobs, doing it for the money is all there is. Very few of us are lucky enough to work for fun or as a vocation. Even as a translator, working in a medium I love, I often wish that I was able to read for fun, and not have to worry about rendering every sentence I read into a form acceptable to others. In music, it seems that the best artists are not doing it for money, but instead embarked upon an artistic quest whose fruits were more likely to be spiritual than financial. It was often hard to tell who was doing it for the money and who wasn't, as several of those not doing it for the money seemed to spend their time travelling around the world and enjoying a lifestyle far beyond most people's dreams, while those who were doing it for the money spent most of their time on unpleasant and gruelling television shows where they were shoved around like performing chimps.

The worse offence of all, worse than murdering someone or being an obvious heroin addict in the eyes of my ex-girlfriend and her friends, was 'selling out'. Selling out was a foggy concept that could mean anything from taking corporate sponsorship to – in some people's eyes – just signing a record contract. One of my ex-girlfriend's circle once organised a charity disco or rave to raise money for some worthy cause or other, and was immediately rounded on for selling out by other members of the circle when he charged a slightly higher than usual amount of money on the door, and so the event was a failure as many people refused to attend it. (I remember this particularly clearly as it was the occasion of another unsuccessful joke on my part. I said that, as nobody was going to the event, there wouldn't be any worries about it 'selling out'. It wasn't a great joke, or a popular one.)

And it seemed to me now, reading the review of *Showtime?* by Carrie and the Legions and remembering those earnest student chats, that the anonymous writer was accusing Carrie precisely of selling out. Clearly, the implication of the piece was, her decision to opt for a more commercial sound – and, specifically, to achieve this sound by working with this producer, Henry J – was a cynical move, a false step which, instead of propelling her towards her true artistic goal, had had the opposite effect and alienated Carrie from her true fans, who were presumably discerning people like my ex-girlfriend and her friends. Carrie, in short, was not only selling out, but also doing it for the money, and this was what had so vexed the writer.

There was another implication. I may or may not have been reading too much into the piece, but it sounded like

Carrie herself was unhappy with the way things had been going. The lyrics of the song quoted in the text were, to say the least, full of doubt, worry and, unless I was very much mistaken, fear. The final line of the review, too – 'It's almost like she knew what was coming' – made me uncomfortable. What exactly was coming? And did she know it was coming? I realised, of course, that there was a simple way to answer these questions. All I had to do was to keep reading the notebook, which was clearly laid out in chronological order, and the story of Carrie and the Legions would unfold in front of my eyes.

I decided not to do this right now. For one, I wanted to mentally digest the things I'd seen so far, and if possible see if it somehow linked up in my mind with all the other, equally confusing, information that had come my way recently. Thoughts of the *Alice* text, the terrifying photographs, and the fact that the girl – who might in fact not be Carrie at all, just a devoted fan – had disappeared (along, of course, with my own inadvertent role as an innocent suspect) were all rolling around in my head, refusing to align themselves and spell out answers to which I didn't even know the questions. Part of me also wanted, perhaps oddly, to indulge in what the psychologists call 'delayed gratification'. It might sound a bit perverse, but I found I was looking forward to reading the next instalment of Carrie and the Legions' career.

And part of me was aware that the train was now approaching the outer suburbs of Paris. Meanwhile, Frant stirred beneath his fedora and made little snuffling noises in his sleep. Perhaps he was dreaming he was chasing unicorns and other imaginary beasts. I didn't know, but I suspected that these noises were a prelude to him waking up, and I didn't want him to see me reading the notebook. I was keen for any interest in my business on Frant's part to be kept to a minimum, and so I put the notebook back in my pocket and waited for Frant to surface from the grumbling land of Nod.

I'm not particularly well travelled, which might strike some people as odd given what I do for a living, but the fact is my income doesn't often enable me to visit the places mentioned in the books I translate. And when I do, frequently they're not as exciting or interesting as the way they're depicted by my writers, which I guess is a testimony to the skill of these authors. I once made the mistake of travelling to Düsseldorf on the strength of a particularly exciting passage in a book called *They Struggle at Night* by a briefly popular German crime writer named Wolf Stern, who had made that city look like downtown Los Angeles in the 1940s. In fact, Düsseldorf turned out to be very much like every other large German city, full of clean concrete buildings with a city centre that emptied at six o'clock every night, and I soon regretted my decision to book a fortnight's holiday there.

But Paris did not disappoint me. Just getting off the train at Gare du Nord your senses are struck by a brilliant metallic tang in the air, a mixture of water and iron that seems to come off the trains even on the sunniest days. Stepping off a train into an unfamiliar location always fills me with optimism anyway, because there is no better place to feel a sense of possibility than a railway station, where people are always beginning new journeys and everywhere is full of the reality of fresh starts. That's what I felt anyway. Euros Frant clearly had a different point of view, as he pulled his trousers tighter round his waist, the better to prevent his money belt being visible to thieves, and tugged a valise with a retractable handle along on little wheels. I'd never seen a man less at ease with the process of travel. He looked suspiciously around him at every passing tourist, visibly flinched when asked to produce his passport, and repeatedly urged me to be careful as I loaded the rest of our luggage onto a trolley and pushed it towards the cab rank.

Once in the taxi, Frant became more relaxed. '*La belle France*,' he said, accurately, as the taxi pulled out into traffic. 'How I love Paris!'

'Have you been before?' I asked.

'Of course,' said Frant. 'My work is respected here, and I am often invited to speak at conferences and literary conventions. In fact, I have recently heard from a very reliable source indeed that my name is in the hat for a little red ribbon.'

I must have looked confused, because Frant shook his jowls at me irritably and said, '*A Légion d'Honneur!*'

'Congratulations,' I said, wondering what derangement of French culture could possibly result in an idiot like Euros Frant receiving any kind of honour from the government.

'Is this our hotel?' said Frant, peering out of the window. '*Arrêtez ici, s'il vous plaît.*'

The driver pulled over outside the hotel and Frant all but leapt out of the cab, leaving me to pay and to bring the luggage.

Inside, I found Frant surveying the lobby with a disapproving eye.

'Pokey would be the appropriate word,' he said.

'We're not staying for very long,' I said, 'and luxury ill befits a scholar.'

I tried to stop the words leaving my mouth but it was too late. I was now starting to sound like Frant, which was not a good thing. Fortunately, he didn't appear to be offended by what I'd said but seemed to be taking it as a compliment.

'You're right, of course,' he said as graciously as he was capable of. 'The ascetic life is always the most appropriate. Come, to our rooms.'

I was amused that he had assumed I could afford separate rooms. In this case, though, he was right; money was for once no object and there was no way in hell I was bunking up with this maniac. Declining the offer of a porter, I shoved our luggage into a lift and we went up.

My room was not attractive. There was a single bed, a bedside table made out of a curved piece of white plastic that was covered in melted troughs where previous occupants had used it as an ashtray, a plywood desk and a television that, for reasons known only to the management, was bolted to the wall in the furthest corner of the room just under the ceiling, and therefore required the user to operate it by raising the remote control in a form of a Hitler salute and clicking it, or would have done had the batteries not expired some time ago. The shower, toilet and washbasin were also moulded from one piece of plastic, and appeared to have suffered grenade damage at some point in the recent past. There was no chair. My one consolation was that Frant's room would be identical. Indeed, a minute or so after I had inspected my surroundings, I could hear him on the phone to reception, demanding a better room with – if his muffled swearing was anything to go by – no success.

I began to unpack. I had scarcely tipped the contents of my bag onto the bed when there was a furious knocking at the door. I opened it and Frant squeezed his way angrily past me and dumped himself like the contents of a trash can onto the bed.

'Your room is much nicer than mine,' he said, which was such an enormous lie that for a moment I imagined him in a bare cupboard, or perhaps an iron maiden.

'All the rooms in this price range are identical,' I said calmly. 'Could you please not sit on the bed, I'm trying to unpack.'

Frant stood up and moved towards the window, which offered a fine view of a nearby office block's heating system.

'This hotel is insufferable,' he said after a while. Clearly he had tired of the ascetic life.

'I agree it's not particularly pleasant,' I said. 'Give me five minutes and we can go to a bar.'

Frant brightened so much at this that I wondered if he might be a drunk. If so, I bet he was a mean drunk. 'There's an excellent place two streets from here,' he said, and gave me the name. 'I'll see you there.'

I finished unpacking my clothes and put my toothpaste and toothbrush in the bathroom. I hadn't brought any soap or shampoo, but the hotel had provided two tiny bottles of what smelled like solvent, so I guessed I could make do with those. I was about to leave the room when I saw the notebook had fallen onto the floor. I bent down and picked it up and was about to put it into a drawer when it occurred to me that it might be better to keep the notebook with me. I was sure even the most dedicated hotel room thief would be unlikely to steal an old notebook, but there was always a chance a cleaner might throw the book away, if, that is, this hotel employed a cleaner.

Before I left the room – I was in no hurry to meet Frant in a bar, reasoning that five minutes not enduring his company was five minutes well spent – I sat on the edge of the bed and opened the notebook once again. I had not yet puzzled out the significance of the first two reviews, and another thought had occurred to me: why had I been unable to find anything about Carrie and the Legions on the internet, when the reviews I'd read suggested that the band were at least worth noticing? I wondered if perhaps these were regional articles or – more likely – pieces from a college magazine. The student papers I'd seen in my own university days had been hotbeds of opinion, testing grounds for would-be writers of the future.

And they would, thinking about it, be less likely to end up reproduced on the internet.

I was slightly disappointed by the results of my logic. If all Carrie's reputation amounted to was some favourable notices in college papers, then perhaps the 'success' alluded to was entirely minuscule. I don't know why, but I realised I couldn't help hoping that Carrie, whatever her music was like, was a talented person whose abilities had been recognised. The reviews certainly seemed to say as much. I decided that as soon as I was able to go online again – my laptop was presumably now in the hands of the police, its hard disk scoured for evidence of murder, and I couldn't get my mobile phone to surf the net in France – I would redouble my efforts to find out more about Carrie and the Legions. But for now, I felt slightly let down by the notebook. Once it had promised me a thrilling tale of either rags to riches or decline and fall, but now it was looking like nothing more than some student posturing. Nevertheless, curiosity is a powerful force and, disappointed though I was, I decided I should stick to my guns and read on in the notebook, so I opened it at the place I had carefully marked with my train ticket stub and turned to the next page. What I saw there transfixed me.

It was a transcription of a press advert. At the top were the words 'THE SONG EVERYBODY'S TALKING ABOUT'. Beneath that were some quotes, presumably from various critics. One said, 'Remarkable', another, 'The tour de force to end all tour de forces'. I mistook the third for a censored obscenity until I realised that '****' was just a score. Beneath these accolades was a photograph which I recognised instantly. Lying on a bed, a rose on her chest and a gun by her side, was the girl I had met in the bar that night. I knew the photograph because she had shown it to me; it was one of the images in her book, the translated *Alice*.

Underneath the photograph was a caption. 'THE MURDERED GIRL', it said, 'THE BRAND NEW RELEASE BY CARRIE AND THE LEGIONS.'

I must have sat on the bed for a few minutes. I would probably have sat there for an hour or more had my phone not begun to trill out its new European ringtone. I woke from my stunned state and answered. It was Frant, with the full address of the bar, which he pronounced in a French accent so exaggerated that I had to ask him to repeat it several times. Eventually, we achieved mutual comprehension and I found I had shaken myself out of my trance-like state.

There was nothing to be done about this shocking image that I wasn't already doing. I was in Paris, the apparent current resting place of my only clue to the whole business of the girl and her disappearance. I still had no idea if what I was doing was right – in fact, I had no idea what I was doing – but the sooner I saw this Von Fremdenplatz book and was able to work out what connection, if any, it had to events, the better. I put the notebook back in my pocket and left the hotel room.

The bar was a lot further away than I had anticipated, and I suspected that Frant did not really know where he was. Unfamiliar cities are easy to get lost in, and one part of Paris – bar, boulangerie, café, bar – can look remarkably like another. I must have walked for about half an hour before I found the place Frant meant, having first picked up a small and annoyingly uninformative tourist map of the city.

Frant was on a stool at the counter. I knew why he was doing this, but he was still keen to tell me.

'I am sitting here because they charge more at a table,' he said. 'This is a traditional Parisian zinc and I don't want to be treated like a tourist.'

As he had placed his fedora on the next stool and removed his brown paisley scarf, I surmised that he was at least making the effort to look more normal, but it wasn't entirely successful. True, he resembled no tourist I had ever seen, unless he was a tourist who was also a poet who dressed in the dark. To fit in even more, Frant was drinking something purple. I didn't ask him what it was, because I was afraid he might tell me, so I ordered a beer for myself and sat down next to the fedora.

'Why are you here?' said Frant suddenly.

'I beg your pardon?' I said. The question had taken me by surprise. Not only was it somewhat direct, but also Frant had never expressed an interest in my motives before.

'The question is a simple one,' said Frant. 'Why are you here? *Pourquoi êtes-vous ici?* Why have you come to Paris?'

'For the same reason as you,' I said.

Frant looked at me quizzically. 'Really?' he said. 'I am here because of a scholarly interest in the Von Fremdenplatz documents. As an author of fabulist texts, this quest pertains directly to my own interests. The text that came into your hands – a text, moreover, whose acquisition you have not fully accounted for – is germane to my work and, if I am successful in using it as a key to the Von Fremdenplatz, will help to secure me my rightful place in the world.'

He paused to sip his purple drink. 'You, however, have none of these motives,' he continued. 'You are a hack translator, a man whose interest in words is entirely pecuniary. Where I bring imagination and creativity to the world of language, you merely offer the workaday skills of a drudge. And yet you have left the security of your ordinary life for this undertaking. Again, I must ask you – why are you here?'

Frant did have a point. There was no way I was going to tell him the truth, obviously, but now I came to think of it, it must seem peculiar from his point of view that I had decided to accompany him. I was sure, too, that Frant must be aware from our previous work together on his awful *Chronac* that I wasn't a fan of his made-up languages and silly fantasies. I knew he was vain enough not to heed any slights but that didn't mean he wouldn't have registered them on some semi-conscious level.

'I agree that I am only a translator,' I said, 'and I acknowledge that I don't have your creative gift. But this whole business strikes me as a once-in-a-lifetime opportunity.'

'How so?' said Frant, and his eyes narrowed slightly.

'The credit for connecting the *Alice* text to the Von Fremdenplatz documents is entirely yours,' I said. 'And the task of translating the Von Fremdenplatz is one I can only assist with. But that said, the discovery of the *Alice* text is mine alone.'

Frant's eyes had now narrowed so much they looked like a snowman's, two little bits of coal under his idiotic eyebrows. I knew I had him now.

'So you mean to profit from this venture,' he said. 'Your once-in-a-lifetime opportunity is an opportunity, in your eyes, to ride on my coat-tails.'

I didn't mention that without me he would still be sitting in his weird apartment surrounded by boxes of unsold books, nor that I was sure he had his own well-developed financial instincts. But if I could make him believe that I was here solely to profit from his genius, that was all well and good. The truth was none of his business.

'I just want to help,' I said disingenuously.

'Very well,' said Frant. 'I'm sure some crumbs from the table will fall in your lap in due course.'

He gave me a disapproving look and the subject was closed. I decided to move on.

'So what's the plan?' I said. 'Shall we go to wherever the Von Fremdenplatz is and have a look at it tomorrow morning?'

Frant gave me a peculiar look. 'You are clearly not well versed in this sort of thing,' he said. 'You cannot just "go and have a look" at the Von Fremdenplatz. That would be like saying that anyone who wishes can just walk in off the street and go and have a look at the *Mona Lisa*.'

'You can just walk in off the street and go and have a look at the *Mona Lisa*,' I said. 'It's in the Louvre.'

Frant pursed his lips into a fishy pout.

'Well, then, the Von Fremdenplatz is clearly more special than the *Mona Lisa*,' he said. 'For a start, it isn't in the middle of some sweaty public gallery for everyone to gawp at. It is not on public display at all.'

'Where is it then?' I said. 'In a private collection?'

'No,' said Frant, then, having actually taken in what I had said, 'Yes, it is in a private collection. It can be seen, but it must be viewed by appointment only. And even then only those with the appropriate professional qualifications will be successful in their application. It took me several hours on the telephone to convince the relevant authorities of the sincerity and importance of my visit.'

'OK,' I said, wondering what the big deal was. The Von Fremdenplatz was just some made-up item after all, with no actual historical or artistic value.

Frant must have sensed what I was thinking because he came out of his huff to say, 'I realise that for the likes of you, for whom all art must be pre-delivered cut and dried, a masterwork such as the Von Fremdenplatz is an unknowable quantity. After all, it has no famous name on the cover, no reviews from high-faluting critics, and has not been accepted by one of the so-called major publishing houses.'

I suspected from the strain in Frant's voice as he all

but spat out his words that he was thinking not so much of the Von Fremdenplatz as his own, even more obscure, unknowable quantities.

'But how can it be a work of art if nobody knows what it is?' I said. 'Yes, it could be a masterpiece as you say, but it could equally be some random nonsense.'

Frant's expression soured. 'Some random nonsense?' he squealed, his face almost as purple as his drink. 'Some random nonsense?! Look!'

He pulled out some sheets of paper from his jacket. They were computer-printed excerpts from the Von Fremdenplatz.

'Observe the wealth of detail!' he all but shouted. 'Realise the effort that has gone into this! Oh, it might be random nonsense to a plodder like you, but to the discerning eye this is a significant contribution to art and culture!'

I took one of the sheets of paper from his trembling fingers. 'To the undiscerning eye,' I said, 'it appears to be a mishmash of old photographs and paintings, with funny writing underneath.'

Frant went up another shade on the purple spectrum. 'All art is useless!' he shouted. 'Oscar Wilde said that!' Signalling for another drink, he turned away from me. I shrugged inwardly – a moment's peace and quiet, however fraught, was always welcome – and studied the print-outs again. There were footnotes appended by a third party, which fortunately for my sanity were written in a real language. While favourable to the Von Fremdenplatz, they were also written calmly and clearly, and made no claims for the documents to be a cornerstone of Western civilisation or anything like that. The anonymous author did, however, make several points in the documents' favour. They drew the reader's attention to the quality of paper used, the attention to detail, and the sheer epic nature of the work – apparently the documents were over 1000 pages long, with a style and orthography both more consistent than that used in the King James Bible.

Even if it was, as I had suggested to Frant, complete nonsense from start to finish, it was complete nonsense on a scale that was both highly professional and almost luxurious in its scope. I could see the appeal of the documents, and how their mysterious nature and – I supposed I had to admit – peculiar beauty might cause people to become fascinated with them. Much to my surprise, I found that I was looking forward to seeing the Von Fremdenplatz documents. I said as much to the back of Frant's head, and was rewarded with a grunt.

A few seconds later, he turned around and said, 'I suppose even a philistine can see the attraction of a diamond in the dust.'

'Yes, quite,' I said. 'Now it's getting late. Shall we go back to the hotel and get some rest?'

'I was just about to suggest that,' said Frant. 'I shall telephone the institute tomorrow morning and confirm our appointment.'

I couldn't be bothered to ask him what 'the institute' was, and anyway I guessed I would be finding out for myself in the morning, so I finished my drink and paid up (Frant's money belt was obviously inaccessible at that moment).

We left the bar and walked down the street back towards our hotel. Frant had clearly decided to forgive me for my earlier remarks and was in an effusive mood, probably because he'd had a lot of purple drinks.

'Do you know what the French call this time of night?' he asked.

I assumed he was being rhetorical and hadn't just forgotten what I did for a living. I must have been right, because almost without a pause he answered himself.

'*Le crépuscule*,' he said. 'Such an odd word, don't you think? It does double duty for both "sunrise" and "sunset", which suggests to me not so much a linguistic idleness on the part of *les Français* as a typically Gallic indifference to an irrelevant distinction. The French are saying, it seems to me, that it makes no odds whether *le crépuscule* occurs at day's end or its beginning. What concerns them it is its intrinsic nature, which is itself contained in the word *crépuscule*, a shadowy, sinister-sounding combination of syllables to my ears.'

I agreed with him about the sunset part, but found it hard to see anything sinister in sunrise, which generally gives way, as its name suggests, to the arrival of the sun and the removal of shadows. But he was enjoying himself and wasn't actually insulting me, so I let him burble on all the way back to the hotel, where he hiccuped, tipped his fedora to me, and said goodnight.

I wasn't particularly tired, so I asked at reception if there was a bar in the hotel. The concierge jerked a finger in the direction of a tiny corner with a potted plant and some tables, and I went over and ordered a martini. I still had the Von Fremdenplatz print-out in my jacket and so I sat down at a small table and flattened them out in front of me. Creased and blurry from Frant's cheap printer, the images on the sheets of paper before me were still impressive in their range and imaginative scope. I couldn't imagine what sort of person would devote years of their life to putting something like this together – and it would clearly have to be years, judging by both the quantity and the quality of the documents.

The print-out was folded in an article from the institute's website about the origins of the Von Fremdenplatz documents. The facts, if that's the right word to describe something so vastly imaginary, were fairly simple. A German professor of linguistics, visiting colleagues at the University of Rouen, was looking for a book in the library there when his eye was caught by a misfiled volume on a low shelf. The book's German title had attracted him and when he removed it from the shelf, he discovered that the volume was not a scholarly or linguistic title at all, but a collection of peculiar images, bizarrely juxtaposed, and linked only by a text in a language he could not recognise. The book had no title as such, only the words VON FREMDENPLATZ embossed on the spine in gold letters. When the professor showed the book to a librarian, she denied all knowledge of it and produced evidence in the form of its apparent absence from the university's library catalogue and database.

The professor claimed the orphan volume and showed it to his friends who, like him, were both puzzled and intrigued by it. They too had no idea what the language was – it clearly had roots in both Romance and Germanic tongues, but its grammar was chaotic and seemingly random and there were other aspects, too, that made translation impossible. For example, there was a great deal of unusual repetition – in one fifteen-word sentence the word *hevlént* appears nine times; this word does not occur anywhere else in the book. Words like *est* and the one I remembered when I saw the *Alice* in the bar, *sunt*, which are normally indicators of the verb 'to be' in many languages, were dotted about in places where no verb should be. Six pictures on the same page – two of different kinds of eagle, one of a ruined castle, two photographs of what seemed to be elderly identical twins of different sexes, and a crude cartoon of a bicycle – were all captioned *Flupe*.

The volume began to acquire some notoriety in academic circles, where scholars began, first tongue in cheek and then in earnest, to attempt to decipher it. Arguments predictably raged as to whether it was an authentic text or an elaborate hoax (hoaxes, of course, are almost always elaborate), and the whole thing was given fresh popularity when German television made a documentary about it. (The Germans felt particularly close to the Von Fremdenplatz, as it was now known, partly because of the nationality of its discoverer, and partly because 'Von Fremdenplatz' is the only translatable phrase connected to the book, meaning, depending on who you believe, 'From Foreigner Square' or 'Belonging to the Place of Strangers'. Needless to say, no such place, square or even person of that name has ever been discovered. And also, it's not strictly in the book, it's just, as it were, on the book.)

Then, just as interest was dying down again, two things happened. First, a French internet publishing magnate with pretensions to being seen as intellectual offered an enormous cash reward to anyone who could translate the book, which created major interest on the Continent. And second, another volume of the Von Fremdenplatz was discovered, this time in the stockroom of a large bookshop in Bordeaux (the finder was a student working a holiday job, who had taken the book to her boss when she'd been unable to find a barcode to price the book with). A month later, more volumes were found, more slender than the others, with the appearance of being appendices to a larger work. Naturally, this created something of a furore in the parallel worlds of applied linguistics and made-up fantasy nonsense. Those who believed that the Von Fremdenplatz was an authentic text claimed variously that it was a message from a parallel civilisation, a leak from an all-controlling secret society, or just a message from God, coded in tongues. Those who saw it as a huge prank pointed out that a similar thing had happened in a story by Borges about a mysterious book that had appeared from nowhere in several different places at once.

It was all getting rather heated, and matters came to a head when one of the smaller volumes was stolen from the college that had purchased it and was later found defaced and smeared with either blood or jam outside a Lutheran church in Utrecht. The meaning of this gesture remains obscure, but it led directly to the internet publishing magnate, who had already withdrawn his prize offer, deciding to buy all the known copies of the Von Fremdenplatz, including the damaged one, and loaning them to a private Parisian museum with a reputation for closeness and dislike of media attention. Whatever these documents were, was the reasoning, they were both fascinating and troublesome and should be kept away from exactly the kind of people who wanted to see them.

All this was some eight years ago. Since then, no further editions of the Von Fremdenplatz documents had turned up and, with the reward withdrawn, public interest waned. There were, of course, many websites devoted to the documents, and an endless stream of bloggers claimed to have found the key to translating the Von Fremdenplatz. But as there were no new developments, people discovered other, trendier obsessions, the steady flow of applications to see the documents was reduced to a trickle and the Parisian museum remained as unvisited as it always had been.

Perhaps, I wondered, this was why Frant's own application to visit the museum had been successful. Now that fewer people wanted to see the Von Fremdenplatz, maybe the caretakers of the collection were less on guard about their charge. Possibly they were just bored and wouldn't mind some company. I had no idea, but having read this much, I found I was looking forward to seeing the Von Fremdenplatz documents, real or fake, as if they were any other fascinating historical artefact.

The barman appeared at my table. 'Would you like any more drink?' he said in English. 'We are closing now.'

I asked for another martini. He nodded and then indicated the print-outs on the table.

'You are going there?' he said. '*L'institut?*'

'Tomorrow,' I said. '*Demain,*' I added. Frant's penchant for saying everything in two languages was rubbing off on me.

The barman shook his head, as if to say rather me than him. 'Crazy people,' he said. '*On fait collection de merde.*'

He left, and I studied the print-outs once more. There was nothing in the article about crazy people but then, as it was from the institute's own website, there wouldn't be. Oh well, I thought to myself as I put down some change for a tip, if there was one thing I was used to, it was crazy people.

CHAPTER SIX

I rarely sleep well when I'm away from my own bed, which I'm sure is a common experience, even among people who aren't staying in hotels where the bed is only slightly less narrow than a plank and the pillows haven't apparently been harvested of their filling. I woke several times in the night, partly out of discomfort and partly because, judging by the noise of sirens outside, my room seemed to be placed just above one of Europe's major police and criminal chase thoroughfares.

I finally drifted off to sleep about five o'clock in the morning and immediately found myself in a familiar dream. I have never to my knowledge ever suffered from what I believe are known as 'recurring dreams', but this one was without doubt such a thing. I was standing in a large open space, exactly as I had been the night I'd met the girl. The sun was shining brightly, in the distance I could see trees and the faint shapes of people, and once again there was nothing else but me there.

This time I didn't want to waste a moment just standing there but when I tried to go and explore I found I couldn't move. I was pinned to the spot. I could move my head and my arms but my feet might as well have been glued to the ground for all I could do to shift them. I was compelled to stay where I was. I wasn't happy about this.

And then I saw one of the dim figures in the distance turn. I can't tell you how I knew it was turning but it just was turning. It seemed to detach itself from the other shapes and was moving away from them. In fact, the figure was clearly moving towards me. Moving at walking pace, for sure, but moving in my direction.

I screwed up my eyes to see more clearly, but I couldn't. Even though the figure was getting nearer, I couldn't make out its features. Closer and closer the figure came, until it was so close that surely I should be able to see its face. Then I realised: the sun was behind it. I couldn't see who it was because the figure was blocking out the sun and was therefore its own shadow. Meanwhile I was trapped and the figure was bearing down on me.

And then I woke up.

Like I say, I hate dreams.

I decided, having given up trying to get anything but French static on the wall-mounted television set, to get up then, and after a surprisingly powerful if intermittently boiling shower, I was nearly ready to go down to breakfast. I was about to unplug my mobile phone from the adaptor when it began to ring.

'It's me,' said Mr Walker-Hebborn. 'Where are you?'

The simple question threw me. I had no idea what was happening back home and wondered what Walker-Hebborn had heard. For all I knew I was on the front page of every newspaper, a blurred passport photograph staring out with killer's eyes under the headline MURDER SUSPECT FLEES COUNTRY. Perhaps there would be an interview with my curiously dry-eyed mother. 'He never liked my dog,' she might be telling reporters. I decided to play for time.

'I've just got up,' I said. 'I'm about to go and have breakfast.'

'Can you come in later?' said Walker-Hebborn. 'I want to talk to you about a couple of things. Well, one thing really.'

My mind was working overtime. Walker-Hebborn's first question suggested that he still thought I was in town, never mind in the country, otherwise he wouldn't have asked me to come in later. He would have said, 'Can you come back?' That said, his request to talk to me was curiously vague, and I wondered if perhaps he was setting a trap. While it wasn't my employer's nature to set traps for his translators, I wouldn't have been surprised if Quigley and Chick were sitting right behind him, issuing instructions. Then again, this was a ploy that would hardly fool a child, so it was entirely possible that Walker-Hebborn really did just want me to come in for a chat.

'I can't today,' I said. 'I've been called away rather urgently. What was it you wanted to talk about?'

Walker-Hebborn released a massive sigh which sounded so natural in its irritation that I realised he was being entirely sincere. I was slightly disappointed, to my surprise, as if on some level I had been actually been hoping to be the focus of a massive police operation. Maybe this is how real criminals feel as they sit in their dens reading about themselves in the papers. But I was clearly no Public Enemy Number One.

I realised Walker-Hebborn was talking. 'Sorry,' I said, 'could you repeat that, please?'

'I wanted you to come in and talk about the preparations for Madame Ferber's visit,' he said. 'She's very keen as you know for you to be present at the signing of the new contract.'

'I thought she never left home,' I said.

'What are you talking about?' said Walker-Hebborn. 'She's a globe-trotter, old Ma Ferber. I admit she doesn't honour us with her presence in these offices much, but I bet you right now she's jetting across the world to another exotic destination, funded by the massive advance she's about to get from us.'

He sounded a little sharp, and I wondered just how much Madame Ferber had requested for the pleasure of remaining with Walker-Hebborn.

'When is she coming in?' I said.

'I don't know,' said Walker-Hebborn irritably. 'Minor details like that don't seem to trickle down to the likes of me. I'm only her publisher, after all. But it will have to be before the end of next week or else her contract will have expired and we don't want some big faceless publishing house to snap her up.'

Again, his voice was rather sharp and I couldn't help feeling he was blaming me for the delay. This was rather unfair, as the last time we had spoken Walker-Hebborn was trumpeting my praises to all and sundry and fêting me as the man who had single-handedly lured Madame Ferber back into the fold. Now he seemed to be suggesting that it would be my fault if she didn't sign up.

'I'll be back before then,' I said, with no factual justification for my statement.

'You'd better be,' said Walker-Hebborn and rang off.

I was displeased with his brusqueness, but consoled myself with the amusing thought that if Walker-Hebborn only knew where I was he would be spluttering with impotent fury. I was not, as he supposed, distant from Madame Ferber and unavailable, but actually in the city in which she resided. I might see her in a café at any moment, or perhaps a gallery. Not that I would recognise her, of course, unless she was the kind of person who liked to preserve their youthful appearance through surgery. I could even – I suddenly realised – simply go round to her home, ring the doorbell and invite myself in. 'Madame Ferber, I presume,' I would say, 'I have the honour to be your translator.' Although in reality she would demand to know how I had got hold of her address and call the police. And, as I only knew her address because I'd come across it in the files while looking for an address for Euros Frant, I couldn't really blame her. Admittedly, I hadn't written her address down, but instead found it had lodged in my mind from her frequent corresponding (that absurd letter crest) but she wouldn't have known that.

I realised I was drifting rather in my thoughts and was almost relieved to hear my mobile ringing again. This time it was Frant.

'I'll keep this short,' he said, 'these calls cost a fortune.'

'Why didn't you call me on the phone in my room?' I said.

There was a pause. 'You have a phone in your room?' he said.

'What did you want to tell me?' I said.

'I have had my appointment confirmed by the institute,' said Frant. 'Meet me in the lobby in five minutes.'

'Should I be ready to check out?' I said. 'After all, we could do this and get the train back the same day. That would save me some money—'

Frant had rung off. I decided to take my small bag of belongings anyway and went downstairs to the lobby where I found him, if not exactly pacing up and down, then looking somewhat agitated.

'Hurry up!' he said. 'The appointment is at ten o'clock. We cannot afford to be late.'

It was nine o'clock and the institute was a five-minute walk from the hotel. I hadn't had any breakfast. Still, getting this over with would enable me to get away from Frant more quickly, and who knew, once that was done I might have some information that would give me an idea how to clear my name with the police.

'All right,' I said, 'let's go.'

'Not so fast!' said Frant. 'I haven't had any breakfast yet.'

As we hastily consumed small, almost fresh croissants and slightly burned coffee, Frant went through a checklist.

'Arrive 10am,' he said, 'find main office on first floor, meet Monsieur Derringer, Head of Artefacts. Present our credentials to Monsieur Derringer—'

'What credentials?' I said. 'I haven't got any credentials.'

'I will have credentials enough for both of us,' said Frant. 'Ten fifteen, Monsieur Derringer admits us to the Document Room and, if he has any manners, leaves us alone for a few hours to study the Von Fremdenplatz properly.'

'That seems rather a long time,' I said. 'I hope we don't miss our train.'

'Always the mundane worrier,' said Frant. 'I hate to disturb your timetable fetishism but we will need time. The Von Fremdenplatz documents are copious to say the least, and we – I – will need time to study them. The translated *Alice* is after all an imperfect Rosetta Stone.'

I said nothing. I could picture myself, sitting on a hard chair in the corner of a small windowless room, watching, bored, as Frant pored over his beloved Von Fremdenplatz, possibly with an actual magnifying glass, going over the same words again and again until night fell and there were no more trains to take me away from him.

Frant opened a small leather zip case and removed some familiar pieces of paper. There was a map detailing the five-minute journey from our hotel to the institute, some sections of the Von Fremdenplatz with several key phrases ringed, and another copy of the *Alice* pages, with similar phrases also ringed. Frant's zip case held a copy of one of his books too (I refused to upset my eyes by looking to see what it was called) and some certificates, which were presumably his credentials (again, I didn't want to see what deluded organisation had seen fit to award Frant qualifications). He licked a finger, laboriously counted all the papers, and put them back in the zip case.

'I'm ready,' he said. '*Traversons le Rubicon.*'

Crossing the Rubicon didn't take very long once I had paid for our breakfasts and Frant had once more taken out his map to determine that we were walking in the right direction. It was a sunny Parisian morning and the sky's wide blueness suggested nothing but hope and possibility. Of course, the sky wasn't going to spend the day with Euros Frant, so it could afford to be full of hope and possibility. But the weather made me feel a bit better, and even Frant was smiling as he turned his map the right way round and headed towards the institute. It was an awful smile, twisted and full of teeth, but at least it was a smile.

As we neared the address on the map, however, Frant began to look more nervous. He dropped his man-bag on the floor and, when I bent to pick it up, snarled at me to leave it. He got it himself and forced another, less convincing smile.

'Please excuse me,' he said. 'Today is possibly the most important day of my academic career and I am perhaps a little on edge.'

'That's all right,' I said. 'It's a very exciting day.'

'Isn't it?' he said, his eyes shining. 'Isn't it, though? Ah! We are here.'

Frant was right and we were standing outside a very large wrought-iron gate, so convoluted in design that it looked like a huge metal doily, suspended across a large stone doorway. Through the ironwork I could see a big courtyard, with old warped flagstones and a path leading to a building of pre-revolutionary vintage. Clearly this institute had been around for a long time.

Frant rang a large and noisy bell. After a few minutes, a very old and very small fat man appeared behind the ironwork. 'We have an appointment,' Frant said. 'Monsieur Frant.' The man turned round and nodded to an unseen accomplice, and the iron doors swung open. Frant and I followed the man into the courtyard, where Frant almost tripped over a particularly knobbly flagstone, and into the building itself.

There a second man awaited us. Tall, shaven-headed and wearing rimless spectacles like a German dentist, he was obviously Monsieur Derringer. Frant introduced himself and, amazingly, me, and presented his credentials. Derringer looked at them and nodded.

'Welcome to the institute,' he said. 'We are honoured that you have travelled so far to see the Von Fremdenplatz documents.'

'We've only come on the train,' I said.

Frant shot me an angry look. 'Among other, equally tiring modes of travel,' he said to Derringer, and I suddenly realised that Frant had got us in here by lying through his teeth. He must have told Derringer's people that we had travelled across the world, possibly from far Cathay, to see the documents; he'd probably also lied about who we were. I didn't really care, I just wanted to get in and get this over with.

Frant was waffling away to Derringer about how it was even more of an honour for us to be here and so forth, and this seemed to smooth over any confusion I'd caused, because now Derringer was rooting about in an old bureau for our passes, which were not the usual rectangular folders of Perspex containing printed scraps of paper, but proper blue enamel badges with the institute's logo embossed on them in gold. We pinned them to our lapels as requested, and without another word Derringer set off at a pace.

'Here we are,' he said at last, after we had walked down several identical wood-panelled corridors, each lined with portraits of people in wigs. We were outside a smallish oak door whose only distinguishing feature was the number 106.

'Room 106,' said Derringer, perhaps unnecessarily, and took out a key. The key was large and ornate, and seemed a bit too fussy for its simple job of being a key. All it lacked was a big gold tassel; I was beginning to think that the institute was a touch too showy for an academic workplace. Frant, however, was lapping it up. I could tell by his almost salivating expression that he had thrown himself into the role of Important Visiting Professor.

'The moment of truth,' he said, before he could stop himself. Derringer raised an eyebrow. 'I mean, soon we shall see the documents and all will be revealed.'

'Really?' said Derringer, 'For most people who come to see the documents, now is generally the moment before nothing is revealed.'

'It's just an expression,' said Frant.

Derringer all but shrugged and put the key in the lock.

The door swung back and Derringer turned on the lights. The room was quite large, with more portraits of people in wigs on the walls. One or two busts in the Romanesque style stood on pillars between the portraits. In the middle of the room was an old-fashioned display case, the kind with glass doors that open upwards at an angle. Derringer walked over to the case and we followed him. He flicked a switch in the side of the case and some more lights came on.

'Gentlemen,' he said, 'I give you the Von Fremdenplatz documents.'

We looked into the case, which contained six leather-bound volumes, each open at a page of illustrated text. The volumes were of different thicknesses, but in each the paper was of the same size and age, and there was no doubt that each of these books was somehow part of a larger, unified whole. The text, though incomprehensible, was exquisitely printed, while the illustrations were beautifully reproduced as if with the latest computer technology. I knew this to be impossible, as the documents had been discovered many years ago, but it was hard to escape the feeling that we were looking at something brand new.

I said as much to Derringer, who nodded. 'For printed matter of this age to look so pristine must have involved the very highest standards,' he said. 'We have examined every aspect of the documents, however, from the ink and paper to the glue used to bind the pages together, but we are unable to determine anything about the process. A private printer must have been used at every stage. If you look at the edging—'

Frant, who was virtually hopping from foot to foot at this point, interrupted. 'Would it be possible to examine the volumes?' he said.

'Of course,' Derringer said, a touch irritably. 'I was getting to that.'

'My apologies,' said Frant. 'I am a trifle edgy. You see, this is the greatest day of my life.'

'I see,' Derringer said. He seemed to be thinking about something.

I wondered if Frant's effusiveness had set off any alarm bells. After all, experts in the field of counter-factual linguistics or whatever it was Frant claimed to be probably didn't go round saying things like, 'This is the greatest day of my life.' Or maybe they did. I don't know.

Nor, it appeared, did Derringer, as after a moment's

hesitation he took out another, much smaller key and opened the display case.

'Wait,' he said, and produced from a drawer three pairs of white cotton gloves. We all put them on, and Derringer removed one of the smaller volumes from the case. He closed the glass door again and carefully laid the volume on top of it.

'Beautiful,' said Frant, and for once he wasn't wrong. The small volume was even more gorgeous close up. The typeface was not one I recognised, although, to be fair, I am no expert on typefaces and have never seen the point of those books that end with epilogues describing the history and origins of Pendalo Garibaldi or whatever font was used. It also made each letter look somehow elegant and effective. The quality of paper was almost ridiculous. It would have looked excessive in a medieval manuscript, let alone a twentieth-century printed book. And the illustrations ... well, if they had looked good in a computer print-out, then on the pages of an actual book they were simply extraordinary. On this page, a mythical beast with the body of a lion and the face of a man – reproduced in glowing autumnal colours from some medieval map or calendar – was placed incongruously next to a photograph of an old man in Edwardian dress, his lined face etched vividly in black and white. On the opposite page, simple line drawings of men and women, full-lipped and wearing biblical dress, illustrated a piece of writing laid out like either a poem or a shopping list. It was impossible to tell what anything was meant to be, but it was all, as Frant said, quite beautiful.

'May I?' said Frant, gesturing at the book with a gloved hand, and Derringer nodded. Frant carefully lifted first one page, then another, and began to leaf slowly through the volume, exclaiming from time to time at each new illustration or block of text.

Then I noticed he was making faces at me. Frant appeared to be signalling with his eyebrows, which he kept hurling upwards in the direction of Derringer. I realised that for some reason he wanted me to distract Derringer, and when Frant pulled out the corner of the *Alice* document, I understood. He obviously didn't want the man to see his Rosetta Stone.

'I imagine the Von Fremdenplatz is the centrepiece of your collection,' I said.

'Oh no,' said Derringer. 'We have many valuable books and documents from all periods of history. And, while this is a marvellous piece of work, it lacks the historical importance of some of our, shall we say, more real acquisitions.' He permitted himself a small chuckle.

Frant frowned and, forgetting that he had wanted me to distract Derringer, said, 'What do you mean, more real? The Von Fremdenplatz is one of the most important documents of the modern era!' His eyebrows were wobbling alarmingly as he said it, and I could tell that he was quite agitated.

Derringer sighed. 'I realise that to someone of your background,' he said, sending Frant's eyebrows reeling, 'these documents are something of a Holy Grail, but to more historically inclined academics they are a cul-de-sac. They have no provenance, no connection to any other aspect of Western culture, and they exist entirely in a vacuum. They may be beautiful and enigmatic, but they are nothing more than curios. Unless, that is, you believe they are gifts from aliens.'

For a moment I thought Frant was going to say that yes, he did believe they were gifts from aliens, but he didn't. Instead he said, 'If the Von Fremdenplatz documents have no connection to Western culture,' he said, 'then how do you explain this?' and thrust the pages from the translated *Alice* under Derringer's nose.

Derringer took them. 'What's this?' he said.

'Evidence!' shouted Frant. 'A direct link between the documents and the so-called real world!'

Derringer must have put Frant's suggestion that this world was not a real one down to the heat of the moment, because he laid the *Alice* pages down on the cabinet next to the open volume of the Von Fremdenplatz and started to look at them.

'This is fascinating,' he said. 'Where did you get this?'

I gave the same edited explanation that I had given Frant.

'Ugh,' said Derringer suddenly, and fell forward onto me. He was unconscious. I moved backward under the weight of his inert form, which gave me a view of Frant putting down a bust of a French philosopher.

'Did you just hit him?' I said, pushing Derringer towards a chair.

'No time to explain,' said Frant, stuffing the translated *Alice* into his man-bag. 'Here.' And he pushed the bound volume into my hands. I took it more in confusion than anything else, and watched in bafflement as Frant grabbed the other volumes from the display cabinet.

An alarm sounded. I looked up and saw a small surveillance camera winking down at me.

'Run!' said Frant, and bolted from the room.

I don't know what you would have done in the circumstances, but I was shocked and confused and I think I would have obeyed any direction right then, no matter how absurd or counter-intuitive. In short, I ran.

The corridors of the institute were dark and winding and it took us a few minutes to find our way out. There were no clattering feet or shouts of command following us, which suggested that security was minimal. Indeed, we made it to the front door without seeing another person. Frant pressed a switch beside the wrought-iron gate and it opened outwards into the street. 'Hurry!' he said, shoving the bound volumes deeper into his coat, and he ran into the road. Still nobody pursued us, and I wondered why no police cars were arriving. But I had no time to speculate as Frant was scurrying up the street and if I had any chance of understanding what the hell was going on, I figured I had to follow him.

Finally, he stopped running after he had ducked into a back alley behind a restaurant. I stopped beside him and we both took a few seconds to get our wind back. There were still no police sirens.

When I had sufficient breath to speak, I said, 'What the hell did you do that for?'

'Isn't it obvious?' said Frant. 'I wanted to acquire the Von Fremdenplatz documents and there was no way Derringer would have permitted that.'

'So you hit him over the head? You could have killed him.'

'I doubt he would have been susceptible to verbal persuasion. And besides, I am not a strong man. I was lucky to render him unconscious.'

'You're insane.'

'Insane? You heard what he said. The institute regards those documents as insignificant pieces of trivia. They would have been quite happy to let them moulder under glass for decades. I had to liberate them.'

'But he seemed quite interested in the *Alice*. I'm sure he would have let you come in whenever you liked and work on your translation.'

'And taken all the credit for it. I know from bitter experience what these academics are like. Masters of infighting who'd murder their own aunts for sole credit on a paper. Think what glory might accrue to a nobody like Derringer.'

'That was still no reason to hit him over the head!'

Frant sighed like a man who has been extremely patient with an idiot. 'I have already explained that I had no other choice. I realise it was an act that closes down some options and makes others difficult—'

'Options!' I almost shouted. 'I'm not sure you have any options! You just assaulted a man and stole a rare document! You're a wanted man!'

'No more than you,' said Frant. For a moment I wondered if he was referring to my previous encounter with the police, and it took me a second to grasp his meaning.

'I had nothing to do with this,' I said.

'Which is why you ran when I ran,' said Frant. 'Which is why you failed to raise the alarm. And which is why you have a stolen book in your coat.'

He was right. There would be CCTV footage. And the French police, not noted for their kindness and liberalism, would be quick to connect me with the murder back home. Frant didn't know it, but I was potentially in even more trouble than he was, and he was in a whole lot of trouble.

'Great,' I said. 'Now what do we do?'

'In the short term, we continue to flee,' said Frant. 'In the long term? The plan is simple. When I have completed my work, I will publish the results of my translation of the Von Fremdenplatz documents. I will of course acknowledge the small part that you played. I will achieve the recognition that I have always deserved for my work. You will also benefit in some measure, perhaps becoming more "in demand" in your job than you are now.'

I felt like saying that as a man wanted for murder, assault and robbery in two different countries I could hardly be more in demand than I was right now, but I kept silent. It had just occurred to me that Euros Frant was stark, staring mad – not just in the annoying, rude way I was used to but in the way that crazy psycho killers are stark, staring mad – and the only way of extricating myself from this mess was to get as far away from him as possible and do some hard thinking. I was after all not actually guilty of murdering anyone (in fact, there was no evidence that the missing girl had been murdered) so there was a slim chance I would be able to make a case for my innocence. Running away never looks good, but I could tell them the truth, which was simply that I had panicked. The current situation was less good, admittedly, but again I had not actually assaulted anyone and I hoped the CCTV would pick up the shocked nuances of my face when Frant hit Derringer with the bust.

In fact, the more I looked at things, the more I became convinced that the only sensible course of action for me to take, however reluctantly, was to turn myself in at the nearest French police station. It would mean answering a lot of questions, admitting that I had withheld evidence, and pleading guilty to one or two more minor charges, but I felt sure that this was my only way out. All I had to do now was get away from Frant. I had already calculated that he was unlikely to want to join me in my mission of expiation.

'I think we should split up,' I said. 'The police will be looking for two people.'

'No,' said Frant. 'We're both in this. Our only chance lies in sticking together.'

'That doesn't make any sense,' I said. 'Two men, looking suspicious, lurking in the back streets of Paris. They'll be onto us like a shot. No, our only chance is to part company and make our own separate ways from here.'

'That,' said Frant, with a hint of exasperation in his voice, 'is exactly what they will be expecting us to do.'

'Well, let's not disappoint them, then,' I said tetchily.

'Are you familiar with the tale of "The Purloined Letter"?' said Frant.

'Yes,' I said, my heart sinking. Here we were, trying to evade capture by the French police and for all I knew Interpol, and Frant was about to deliver a lecture on crime fiction.

'Then you should be aware of the concept of "hiding in plain sight",' he said. 'In that story, in which the letter of the title is missing, it is discovered concealed in the most elegant hiding place imaginable, namely a letter rack.'

'I am aware of it,' I said, 'and it's different to this. A letter hidden in a letter rack is invisible, unless of course you're a policeman with half a brain and it occurs to you to look in the letter rack anyway because what the hell? People put letters in letter racks. But we're not letters, are we? We're two foreigners with a rare book in your coat and we look sweaty and suspicious. If I was a cop, I'd arrest us just for looking guilty.'

'This is not a time for flippancy,' said Frant.

'I'm not being flippant!' I said. Then I gave in. Frant was so bonkers that anything I said would have no effect on him. And if I really wanted to turn myself in to the police then arguably the best way to do it was simply to hang around with him. Sooner or later we would be arrested and all this mess would be over. I was tired and I could barely think. I wanted it all to stop.

'In that case,' I said, exhausted, 'if you really want to hide in plain sight, I know where we should go.'

'Where?' said Frant.

'The hotel,' I said. 'According to your logic, they'll never think of looking for us there.'

Frant looked at me from under quizzical eyebrows. 'That may be the first intelligent thing you have ever said,' he said. 'Let us go, then, you and I.'

Back at the hotel, I was surprised to discover that my plan seemed to be working. The lobby was not crawling with police, our rooms had not been turned over, and there weren't even any messages for us.

'The police will eventually work out that we are here,' said Frant, 'but we have a valuable breathing space.'

'To do what?' I said. 'We still have to get out of here. And when we do, what next? Do we assume false identities for the rest of our lives?'

'All this will blow over,' said Frant. 'When the reason for my actions is discovered, there will be great international sympathy and I will be excused. As my assistant, there will also be room in people's hearts for you.'

He really was raving mad, and I was stuck with him. In a court, Frant's actions would in all probability be defensible with a plea of insanity, whereas I was someone who, although a complete idiot and a gullible fool, was apparently in my right mind when I acted as Frant's accomplice. It was not a comforting scenario.

'I need a drink,' I said. 'I'm going downstairs.'

'Is that wise?' Frant said.

'Hide in plain sight, remember?' I said and stood up. Something fell from my pocket. It was the notebook. I reached down for it, but Frant had already picked it up.

'What's this?' he said, opening it. 'A diary?'

'That's mine,' I said. 'Please hand it over.'

'Carrie and the Legions,' Frant read out. 'I should have known you were a fan of rock music.'

'Oh yes,' I lied. 'I can't get enough of it. Please give me my notebook back.'

'Really, at your age,' sniffed Frant. 'But then I suppose nobody grows out of anything these days.'

He handed me back the notebook and went into the bathroom. I was about to put it back in my pocket when it occurred to me that I might not get an opportunity to look at it again for some time, as being on the lam offers few chances for reading. I opened it at the review I'd read last and turned to the next page. To my surprise, this wasn't a review at all, but an interview between 'C', whom I assumed to be Carrie, and 'Q', obviously an anonymous interviewer. It looked quite long, too. I folded the corner of the page to mark it and got up.

'I'm going to the bar,' I shouted at the bathroom door, and went downstairs.

Q: I'm here with Carrie, singer with Carrie and the Legions. It's just Carrie, right?

C: Right. I have other names but I'd rather not divulge them here.

Q: OK. Is that because of the hostile reviews of your last album?

C: Ha ha! I certainly did cop a lot of flak for that one, didn't I? But I think there were some brave choices on that record. I was striving for a new direction and I know some people think I failed, but I consider it a worthwhile experiment.

Q: Will you be working with Henry J again?

C: Wow, you really cut to the chase, don't you? I have no plans to work with any one particular individual right now. Henry is busy on other projects, anyway.

Q: Do you feel that Henry J was the wrong person to collaborate with?

C: Henry's a great guy. The stories you hear about him are true, ha ha, in that he is something of a perfectionist and if he wants something and you don't, he will probably end up getting his own way.

Q: Is that what happened to you? Because the hand of Henry J is all over *Showtime?*.

C: And that's what I wanted on that particular record. I was happy to put myself in his hands. But now I feel it's time to move on.

Q: Do you regret working with Henry J?

C: Like I said, I feel it's time to move on.

I was starting to make sense of the notebook. This was obviously an interview conducted in the wake of Carrie and the Legions' record *Showtime?* which had not been a success. The interviewer was suggesting, as far as I could tell, that the failure of *Showtime?* was the fault of Carrie's collaborator, the record producer Henry J. Reading between the lines, it was clear that Henry J was a man with a forceful personality, and he had imposed this personality on Carrie's record with negative consequences. I wondered if Carrie was telling the whole truth when she said that she had been happy to put herself in his hands. I knew next to nothing about her but I was sure that she was the kind of woman who surely found it difficult to surrender her independence to anyone, and in fact would go to great lengths not to do so. So I wondered what circumstances would have led her to let someone take over the reins. Money, I imagined, although from the reviews Carrie seemed to be a person of great integrity. Nevertheless, as I knew from the music papers my ex-girlfriend had been so fond of, integrity was something that people in the pop and rock industry were giving up every day. It was, I was aware, a cut-throat industry.

Frant still hadn't made an appearance, so I took a chance and read on.

Q: I'm sorry, I only have a couple more questions.

C: That's fine. I hope you're going to ask me about the new stuff.

That's the thing about you guys – it's all about raking over the past. You never want to know what people are going to do next.

Q: As it happens, that was my very next question. Now that you've severed your ties with Henry J—

C: You had to get him in one more time, didn't you?

Q: What are your plans for the future?

C: OK. Well, my immediate plans are to take a break, think about stuff, search for a new label, and record my new songs. At the moment, you could say I'm working with a blank slate and that's how I like it. It's time to move onwards and upwards.

Q: 'New songs'. Can you give us a hint of what these songs are and how they might sound?

C: All I can say right now is I'm feeling optimistic. I've got some great ideas and I have to say that I've got a feeling that the next record is going to be the one. This could really work out for me, you know?

And there the interview ended. I turned the page, and it was blank. The next page was blank too, and the next one after that. I flicked through the notebook, and it was all blank. The interview I'd just read was the last piece in the notebook. I found that I felt a little depressed. As well as being the nearest I had to evidence of Carrie (if that was her name)'s existence, I had also become involved in her narrative. But at least I had more information now. I knew the name of her collaborator – the egotistical Mr J – and of one of her recordings. I could go online and perhaps find out more.

'Daydreaming again?' said a voice and I looked up to see Frant standing over me, a sardonic expression on his face. I realised that my dislike of the man had increased even more in the last few hours, and once again I wondered how it was that I had ended up shackled to this appalling lunatic as though we were in some nightmarish three-legged race.

I put the notebook away.

'Do you have a plan?' I said, barely restraining the sarcasm in my voice.

'Of course,' said Frant. 'There is a man I know with whom we can go and stay.'

'Is that safe?' I said.

'Of course,' said Frant again. 'He has friends who will be able to get us out of the country undetected. Once we are in the United States, we will be able to return to a state of equilibrium and sort out this whole unfortunate business.'

'The United States?' I said, and then, because I couldn't help myself, 'Of America?'

'Of – yes,' said Frant, managing to avoid starting a sentence with 'of course' for a third time. 'Europe is not safe, what with extradition treaties and so forth. Besides, there is a much more sympathetic attitude to the whole Von Fremdenplatz issue there.'

'Let me get this straight,' I said. 'Even though you have assaulted a senior French academic—'

'Senior, my foot,' said Frant. 'The man was nothing more than a glorified caretaker.'

'And stolen some rare documents, you think you can not only get away with it, but also escape to the United States and everything will be forgotten?'

'Yes,' said Frant, 'I do.'

I looked at him with amazement and dislike. 'They've got our faces on CCTV,' I said. 'You filled out an application form. They have our names and our addresses.'

'No,' said Frant, 'they don't.'

'What do you mean, they don't?'

Now it was Frant's turn to give me a look. 'Do you seriously think that if I had put down who we really were that we would have been admitted to the institute?'

I felt a chill. 'What do you mean?'

'I mean this. You are a hack translator, a middleman between an author and his public. You had the key to the Von Fremdenplatz in your hand and you were unable to recognise it. That scarcely qualifies you to examine a parking ticket, let alone one of the most important documents of all time.'

I let the insult go. It could join all the others at the back of my mind. 'But what about you?' I said. 'Your entire life has been devoted to the pursuit of this … kind of thing. If anyone is qualified to examine a made-up document in a pretend language, then surely it's you.'

Frant nodded. 'You are right, despite the sarcasm. However, while I am perfectly placed to decipher the Von Fremdenplatz, I am not welcome in the halls of academe. I do not have a fancy degree from the Sorbonne. I have never sat at the high table at Oxford or Cambridge. I do not publish incomprehensible, dull papers. I am a writer, I am a creator, I am an artist.'

'I see,' I said, before he could go on to say that he had studied at the school of hard knocks and the university of life. 'So how did we get in to see the Von Fremdenplatz?'

'I forged our credentials,' said Frant.

'You what?' I said.

'One of the advantages of working with the literature of the fantastic is that you develop a certain facility for creating convincing alternatives to reality,' said Frant.

'You mean you know how to make things up and make them look real?' I said.

'There is no point creating a work of parallel history or a volume of alternative literature if it looks like you just bought it off Amazon,' said Frant. 'Had, for example, your doltish publisher seen fit to publish my *Chrona* the way I wanted, I would have insisted that it resemble exactly a fourteenth-century almanac, in agedness, paper quality and even smell.'

This made sense. Walker-Hebborn was reluctant enough to commission full-colour covers for his paperbacks so I could hardly see him agreeing to forge a medieval manuscript on authentic parchment with, presumably, manure rubbed into it.

'And compared to recreating a pre-Industrial Revolution document,' continued Frant, 'forging a couple of references is a piece of cake.'

'But they had our names on,' I said.

'Did they now?' said Frant, eyebrows aslant with wryness.

'Oh God,' I said, 'you gave us false names.'

'You are Mr Panza,' said Frant, 'after the rustic simpleton sidekick of Don Quixote. And I am Mr Loki, after the Norse trickster god. Appropriate, do you not think?'

'You applied to see the documents under the names of Mr Panza and Mr Loki?' I said. 'We sound like a music-hall act.'

'It worked, didn't it?' said Frant. 'And now you see that our dilemma is lessened. They may have our descriptions, but they do not know our names. Doubtless the police are looking for us, and checking recent arrivals to Paris, but there must be plenty of people matching our description to sift through. Hence the comparative safety of this hotel.'

I looked at Frant's fedora, scarf and eyebrows and doubted that there was anyone matching his description. 'So all that hiding in plain sight bit was nonsense?' I said. 'They never even knew we were here in the first place.'

'I just wanted to get back to the hotel and rest,' said Frant.

I got up and walked around for a bit. I was processing far too much information, none of it particularly good. True, the French police didn't know who we were, but surely it wouldn't take them long to find out. And I was now on the run under a false name. Things hadn't really changed.

'How are we going to get out of the country, though?' I said.

'Leave that to my friend,' said Frant. 'He has some experience of ... moving that which is not intended to be moved.'

'Please don't say he's going to smuggle us out of the country,' I said.

'Very well,' said Frant. 'Although that is exactly what he is going to do.'

'But why?' I said. 'We both have valid passports. Why can't we just go home? We can find ourselves good lawyers and sort this out.'

'I doubt that,' said Frant, 'After all, as you well know, I am the one who committed the assault. As you said, they have me on camera. As for you ...'

Frant sat down next to me.

'As for you,' he said, 'you can't go back, can you? Not when you're the principal suspect in a murder enquiry.'

CHAPTER SEVEN

I stared at him. 'I don't know what you're talking about,' I said.

'People always say that,' said Frant. '"It wasn't me." "I don't know what you're talking about." "You can't lay that on me." Well, in this instance, my dear Sancho Panza, you know exactly what I'm talking about.'

'Please don't call me Sancho Panza,' I said. 'How did you know?'

'It wasn't the greatest piece of detective work,' said Frant. 'I first became suspicious when, after refusing ill-manneredly to accompany me to Paris, you then called back within the hour having had a complete change of heart in the matter.'

'And so you thought, Oh, I get it, he's clearly on the run from a murder charge?'

'No,' said Frant. 'As I said, I merely became suspicious. But my suspicions were confirmed when I read this.'

He took out a crumpled copy of a free newspaper, the kind that are doled out to commuters by the kilo during rush hour. I expected to see my face plastered all over the front page. Instead, Frant opened the paper to an inside page. 'Murder investigation continues,' he read flatly. 'A new suspect has been announced in the blah blah blah ... then it's a description of you, and your relationship to this girl ... oh, here it is ... The suspect is known to have in his possession a notebook belonging to the missing girl.'

He showed me the newspaper. There was a small, out-of-date photograph of me next to the article, which they must have got from my mother, or possibly my ex-girlfriend.

'It was the notebook, you see,' said Frant. 'You were so secretive about it and I couldn't see why. And then I read this article, and it all fell into place.'

'I imagine it helped that they printed my name and my photograph,' I said.

'Yes,' said Frant stolidly, 'but the notebook was, as they say, the clincher.' He took the newspaper back. 'So,' he said, 'perhaps you'd like to tell me everything.'

I told him everything. I wish I could have said that it was a weight off my mind. That's what criminals say, I believe, when they confess. But I'm not a criminal, I suppose, so it wasn't a confession. Anyway, I started at the beginning, in the bar, with the girl, and went all the way up to the police arriving at my apartment. I left out one or two details, like the fact that there were photographs of the girl in the book, and the fact that she had come back to my apartment and then fled into the night. I had so little dignity left, I was keen to preserve some shreds of it.

As I told my edited story, Frant nodded as though wise throughout.

'I see,' he said. 'And you thought it best not to tell me that I was going abroad with a wanted man? Thereby putting my mission in jeopardy?'

I refrained from pointing out that I was at least an innocent wanted man, while he was guilty of actual crimes, like theft, and hitting a man over the head with a bust. But I didn't. I was fed up of the whole thing. I just wanted to hand myself in to the police and get it over with. Again, I didn't say this to Frant as I was sure he would see things somewhat differently.

'This changes nothing,' Frant said. 'Angry though I am at your deceitfulness, we still have to carry on.'

'Can't you just leave me here?' I said. 'You would surely travel lighter alone.' Now I was talking like him.

'Oh no,' said Frant. 'If you fell into the hands of the police, you'd crumple like an autumn leaf. No, I must needs keep you by my side.'

'All right then,' I said, thinking that once we were on the move, I could still give him the slip. 'Let's go.'

'Good,' said Frant. 'You settle our bill, I'll keep an eye out for the police.'

I stood up, but Frant put his hand on my sleeve.

'I'd like to see that notebook, please,' he said.

'Why?' I said.

'Because obviously this girl is key to everything,' said Frant. 'She is the person from whom everything devolves. She has the translated *Alice* – all of it, not just a few copied pages. Did you not think to try to track her down?'

'Of course I did,' I said. 'But she has vanished. That's what "disappeared" means. It means "gone". And she hardly left many clues. All I have is those pages of the *Alice* and that notebook, which is just reviews of rock concerts.'

I passed him the notebook and he flicked through it. He looked disappointed, as though he had expected to find the girl's name and address at the back. Frant handed it back to me, and immediately I felt relieved. The notebook was after all my only real link to the girl.

'Oh hell,' said Frant suddenly. He was looking at the hotel lobby. A police car was parked outside on the pavement. 'Let's get out of here.'

'How?' I said.

'Plain sight,' said Frant. 'Follow me.'

And he got up and walked out. I followed him. Frant turned right, away from the police car, and walked down the street, casual as anything. By the time the police would have entered the hotel and summoned the desk clerk, we were two blocks away.

'And we haven't paid,' I said to Frant.

'I think we have more important things to worry about,' Frant said. 'Taxi!' he added loudly, and a cab pulled over.

'It seems to me,' said Frant, 'that you have mishandled everything.'

The taxi was stuck in a parody of Parisian traffic, surrounded by honking static vehicles. It smelled of cigarettes and an unidentifiable foodstuff.

'Please explain,' I said tightly.

'Your first action should have been to ask the girl where she got the book,' said Frant. 'Then you should have ascertained her name and telephone number. After that, when she disappeared, you should have gone straight to the police, told them everything, and given them the notebook.'

'I see,' I said. 'Thanks for the advice.'

'You're welcome,' said Frant. 'Ah, here we are.'

He rapped on the Perspex window separating the driver from his passengers.

'*Ici, s'il vous plaît*,' he shouted.

The cab pulled over and Frant got out. I paid and followed suit. We were on a nasty grey street outside a grey-walled bar.

'Where are we?' I said.

'Patience,' said Frant irrelevantly, and went into the bar.

The bar was empty apart from a couple of very old men who were engaged in conversation with two young girls. A

CD jukebox played something with loud drums and louder accordions. Frant approached the bar.

'*Une bière et un apéritif,*' he said to the barman.

'I don't want a drink,' I said.

'The beer is not for you,' said Frant. 'It's for my friend.' Frant sat on a bar stool and sniffed his aperitif. 'He should be here any minute,' he said.

'Who?' I said.

'I told you,' said Frant, 'my friend.'

Frant was obviously enjoying being mysterious so I ordered a coffee and a sandwich and took out the notebook again.

'I don't know why you don't just throw that away,' said Frant.

'It's interesting,' I said. 'I never knew much about rock music, but it's a whole fascinating world.'

'I doubt that,' said Frant. Just then his phone started ringing. Its ringtone was the Anvil Chorus from some opera or other and to my tired mind it sounded louder than the jukebox. As Frant fumbled for the mobile, the sound of an enormous choir singing along to clanging anvils mixed in with accordions created a special audio hell. Finally, to my intense relief, he got the thing out and answered it.

'Yes?' he said. '*Oui?*' he added, presumably for clarity.

I couldn't hear a voice at the other end, but whatever it was saying, it wasn't good. Frant's eyebrows began a small Mexican wave, and his eyes narrowed.

'*Quoi?*' he said, ungrammatically. '*Qu'est-ce que c'est que vous dites?*'

I had a feeling that Frant's friend wasn't going to come through. Frant swore a few times in French and English then put the phone away.

'We are betrayed,' he said.

'What do you mean?' I said.

'My friend has gone to the police.'

'Excuse me?' I said. 'I beg your pardon? What?'

'You heard me,' said Frant.

'I know,' I said, 'I'm just a bit confused. Are you telling me that this mysterious friend of yours, who half an hour ago was willing to provide us with tickets and visas and false passports and God knows what else—'

'We don't need passports,' said Frant sullenly. 'I explained that.'

'Whatever,' I said. 'All that and now he's turned round and gone to the police?'

'Apparently they were leaning on him,' Frant said.

I said nothing. I wondered what kind of business Frant's associate ran. Perhaps he was constantly running fake academics and fantasy writers in and out of the country on a kind of underground railway for idiots. More likely he had other, equally dubious sidelines and this had led the police to him.

'So are you saying that this man has traded us in?' I asked.

'I presume so,' said Frant. 'And while I was careful not to mention the Von Fremdenplatz documents by name—'

'Oh no,' I said, perhaps a little too sarcastically, 'you should never mention the Von Fremdenplatz documents by name.'

'I fear the police may have our names.'

'Oh great,' I said.

'Which of course they will have transmitted to the American authorities in case we decide to flee independently.'

'You're joking,' I said. 'So now we're wanted by the police of two continents.'

'It would appear so,' said Frant.

I took out my phone.

'What are you doing?' Frant said.

'I'm turning myself in,' I said. 'I can't take this any more.

I'm tired, I'm on the edge of my nerves and I'm wanted by the police of two continents.'

'Yes, you said that,' said Frant absently. 'I strongly advise you not to call the police.'

'Why?' I said. 'What could possibly be worse than the situation we are now in?'

'Well, you could be in jail,' Frant said.

'I am going to be in jail,' I said. 'Of that there is no doubt.'

'I hadn't finished,' said Frant. 'You could be in jail and never know what happened to the girl.'

I put the phone down on the bar. 'What girl?' I said, trying and failing to sound casual.

'You know very well what girl,' Frant said. 'The girl with whom you are clearly obsessed. The girl whom you met in the bar, the girl whom you so clearly offended that she ran away, the girl for whom you are still carrying a torch and the girl for whom you have done all this and come so far.'

I don't think I had ever heard anyone say 'whom' so much in one sentence. 'Are you saying,' I said, 'that you know what happened to her?'

'No, I'm not saying that exactly,' Frant said, and I picked up the phone again. 'I do not know where she is. What I'm saying is I know where she was.'

I put the phone away. 'Please explain,' I said.

'First,' said Frant, 'I want you to tell me everything you know about her.'

'Why?' I said. 'No,' I added, after very little thought. I don't know why, but I didn't want Frant anywhere near her, if you see what I mean.

'If you don't want me to help you ...' Frant said.

I didn't want him to help me, he was right. On the other hand, what other hope did I have? I didn't know her name, her whereabouts or anything. I had come this far and I was more in the dark than ever. The only lead I had was in the mind of the man sitting opposite me, a man who had unwittingly done his level best to ruin my life. I had no choice.

'I met her in the bar, as I told you,' I said. 'We had a few drinks and went to my apartment.'

'Where you made love?' said Frant.

I flinched. 'No,' I said, 'if you must know.'

'I must know,' agreed Frant, 'else how can I build up a picture of this girl?'

'And when she was in the bathroom I was unable to stop myself sneaking a look at the book,' I went on.

'There is nothing to be ashamed of in that,' said Frant. 'If the discoverer of Nineveh and Tyre had been a stickler for manners, there would be no winged lions in the *Musée Britannique*.'

'It's not called that,' I said.

'When in Rome,' said Frant. 'You merely displayed a scholar's instinct for the truth. If only' – and here he turned to the window to stifle a sigh – 'if only you had taken the actual book.'

'Whatever you say,' I said. 'When I was discovered, she flew into a rage and left. I never saw her again.'

'And since then you have been obsessed by her,' said Frant. There was, for once, no hint of mockery in his voice. 'But does it not occur to you that all this seems perhaps a touch too easy?'

I was unable to think of anything easy about the last few days. Words like 'hellishly difficult' and 'unpleasantly dangerous' sprang to mind instead.

'What do you mean?' I said. I didn't like the way this conversation was headed.

'I mean,' Frant said, 'that with all due respect, here you are, a simple fellow, neither attractive nor unattractive, with few attributes of note ...'

I really didn't like the way the conversation was going now.

'And here is this woman whom you assure me is the essence of female-hood,' said Frant, 'virtually jumping over the other customers at the bar to bed you.'

'We had both had a few drinks,' I said defensively.

'No doubt,' said Frant. 'That would have been necessary. Nevertheless, this beauty, this modern siren, turns up in a bar with a book in a mysterious language that she cannot understand and who does she run into? A translator.'

'I did wonder about that,' I said.

'A translator, moreover, as I have said, whom she finds desirable,' said Frant. 'Hearts and minds are engaged and, if you don't object to the simile, the fish is hooked. You are the fish,' he explained.

I was shaken, although I was trying not to show it. But still nothing made sense.

'Why, though?' I said. 'I couldn't translate the book. It's not my area.'

'No,' said Frant, 'but I could, and you knew me.'

'How would anyone know that?' I said. 'I have never told anybody about translating your work,' I said. 'And then there's the notebook.'

'Ah yes, the notebook,' said Frant.

'I suppose you're going to tell me that the notebook is irrelevant,' I said, 'just some childish drivel that has nothing to do with the wonderful world of fantastical languages.'

'It is in that sense irrelevant,' said Frant. 'However, in the matter of finding the girl, who is unarguably the key to all this, it is of the utmost relevance.'

'But it's just a collection of rock music reviews,' I said.

'Give it to me,' Frant said.

I looked at him askance.

'Just give it to me,' he said. 'I'm not going to hurt it.'

I took out the notebook and laid it on the counter, my hand covering it. Frant prised my hand off and from his pocket took out the folded print-out of the translated *Alice*.

'The difference between you and me,' he said, 'is that you are a translator. You work with the much-handled grubby coin of everyday language. Familiar words and phrases from other tongues are your sole stock in trade. You never have to worry about the out-of-the-ordinary because you never come across it.'

You obviously haven't worked with Madame Ferber, I thought. 'What are you trying to tell me?' I said.

'I, on the other hand, do not merely translate the fantastical, I write it,' said Frant. 'I have created words, and dialects, and entire languages. Every day for me is a challenge, every blank page a mountain to climb. A mountain to be populated moreover by gryphons and manticores and gallimaufries.'

'Please get to the point,' I said, wondering how gallimaufries had suddenly got into it.

'What I'm saying is that I am expert at noticing things, whereas you are not,' Frant said. 'Look.'

And he placed the *Alice* pages next to the notebook.

'Pick them up,' he said. 'Study them. Compare.'

I did. I skimmed over the *Alice* text as best I could. I flicked through the pages of the notebook, in which there were no new reviews or interviews.

'No,' I said, 'I don't see anything. The two things are completely different. One's a printed document, a palimpsest of a famous text. The other is a collection of handwritten transcripts of music paper articles. They're as different as chalk and cheese.'

'Really?' said Frant. 'Perhaps to the untrained eye ...'

He took a metal pencil from his pocket, twiddled the end and drew a tiny circle on the *Alice* print-out. I peered at it.

Inside the circle was a tiny symbol. I took a closer look. The symbol was a monogram, the letters CCLF.

'So?' I said.

Frant sighed and opened the notebook. He took his propelling pencil and again drew a tiny circle, this time on the inside back cover of the notebook. I picked it up, even though this time I knew exactly what I was going to see. Sure enough, in slightly clearer letters – this not being a print-out – was a stamp bearing a tiny monogram. The letters CCLF.

'A connection,' said Frant, looking about as pleased with himself as it was possible for a man to be without actually bursting.

'OK,' I said. 'All right. I'm impressed. But it's useless if we don't know what it means. And we don't.'

Frant really did now look as though he were about to explode.

'You might not know what it means,' he said. 'But I do.'

I sat for a moment, full of frustration, anger and hope.

'Please tell me,' I said, 'what does it mean?'

'The acronym?' said Frant. 'CCLF?'

'Yes,' I said, after unballing my fists. 'What does it mean?'

'That's easy,' said Frant. 'Combined Colleges Literary Facility.'

I stared at him for a moment. To say that I was disappointed would be something of an understatement.

'Is that it?' I said. 'Combined Colleges blah blah blah? That could be anything.'

'It could be,' said Frant. 'But it's not.'

'Then what is it?' I asked. 'Please, just tell me. I'm all ears.'

And Frant, for once, explained.

The Combined Colleges Literary Facility, despite its grand name, was one of the smaller cogs in the wheel of academic organisation.

'What the CCLF does is put scholars at College A in touch with departments relevant to their research at Colleges B and C,' said Frant. 'And while once this was an important remit, nowadays with the introduction of the internet and the placing of so much data online, the CCLF has become almost a vestigial office.'

'And you worked there?' I said.

'I dropped in from time to time to offer suggestions and help out,' said Frant, meaning, I guessed, that he did some part-time work to pay for his hats. 'But despite my best efforts, the CCLF has no power to speak of and very little relevance to modern scholastic life. But it continues to exist.'

'What's it got to do with me, though?' I said.

'The girl,' said Frant. 'She has in her possession not one but two items bearing the facility stamp. One is a mere item of stationery – the notebook – while the other – the *Alice* – is arguably one of the most important documents of the modern age. To have access to one of them might be a coincidence, but to be in possession of both leads me to a solitary logical conclusion.'

'What?' I said, perhaps irritably.

'This girl, whoever she is, works in the facility,' said Frant. 'That's how she came by a notebook with the CCLF stamp in it.'

'But what about the *Alice*?'

'That is more of a mystery, but not such a large one. After all, the CCLF is an obscure facility, almost a dead-letter office. Documents and books must often lie uncollected and uncatalogued on shelves and in obscure corners for years on end. You can imagine the treasures, and the mundanities, littering such a place. It makes perfect sense to me that some secretary might have ordered up, say, copies of *Alice's Adventures Through the Looking-Glass* and then found among them, like a cuckoo in the nest, our translated *Alice*. Not knowing what to do with it, our hypothetical secretary would have stuck it in a cupboard or at the bottom of a drawer.'

Frant looked more pleased with himself than usual, clearly enjoying playing the detective.

'The photographs,' I said. 'How do they fit in?'

Frant gave me an odd look. 'What photographs?' he said.

I was puzzled for a moment and then I realised that I hadn't told him about the photographs of the girl. I could picture them as clearly as ever. For a moment I thought about telling Frant about the photographs, but in a second moment I decided not to. It had nothing to do with his stupid books, anyway.

'Nothing,' I said. 'I mean, the photos in the Von Fremdenplatz. Maybe there's a clue there.'

'Ah,' said Frant, and began a monologue about how nobody could figure out where the photographs in the Von Fremdenplatz documents came from, never having been traced to any one particular photographer or agency. It was all thrilling stuff if you're not a suspect in several criminal enquiries, so after a couple of minutes I decided to return Frant to the real world.

'Are you saying that we can find the girl?' I interrupted.

'I told you,' Frant said irritably. 'I only know where she was, not where she is. But yes, the CCLF is a small place, and there cannot be many engaged there. A personal visit should swiftly unveil her employment details.'

'Only thing is,' I said, 'we can't exactly pop by for a chat right now, can we? What with being on the lam and so forth.'

'Nevertheless, we can call them when we have a quiet moment,' said Frant. 'I have, as you must infer, had many dealings with the CCLF, requesting transfers of books, and I can assure you, in that department at least, my name opens doors.'

I was spending a lot of my time with Frant refraining from pointing things out, it seemed. Now I refrained from pointing out that his name might open doors but he had been unable to do what this girl had done, namely stumble across the translated *Alice*. Life's little ironies, I reflected. Then again, I could easily imagine Frant stumbling across a jumbo edition of the Von Fremdenplatz documents, bound in luminous pink vellum with a neon sign saying HEY FRANTY! TAKE A LOOK AT THIS, and not recognising it for what it was.

'OK,' I said. 'We can call them up when we have, as you say, a quiet moment, and ask them about the girl. Fine. The problem as I see it is this: we don't have a quiet moment.'

'We could have done it if you hadn't talked all that nonsense about photographs,' grumbled Frant. 'But I concede your point. It is time to move on before the net closes around us.'

I looked around the bar. The old guys with the two girls had gone. In their place were some frightened-looking young guys, American by their get-up, who obviously thought they'd wandered into the wrong part of town. A couple of tables away, a man with an eyepatch and one ear was doing nothing to disabuse them of this notion, as he leered away at the blondest of the guys.

'I think we're still in a quiet moment,' I said.

At that exact moment, the air was rent with the scream of sirens. A loudhailer sputtered something angry and official in French.

'No longer, alas,' said Frant.

We froze in our seats. There was little point making a break for it, as the police would have covered all the exits. In a futile gesture, I pushed the copy of the Von Fremdenplatz even further under my coat. The door of the bar burst open and three or four French cops strode in, looking determined.

I was about to stand up and save them the bother of

clubbing me to the ground when suddenly the man with the missing ear and the eyepatch jumped to his feet and ran for it. In no time, the policemen had overwhelmed him and were dragging him out of the bar.

'Dame Fate fears that we cannot take a hint,' said Frant. 'The interlude is over. We must now, finally, flee.'

'Flee where?' I said, as we sloped out into the darkening evening outside. 'Your contact is gone and we must be all over the news by now.'

'I wouldn't worry about that,' said Frant. 'In a couple of days' time, my friend will be out on the street again and we can pick up where we left off. The trail will have gone cold, the institute will simply write off the missing copy of the documents just as any museum would a theft, and life will go on as before. We simply need to hole up for a while.'

This was the most optimistic version of events possible. For all Frant knew, his friend might now be a police informer. And even if the institute did decide to claim the insurance on the Von Fremdenplatz and put the theft down to experience, I doubted that Monsieur Derringer would be forgetting Frant's assault on him in a hurry. But I had no other plan apart from turning myself in, and, while this was still the most sensible option, it would prevent me from calling this CCLF place and finally establishing the whereabouts of the girl.

'Hole up?' I said. 'We don't have anywhere to hole up. They'll be watching the hotels and the pensions, and I doubt you want to sleep in a bus station. Are you saying you have friends here?'

Frant looked offended for a moment. 'I have friends everywhere,' he said, 'just not ones I can stay with.'

I bet, I thought.

'Well, I don't know anyone in Paris,' I said. 'I guess it's the bus station or nothing.'

And then it hit me. I couldn't believe I hadn't thought of it before. I guess the mental distance between the abstract idea of what I knew and the reality of our situation had been too great to make the jump. I visualised a piece of paper. A letterhead in the form of a fat-headed lion, with an address underneath.

Madame Ferber's address.

'Oh my God,' I said. 'I do know someone in Paris.'

'What?' said Frant, with a rare eagerness. 'Who? Why didn't you say so before?'

'I don't really know them,' I said. 'In fact, I've never met them. We've just spoken on the phone.'

'That is not ideal,' said Frant. 'Then again, given your bizarre character, perhaps it is to our advantage. In any case, we have nowhere else to go.'

He buttoned up his coat and pulled his hat down until its brim sheltered his eyebrows. He looked both ridiculous and deranged. He was ridiculous and deranged.

'Off we go, then,' he said.

I hesitated. I realised that I was in a great deal of danger, and more than anything else in the world what I needed right now was a safe haven, somewhere I could gather my thoughts and plan my next move. On the other hand, I was lumbered with Euros Frant, a man who was dangerous and unreliable, as well as ridiculous and deranged. Madame Ferber, moreover, was a recluse and an artist, a person who valued her privacy almost as much as she valued her talent. I couldn't just turn up at Madame Ferber's with this nutcase in tow. It wasn't as though she had given me her address and said, 'Please drop by any time you find yourself in Paris, especially if you have a nutcase in tow.' I wouldn't even know her address if I hadn't accidentally memorised it during what I was sure was an illegal document search at Walker-Hebborn's office.

All in all, it was entirely clear that this was a terrible idea and I should abandon it at once and find a fresh alternative. So it was a surprise when I heard myself saying, 'Let me telephone ahead first.'

'There isn't time,' said Frant. 'The police may be upon us at any moment.'

'We can't just turn up,' I said. 'And besides, she may be out.'

'She?' said Frant. He looked pleased, in an unpleasant way. 'The enigmatic translator has a lady friend, does he? Or perhaps he is merely carrying a torch for an unattainable femme fatale.' He paused. 'Another unattainable femme fatale, I should say.'

Not for the first time, I wondered why I hadn't just taken the bust from Frant's hands in that room at the institute and battered him to death with it.

'She is one of Walker-Hebborn's authors,' I said. 'We were supposed to be meeting soon.'

'Riveting,' said Frant. 'I am entranced by your rustic monologue. Can we get a move on, please? If that's not too much trouble.'

Again and again the white porcelain bust came down on Frant's forehead in my mind.

'I need a map,' I said.

Frant leaned against a wall, smoking a French cigarette, while I tried to work out from his free hotel map where Madame Ferber lived. I hadn't known that he was a smoker, but then I hadn't known that he was a violent maniac either, so it wasn't a huge surprise. Finally I located Madame Ferber's street, and was relieved to discover that it wasn't very far from where we were.

'We can walk it in half an hour,' I said to Frant.

He rolled his eyes, as if somehow I was responsible for our destination not being two metres away, and dropped his cigarette on the ground, where it fizzled out in a small puddle.

'Tell me,' said Frant as we walked on, 'this female acquaintance of yours, the so-called authoress … what is her name?'

'You can't guess?' I said.

'I take very little interest in the muddy wheels of commerce,' said Frant. 'Fame and celebrity are nothing compared to the broad sweep of history.'

'Yes, but she's a fellow Walker-Hebborn writer,' I said, boldly putting Frant and his absurd scribbling into the same boat as one of the most successful writers of our time. 'I translate her, so she's obviously foreign. She's a woman, and she lives in this part of Paris so she's successful. Surely those facts would narrow it down a bit?'

'I have no interest in puzzles,' said Frant, a man who had devoted his entire life to writing books in pretend languages and had come to Paris to unlock the secrets of a made-up book. 'Please just tell me who it is.'

I stopped, exasperated. 'Madame Ferber,' I said.

Frant looked blank.

'A.J.L. Ferber,' I said.

Frant looked, if anything, blanker.

'*She Walked Among Men*?' I said. '*Society's Elephant*? *Piquant Morning*?'

Frant shook his head.

'I can't believe you haven't heard of her,' I said. 'She's enormously successful. *There Is No Mountain* was made into a film. It did pretty well.'

'I don't go to the cinema,' Frant said, which I must admit didn't surprise me. Frant looked like someone who'd be upset if he found out about the talkies.

We walked on. I was struck by a thought.

'When we do meet Madame Ferber,' I said, 'it might be a

good idea if you don't mention that you haven't heard of any of her books.'

'You said half an hour,' complained Frant.

'It's this map,' I said. 'The scale is all wrong. This street looks quite short on the map, but it's not.'

The street, which occupied a couple of centimetres on the map, was in reality very long. Block after identical block of apartments stretched out ahead of us, each one a tribute to some imaginationless architect of the early 1900s. I found myself longing for a nice modern steel and glass office block to break the monotony of our journey.

Suddenly Frant stopped. He looked agitated.

'Are you all right?' I said, more out of form than concern.

'Yes!' he suddenly shouted. 'I'm fine! Just a stone in my shoe.'

'Maybe you ought to take it off then,' I said.

Frant looked at me, and turned away to fiddle with his shoe, which was latticed with enough laces to satisfy a Belgian seamstress. I walked away from him, just to have some space as the Americans say, and then I saw her.

It was the girl from the bar. And she was here. I hadn't seen her since that night. She looked different to when she'd been in the bar but it was definitely her. That night, she'd been tense, aloof, almost mysterious. And, even though the first time I'd met her she had been surrounded by the allure of low lights and mirrors, and now I was facing her, my heart was pounding like industry. Funny, I thought, all this time I had wanted to see her again, and now here she was. It was the most banal of thoughts, but it was also the most thrilling.

Now she did meet my eye, with a haunted gaze. She was still beautiful, but she was also – and this might have been the night light or it might have been my mind's eye – no longer ethereal.

Every inch of her face seemed filled with emotion – and not the poetic emotions of a foreign film, but the harsh, real emotions of someone who has lived life and that life has gone awry.

Standing in the shadows of an alleyway, the girl from the bar – who might or might not be Carrie – looked at me as though she had done something badly wrong. I had no idea what that might be. If anything, I was the guilty party. I'd gone through her private possessions, I'd withheld information and evidence from the police that might have been used to find her, and I'd fled the country on a mission which, though designed to help, had been a waste of time and effort.

But here she was now, in a Paris alleyway, looking straight at me. I turned to Frant, who had finally done up his shoelaces.

'It's her,' I said.

'Who's her when she's at home?' Frant said.

'The girl you were just staring at,' I said. Frant shrugged, as if to say that he was always staring at girls. The girl was still there, hesitant in a doorway. 'The girl from the bar. The girl whose disappearance brought me here.'

'Well, don't just stand there,' Frant said, standing up. 'Hey, miss! We need to talk to you! My friend is accused of your murder!'

The girl looked at Frant, and then at me, as if to say, 'Is this true?'

I looked back and nodded. Still nobody moved.

'Oh, for goodness' sake,' said Frant, and strode towards the girl.

In a moment she was gone. Frant ran to the alley, but he was too late. She had vanished completely.

'How vexing,' said Frant. 'I wonder why she didn't want to talk to us.'

'Is that what you wonder?' I said icily. 'You don't wonder why she's in Paris, or why she should turn up now? You don't wonder how she's suddenly come back to life, or evaded her so-called captors?'

'I did consider all those things,' said Frant, 'but found them less relevant. Nevertheless, you should be of good cheer.'

'Why?' I said. I may have sounded bitter.

'Because now that this girl has re-emerged, you are freed from any charge of murder or kidnap,' said Frant. 'Once it is established that she has been seen, unharmed, unmarked and alive, all will be well.'

'And how do we establish that?' I said. 'Nobody will take our word for it. Perhaps you should have taken a photograph.'

'I don't have a camera,' said Frant.

'On your phone – never mind,' I said. I didn't want to have to explain mobile phones to Frant. I didn't want to have to explain anything to Frant. I just wanted to get away from here.

'She has been seen by us,' said Frant. 'Therefore she has been seen by others. You are in the clear.'

'Yes,' I said, 'as soon as we convince the famously liberal French police that you brained a man through pure chance and we accidentally stole rare documents.'

'These things happen,' said Frant. 'As I said, once we are in a safe haven, we can plan our next move.'

'I don't want to plan our next move,' I said. 'I want to look for the girl.'

'The girl can wait,' said Frant, 'And stop sulking. We need to get off the streets.'

A lone police car cruised by. Was it my imagination that its occupants were peering unusually keenly at passers-by through their sunglasses?

'Now,' said Frant.

After some false starts, we finally discovered the door to Madame Ferber's apartment. There appeared to be no doorbell, and it took us another few minutes of searching before we located a grimy plate of buzzers set into the wall. The names next to each buzzer had been erased over time and there was no way of telling which apartment was which.

'Count them,' Frant said. 'Assume that the bottom basement is one, and work your way up.'

'I was just about to,' I said. Madame Ferber lived in Apartment 57, and I ran my fingers up the plate to the fifth buzzer.

I was about to press it when I hesitated.

'Ring her, damn it,' said Frant with unusual fervour.

'I was just thinking,' I said. 'Is this the wisest course of action?'

'It is the only course of action,' said Frant. 'We have nowhere else to go.'

'We could try the British Embassy,' I said. 'We could call my publisher.'

'You could call your mother,' Frant said rudely. 'It would be just as effective.'

He pushed me out of the way and rang the buzzer. There was silence.

'She's out,' I said. I turned to go, and just then a familiar voice came from the intercom.

'*Oui?*' said Madame Ferber.

'It's me,' I said, 'your translator. Jacky.'

There was a long pause. Then the door buzzed open.

I looked at Frant. 'If this goes wrong,' I said, 'it's your fault.'

'I take full responsibility,' Frant said, and pushed the door.

CHAPTER EIGHT

Inside the apartment block, there was no sign of dirt or untidiness. The lobby was an immense affair, with green-veined marble steps and bronze banisters leading away from a charming hallway decorated with low tables and artificial flowers in tall ruby glass vases. To one side was an old-fashioned lift, all metal grilles and carpeted floor. Frant headed for this without a glance around.

'Hurry up,' he said. 'We don't have much time.'

'I thought this was your safe haven,' I said.

'We're not in it yet,' Frant said, and rattled the lift doors open.

I followed him into the lift as he jabbed at the fifth-floor button. Nothing happened.

'You have to close the doors by hand,' I said, and pulled them shut.

Frant glowered at me and jabbed at the button again. Now the lift began, clanking, to go up. It took a long time. At each floor, it stopped and we had to help an elderly lady or enormous man wrench open the doors so they could inch their way into the lift, and then clash the doors shut again before we could proceed. All this sent Frant into a fury of teeth-grinding and sweaty-eyebrowed tension, and I could see that he was on the edge of his nerves. Obviously the long day's travails were starting to get to him. I can't say this distressed me greatly. I felt it was his turn to do a bit of suffering.

At last the lift reached the fifth floor. Frant tore open the doors like a strongman ripping a telephone directory asunder and burst onto the landing. I followed a moment later, and we found ourselves standing right outside Apartment 57.

There was no name by the door, but then what was I expecting? A big sign saying 'A.J.L. FERBER, RECLUSIVE AUTHOR, LIVES HERE'? I knocked on the thick wood door. After a few seconds of silence, I knocked again. This time I heard a tiny sound, as of a sliver of metal being pulled back. I suspected that Madame Ferber was at the spy-hole. Frant must have thought the same as he stood to one side, presumably to avoid being seen. This was wise, I felt, as the sight of Euros Frant, fedora, eyebrows and all, through the fish-eye prism of a spy-hole, would alarm even the most imperturbable of people. Especially now he was muttering, 'Come on, come on, come on,' in an agitated undertone.

Suddenly the door opened and a woman appeared.

'Madame Ferber,' I was about to say, when I stopped. The woman at the door was young, pretty and dressed in a manner that, I presumed, was stylish but not fashionable. While I do not mean to imply any disrespect to A.J.L. Ferber, I very much doubted that this was her.

'I am Camilla Carr,' said the young woman. 'How may I help you?'

'We've come to see Madame Ferber,' said Frant loudly.

I elbowed him aside and told Camilla my name. 'I'm Madame Ferber's translator,' I said. 'I am more than sorry that we have been compelled to disturb you, but we had no choice.'

'Madame Ferber is not here,' said Camilla. 'If you are able

to return tomorrow, perhaps we could make an appointment to see her?'

'We need to see her now, dammit,' said Frant, who was becoming more and more aggressive.

'I'm sorry about my friend,' I said. 'We will return tomorrow.'

'Thank you,' said Camilla, and was about to close the door when a voice said, 'Wait. Let them in.'

Camilla stood aside without even a shrug and I walked in after her. Frant was about to follow, but I frowned and motioned for him to stay put. In his current state he was like an overexcited puppy. To my surprise, he nodded energetically and indicated that he was happy where he was.

The apartment's entrance hall was lit only by heavily shrouded lamps. There was a Persian rug on the dark wooden floor, and a small mahogany chair that looked hefty despite its size. Beside the chair stood a woman. She was wearing a long, almost purple dress, a tangle of gold and pearl necklaces, and flat shoes that did little to disguise her unusual height. Her face, which right now looked pretty stern, was handsome in the way the Edwardians used it of women; she had a strong chin, a Roman nose and very dark brown eyes. Her hair was completely white, and braided.

'I am A.J.L. Ferber,' she said, in a voice familiar to me from many telephone calls. In person, her accent was a little less clipped, but I still found myself wondering if she was Swiss, Austrian or German. I decided that now wasn't the time to ask her, though. She didn't look at all pleased to see me.

'What is the meaning of this intrusion?' she said, not sternly but not kindly either. 'Is this some pre-emptive strike by Mr Walker-Hebborn? I have already indicated that I will, under duress, visit him next week.'

'It's nothing to do with him,' I said. 'This is entirely my fault.'

'I see,' said Madame Ferber. 'Well, I presume that you have

not come for my autograph. And you could hardly be here to steal the draft of my latest *oeuvre* because you have already translated that for me. Is this a social call?'

'Maybe you could let the young man tell you himself?' said Camilla, and a smile passed between Madame Ferber and her. I was impressed; in person, the most demanding author on Walker-Hebborn's roster was proving to be far less terrifying than I had imagined. But then Madame Ferber turned back to me.

'Camilla is right, and I do not take kindly to unannounced visitors. Why are you here?'

'It's a long story,' I said.

'I rather feared it might be,' said Madame Ferber, which was rich coming from someone who didn't get out of bed for less than a million words. 'Perhaps you should sit down and tell me it properly.'

Camilla opened the door to a large sitting room and Madame Ferber and I entered.

'Tea, please,' said Madame Ferber to Camilla and we sat down.

'What about your friend?' said Camilla, looking at me, and Madame Ferber frowned.

'You're not on your own?' she said. 'That would explain the blustering earlier.'

'He's fine where he is,' I said. 'You might get him a glass of water.' I could bring Frant into the conversation when I'd explained everything else. And there was plenty of explaining to be getting on with. Camilla left the room.

Madame Ferber lit what I could only assume was a small cheroot and blew smoke into the chair. 'Tell me everything,' she said.

And once again I unfolded the whole saga, from bar to *Alice*, from police to escape and, because there was something about Madame Ferber that discouraged both omission and dishonesty, from Frant's assault on Monsieur Derringer to our current flight to her apartment.

Throughout the story, Madame Ferber sat in silence, her expression unchanging. When I had finished, she didn't speak, but continued to sit in even more silence. I hoped she was thinking. I hoped she wasn't considering whether or not to call the police. And I couldn't help wondering, in a weird and pointless way, if my revelations would affect her relationship with Walker-Hebborn Publishing. It certainly wasn't the best way for a translator to introduce himself to one of his authors.

Finally she spoke. 'You seem to have been, as my mother would have said, in the wars. I have no doubt that you are the source of some of your own difficulties but things would appear to have got out of hand in a manner not of your choosing.'

'I think so,' I said. 'Right now, I would be happy to turn myself in to the police and get all this over with.'

'I do hope that isn't the confessional urge of the fugitive speaking,' said Madame Ferber.

'I just can't think of any other way out of this,' I said. 'I'm sorry I came to you but there seemed nowhere else to go.'

'Never mind,' said Madame Ferber. 'Possibly you have done the right thing. After all, you are not the idiot who assaulted that man, and most of your reactions have been those of a misguided and panicky innocent.'

I said nothing. I wanted to believe that she was right.

'I should imagine,' said Madame Ferber, 'that with a few tiresome calls to the right people, I can alleviate some of the difficulties you speak of. But that doesn't concern me right now.'

'What does concern you?' I said.

'Your companion,' said Madame Ferber. 'The curiously silent Mr Frant. He was, according to you, furiously keen to seek asylum in my apartment, yet now he is here, he seems equally keen to keep out of my way.'

'He just doesn't want to impose,' I said, but even as I said it, it sounded ridiculous. If there was one man on earth who generally did want to impose, it would be Euros Frant.

'I find that hard to believe,' said Madame Ferber. 'But then so much of your story is … well, that is what it is like. A story.'

'It's all true, I assure you,' I said.

'Please. I did not mean to offend. But consider. You are a man who does not live a life of high drama. Excitement for you is confined perhaps to the pages of other people's novels.'

'That, and the pleasure of making them comprehensible to the general public,' I said. I was surprised at myself. I had just talked back to Madame Ferber. Walker-Hebborn, had he been able to see us, would have been chewing his own knuckles in horror and disbelief.

'I see you have learned to stand up for yourself,' said Madame Ferber. 'An excellent trait in a translator. Unlike some, I have always thought of translators as to a small degree collaborators in an author's work, rather than a linguistic bureau de change, converting one tongue to another.'

Now I was surprised and pleased. 'Thank you,' I said. 'It makes a change from Mr Frant's attitude to my job.'

'Yes,' said Madame Ferber. 'Mr Frant again. Have you ever been to Frant? I have. Pretty place.'

She tailed off, and appeared to go into some kind of reverie. I wondered if she was about to fall asleep, when suddenly she rang a bell. She had to ring it again, and finally Camilla came back into the room.

'Mr Frant wanted a croissant with his glass of water,' she explained.

'I am sure he did,' said Madame Ferber. 'Camilla, Jacky will be staying with us for a while.'

Camilla looked startled, and so, I imagine, did I. I hadn't heard my own name for days, which says a lot about the fractured nature of my recent existence.

'What about Mr Frant?' said Camilla.

Madame Ferber gave her what my mother used to call an old-fashioned look. 'This young man is my translator. He is familiar to me and, whatever his apparent crimes, I feel I should give him a chance and, as the Americans say, "some space" to extricate himself from the situation in which he finds himself. I am under no such obligation to Mr Frant.'

'I don't like him much myself,' I said. 'But he's all mixed up in this too and I feel obliged to him—'

'I fail to see why,' said Madame Ferber. 'Nothing he has done or said suggests a shred of obligation on your part. Also there is just something about him I don't like. Did you notice, Camilla,' she said, turning to her companion, 'he has the same last initial as I do?'

'Yes,' said Camilla. 'We wondered if that would be the case.'

I looked at them, baffled. 'I don't understand,' I said.

'No,' said Madame Ferber. 'Anyway, that is my offer. One hates to be dramatic, but your future rather depends on your answer.'

I wasn't happy. It was an impossible situation. On the one hand, I was trying to help a man for whom gratitude and thanks were alien ideas. If I did help him, it would almost certainly harm my relationship with my employer's most important client. I realise it sounds absurd worrying about career details at a time like this but the mind, as they say, is a monkey, and a pedantic, nervous monkey at that. Yet I couldn't just abandon Frant to the authorities. Knowing him, he would assault several policemen during the course of his eventual arrest and be so unpleasant to everyone involved in his case that he would end up on the guillotine. I didn't know if they still used the guillotine in France, but even if they didn't, I suspected they would make an exception for Frant.

There was another reason, too. The girl. Despite Madame Ferber's kindness and the fact that she was as it were the only port in the storm, she wasn't the one who could help me find the girl. The person who could do that, regrettably, was Frant. In every aspect of the situation, from the *Alice* to the place where she had acquired the notebook, Frant had been peripheral to her actions. I had no idea what connection the girl had to the world that Frant moved in, but it was his world and, unpleasant though it was, he was my only link to her.

I said as much to Madame Ferber, and she looked weary.

'Then I am afraid I have no choice,' she said. 'It is a terrible pity, because I find that I like you, dogged young man. Camilla, please show him out.'

I was surprised at Madame Ferber's abruptness, but realised at once that she had acted correctly according to her lights. She had offered me a way out and I had, effectively, refused it. I stood up.

'Thank you, Madame Ferber,' I said.

'Camilla will show you to the door,' said Madame Ferber.

But Camilla was absent.

'Camilla?' Madame Ferber said, a note of uncertainty in her voice.

There was a thump, and a scream and Camilla staggered into the room, propelled by an unseen force. The door burst open and Frant stood there, covered in croissant crumbs. Ridiculously, he was holding a gun.

'Where did you get that?' I said. It wasn't the most relevant question, but it was the first one that came to mind.

'Shut up,' said Frant, his usual charm to the fore. He waved the gun around, vaguely but dangerously. 'Everyone sit down,' he said.

'Frant, for God's sake! Stop acting like a gangster!' I shouted. 'There's really is no need for this.'

Madame Ferber had been silent so far. Now she looked at him. 'Get out of my apartment,' she said. 'Put that gun down and get out of my apartment.'

Frant ignored her. He was too busy peering at his gun and I realised he was looking for the safety catch. He obviously had little or no experience with weapons and I couldn't work out if this was a good thing or a bad thing. I was just deciding on 'bad thing' when Camilla lunged at him and, with a forearm like iron, jabbed Frant in the throat so hard that he fell back against the wall. I could only stand in confusion as she grabbed Madame Ferber's hand and pulled her towards the door.

Madame Ferber hesitated.

Camilla saw her look at me. 'Why did you have to bring him here?' she said, giving me a look of hate. 'You're as bad as he is.'

Madame Ferber shook her hand off. 'I can't help you now,' she said to me.

Camilla was looking for something on the wall. She found it, a small red dot under a light switch, and pushed it.

'Panic button,' she said. 'The police will be here in three minutes.' And she pulled Madame Ferber out of the room.

Madame Ferber cast me one backward glance. 'I'm sorry,' she said, and was gone.

Silence fell in the apartment, broken only by a faint gurgle from Frant as he tried to stand up while holding his crushed throat. Eventually he got to his feet.

'Quickly,' he croaked horribly. 'We haven't got much time.'

*

When I was a child, I had what my mother used to call unsuitable friends. Even at the time, I thought this was unfair because I never thought of them as my friends. They were all different – some were bigger boys, some were runts, one was a girl – but they all had one thing in common: they were all fairly unpleasant. One was a small boy called Hendrick. His parents were perhaps the only Dutch people in the world who didn't speak English fluently and this may have been the root of Hendrick's oddness. More likely I think he was just naturally horrible. I was always being left with Hendrick because my mother felt sorry for his parents and used to visit them and talk to them in loud English. Hendrick and I would go to his room, ostensibly to look at his collection of weird Dutch soldiers, and as soon as the door closed he would jump on my back and thump me repeatedly in the kidneys until I began to cry silently. I had to cry silently because if I made any noise, Hendrick would bite me on the stomach. I said nothing of this to my mother because I reckoned that if she felt sorry for Hendrick's parents, she would by extension be sympathetic to Hendrick and his horribleness.

Then there was Job-Job. I think his real name was Jonathan but he was Job-Job to everyone but his mother. Job-Job was a few months younger than me and we met in a play park one summer holiday. After that, Job-Job followed me wherever I went for about three years. He would follow me home where my mother, assuming we were friends, would invite him in for milk. He followed me when I went for walks, or to Cub Scout meetings. And once he followed me to school – Job-Job attended a different local school because he was a Catholic – which caused chaos because he managed to attend four or five classes before lunchtime when his imposture was finally rumbled. I got the blame for this but it led to the end of Job-Job's lamb-like devotion when his furious parents blamed me for everything and sent Job-Job to a far-off boarding school where he could follow other boys to his heart's content and nobody would ever notice.

Louise was perhaps the saddest. A tomboy, she was, like Hendrick, prone to sudden bouts of astonishing violence, but with her it was always much more random. In the middle of a conversation, she would suddenly come at me like a dervish, fists flailing, until I was bruised and stunned. I remember once we were catching butterflies and one escaped her net. I said something reassuring to her, like, 'There's another one over there', and she jumped me and kicked me in the ribs. I never said anything to my mother about these incidents, blaming them on imaginary bullies, partly because I was scared of Louise and partly because I felt sorry for her. When she wasn't attacking me, she would tell me about her family in long, confused stories that were clearly complete fantasy.

Her father, she claimed, was a test pilot. His absence from her life was explained by the fact that he was such a good test pilot he had been asked to go to America for a year and teach other test pilots to be as good as him. Her mother was a secret agent, and that was how she had met her father, delivering some confidential (Louise said 'compidential' but I was good at words and knew what she meant) papers concerning a new aeroplane. They had fallen in love and when her father's contract expired, her mother would leave the secret service and they would move away and live in a big house together. I would nod wisely, or wince if she was hurting me at the time, but I knew these stories were nonsense. I'd seen Louise's house and it was a rundown place with rubbish on the lawn and a broken window. But Louise was waiting for the day when her father would return home on a motorbike with a flight jacket and a suntan, and I wasn't going to disillusion her.

After a while, my mother began to notice that whenever I came home from play, I would be injured in some way. At first she blamed herself but as time went on – this would be shortly after my father went away – she decided that there was a degree of what lawyers call 'contributory negligence'. I was deliberately hanging around with bad children, getting into fights and ripping my clothes for fun. The fact was, though, that I had never asked to be friends with these children. I was, looking back on it, someone that bullies and oddballs gravitated towards. I was, essentially, born to be their punchbag.

As the years went by, and I gained a degree of self-awareness and confidence, I learned to recognise these people. At school and at college, there were young men and women looking for someone to have a hold over, but I always managed to avoid them. I became expert, in fact, at dodging these unsuitable friendships, to the extent that if somebody showed signs of becoming a rod for my back in later acquaintance, I would almost immediately give them a wide berth. Sometimes I might look back and think, Maybe they would have turned out to be nice people after all, but nine times out of ten I would see them with their new friends, the people who had fallen victim to them, and consider myself better off.

Now I stood in the hallway of an opulent apartment in Paris, through whose doorway one of my employer's most valuable clients had just fled, thanks to my incompetence, and I looked down at the expensive carpet, where Euros Frant was massaging the muscles in his throat back into place, and I realised that, once again, I had managed to fall into the hands of yet another, in my mother's phrase, unsuitable friend. Not that Frant was my friend, you understand, as even at their worst the likes of Hendrick and Louise had afforded me the odd companionable moment, but he was the only person I had spent any considerable amount of time with for several months and we were, in a way, bound together by the coinciding of our different missions. I had even, it now occurred to me, confided in him. He was in every surface appearance a friend. I had no doubt that, in the language of the press, he was certainly an accomplice and a fellow suspect.

Camilla's final angry words came back to me. I was as bad as he was. Frant and I were, in short, bound together, and I didn't even like him. It was arguably at this point, then, that I should have just said to hell with it and run away. But it was also at this point that I found myself unable to. I looked at the figure on the floor, trying to get to his feet with his throat in one hand and a gun in the other, and I said, 'Let me help you up.'

'I'm fine,' said Frant in the voice of a cartoon duck. He pocketed the gun – I saw he had failed to release the safety catch – and got to his feet.

'Where the hell did you get that gun?' I said.

'I found it in a drawer by the front door,' said Frant. It sounded stupid enough to be true.

'I really think we should get out of here,' I said. 'The police are on their way.'

'I don't know if you've noticed, but the police have a strange habit of always being on their way and never actually arriving,' said Frant. He went over to the panic button that Camilla had pressed and prised it from its housing with a letter opener. The two wires protruding from the back of the button were not connected to anything. 'Quite literally a false alarm,' said Frant, and coughed horribly. Then he crossed the room. I followed him in as he pulled out drawers and threw cushions onto the floor.

'Please stop doing that,' I said.

'Oh!' shouted Frant. 'Excuse me! Have I crossed a line? Apparently it's all right to rob people and attack them and pull guns on them but throwing some cushions around! Beyond the pale!'

I didn't bother pointing out that he was the one robbing and attacking people and even if he wasn't, it still didn't make it all right. I was very tired. I put one of the cushions back on the sofa and sat on it. Frant had now moved on to shoving pictures to one side on the wall, like a burglar looking for a wall safe, I thought, until I realised that he actually was a burglar looking for a wall safe, and I was just sitting there watching him.

'What are you doing?' I said. 'This is Madame Ferber's apartment. You should stop, now.'

'Shut up,' Frant said. 'Do you think I give a fig for Madame Ferber? She always was a third-rate authoress, anyway. These drapes and furnishings were not the fruits of talent, I can assure you.'

A thin chill went down my spine. 'You told me you'd never heard of her,' I said. 'You denied knowledge of her books entirely.'

'Of course I did,' said Frant. 'I was playing my cards close to my chest. Do you think that if I had expressed my true knowledge of Madame Ferber's rotten books, you would have been so eager to take me to her apartment?'

'I wasn't in the least eager,' I said.

'You were so keen to show off your threadbare acquaintance with the famous writer that you all but carried me here,' said Frant, tapping at a dado rail. 'Look at me, the great translator, best of friends with the legendary A.J.L. Ferber. Oh, she's such a recluse, you know, but I'm sure she'll have time to see me.'

I didn't argue with him. There was no point. He had a gun and he was an idiot. Instead, I got up, closed some drawers and straightened some paintings. Now Frant was peeling up the corners of the carpet.

'Have you actually read any of her books?' he said.

'Of course I have,' I said, 'I'm her translator. It's one of the essential requirements of the job.'

'I don't mean follow them line by line like a child working out a code in a puzzle book,' said Frant. 'I mean actually read them. Comprehend their meaning beyond the odd sentence. Garner a sense of the message and philosophy behind each novel.'

I said nothing. Of course, as a translator you don't really have to indulge in the luxury of enjoying the book that you're working on. I had always said to myself that one day I would sit down and really have a go at one of Madame Ferber's novels, but what with one thing and another I'd never actually got around to doing so.

I must have said as much to Frant because he paused in the act of prising up a loose floorboard and said, 'There's really no need. She combines the most turgid moments of Henry James's later prose with the least interesting insights of Ayn Rand. All mixed in with a mysticism that would make Kahlil Gibran feel queasy.'

There was something tugging at the back of my mind about Frant's rather too pat summary. I wondered if I'd read it somewhere else. It wouldn't surprise me, as Frant had never struck me as particularly inventive, even for someone who did write books in imaginary languages.

'I'm afraid I've never read any of those authors,' I said. 'And surely all great writers are influenced by other people? You yourself owe a huge debt to Tolkien and Umberto Eco.'

That struck home. 'I don't know what you're talking about,' said Frant, and stood up. Whatever he was looking for was continuing to elude him.

'Can we go now?' I said. 'I have no idea what we're doing here.'

'We can go when I've found it,' said Frant, and to my alarm he picked up a poker from the fireside.

'Found what?' I said.

'What I came here to get,' Frant said, hefting the poker in his soft writer's grip.

'We came here because it was my idea,' I said. 'We came here to find a safe haven, as I remember it. You didn't know we were coming here—'

'Just like I didn't know who Madame Ferber was,' said Frant. He got down on his knees by the fireplace and started jabbing the poker up the chimney.

I realised that I was completely out of my depth. I was beginning to suspect that somehow I was being led along. I felt depressed and used. Finally, I felt that I couldn't go any further. I got to my feet and wondered if I should just leave without saying goodbye to Frant. It would be easy. I could simply sidle over to the door and walk out. Then again, he had a gun.

'Ah,' said Frant. The jabbing had dislodged something. He prodded the chimney some more and great lumps of soot fell into the fireplace. Frant shoved again, harder, and this time something quite large dropped into the grate.

'Get me a newspaper,' said Frant.

'I want nothing more to do with this,' I said. 'I'm going to the police, right now. I'm sorry, Frant, it's over.'

'All right,' said Frant. 'Just pass me some newspaper and you can go.'

I paused. 'Damn you,' I said. Then I added, 'Why have I got to get the newspaper?'

'Because we're in this together,' said Frant. 'Because this concerns you as well. And because I've got soot on my hands.'

I passed Frant a copy of the *Herald Tribune* and he wrapped it around the large item. He wiped it down and I could see it was a black metal box. He picked it up.

'It's locked,' he said. 'Look in the bureau drawer.'

I went over to the desk, opened it and inside the first drawer was a small bunch of keys. I gave them to Frant and he selected the smallest. It fitted the lock. Frant opened the box.

'Your hands are clean,' he said. 'Yours is the honour of removing the package.'

Inside the box was something small wrapped in clean white tissue paper. I lifted it out carefully and set it on the bureau. Frant wiped his hands on the curtain and came over.

'Unwrap it,' he said.

I removed the thin layers of paper. Inside was a book, bound in red cloth with gold lettering. I picked it up. The lettering read *Il Abentres D'Alissa Paro Illo Specolo*. Even I could translate that. *Alice's Adventures Through the Looking-Glass*.

'I've seen this book before,' I said.

'You've seen a copy of it,' Frant said. 'A copy lost or misfiled in a London student library office. This is the original. This,' he said, taking the translated *Alice* from me, 'is what we came to Paris for.'

I stared at him. 'We came to Paris for the Von Fremdenplatz documents,' I said. 'You remember. You hit a man over the head with a bust and ran away with three of the bound volumes.'

'I have to get them all back,' said Frant.

'All the *Alice*s?' I said. 'How many are there?'

'All the *books*. Open this.'

I realised he meant the book. I opened it to the title page. It was all gibberish to me. Familiar gibberish, but gibberish nevertheless.

'Read it,' said Frant, his eyebrows all but crawling across his forehead in agitation.

'*Il Abentres D'Alissa Paro Illo Specolo Y Quasta El' Trovada*,' I said, wondering absurdly if I was getting the accent right. This was a language that nobody had ever spoken, and for good reason. '*Paria Lewis Carroll. Nove Translati Paria Jeremy Andrews Y Anna Ferber ...*'

I looked at Frant. His eyebrows were virtually tangoing.

'Madame Ferber?' I said. 'I'm guessing, but this blurb means that Madame Ferber was one of the translators of the *Alice*?'

Frant nodded. 'Along with Jeremy Andrews,' he said.

'But if she translated the *Alice*—'

'With Jeremy Andrews—'

'Then why didn't she mention it when I was telling her about the girl and everything?'

'Interesting question,' said Frant, taking the *Alice* back. 'You tell me.'

'I don't know,' I said. 'I am completely and utterly confused. I thought she was – well, I thought she might be my friend.'

'She is nobody's friend but her own,' said Frant. 'She is Ferber, the betrayer of men. But now we have her. The web is closing in.'

I didn't understand what he meant about Madame Ferber but he was right about the other thing. I had no idea if a web could close in or not, but I supposed that if it could, one was closing in on us all right.

'What do we do now?' I said. 'I still think we should take this to the police.'

'No,' said Frant. 'Not when we are so close. Besides, you want to see the girl again, don't you?'

For a moment I actually had to think about it. Tiredness does that to you. You're focused on something for the longest time until in a way you take your focus, your obsession if you like, for granted, and you put it into a little room at the back of your mind, as if for safe-keeping. And you lock it up there and you get on with things and one day, when you're finally getting close to your goal, you realise you've almost forgotten what you signed on for. That's how I felt, anyway. I didn't even know if I was any nearer to finding the girl, and when I thought about it, I grasped how absurd my quest might seem to her. After all, as I said, a long time ago it feels like, we didn't exactly part on the best of terms and what to me seems perfectly natural might be totally weird to her.

But then we had seen her in the street. That was the bit that really seemed like a dream. I have never hallucinated in my life. I've only been drunk a couple of times and I didn't have visions or see things then, I just fell asleep. I had no idea why she was in Paris. Maybe it was simply a good place to hide.

'I need a moment to think,' I said. Frant was about to say something, then thought better of it.

I sat down on the settee. 'I came here to find the girl,' I said. 'I don't, with all due respect, care about the Von Fremdenplatz documents or the *Alice* or any of this. I care about finding the girl. I don't know how Madame Ferber is involved with this, if she is, or if she can help me find the girl. I guess if she could help me, or she wanted to, she would have said something, instead of keeping quiet all the while when I was telling her everything.'

'She is not your friend,' said Frant.

'Please be quiet,' I said. 'Because there's you, as well, isn't there? You bring me here to look at the documents, you say, but when we get here, you batter a man unconscious, steal a book and then ... Oh my God. You made me come here, didn't you?'

Frant said nothing.

'You knew Madame Ferber was here all the time,' I said. 'You knew I would lead you to her.'

'How could I?' said Frant. 'I didn't know that you knew her.'

'No, but you could easily work it out. You just have to look inside one of her books to see my name where it says "Translated by". Or maybe when you came to Walker-Hebborn with your manuscript, you realised she was one of his writers and you worked it all out from there.'

'I don't see why I would need you to lead me to her,' said Frant.

'Because she's Madame Ferber, the famous recluse,' I said. 'She doesn't see anyone, let alone people who've got a grudge against her. She wouldn't have seen me unless it was an emergency.'

'It was an emergency,' said Frant. 'We were – we are – on the run from the authorities. Unless you're saying that I staged that too. And that for good measure I also arranged for you to be framed for murder.'

I thought about that. Frant had a point. 'I don't know,' I said. 'But I do know that our coming here is not a coincidence.'

'It doesn't matter what it is,' said Frant. 'Anna Ferber is an evil woman. That's all you need to know.'

I think that's what did it for me. If all your life you've been told by people not to ask questions and don't worry about it, it can get wearing. When you ask questions like, 'When is my father coming home?' or 'Are you seeing someone else?' and you never get real answers, just a pat on the head and a kind word as if you're the kind of person who's unable to understand important things, like you're not all there or something. I was tired of being the child left outside the door while an argument was going on in the other room. I was sick of being the man everyone talked about behind his back because his girlfriend wasn't really his girlfriend. I hated being the person in the office who got looks even though he was the only one the famous weird author would talk to.

'I don't think she is evil,' I said. 'She may not have been entirely straight with me, but neither have you been. And she hasn't attacked anyone or pulled a gun on them. So if you don't mind I'll make my own choices about who's evil and who's not. And you can help me, Frant.'

Frant looked at me through narrowed eyes. 'What do you mean?' he said.

'You can tell me what exactly is going on,' I said. 'No more lies. I want to know how you know Madame Ferber. I want to know how she wrote a book in the same language as the Von Fremdenplatz documents. I want to know how the girl comes into it. And,' I said, almost as an afterthought, 'I want to know why we saw the girl from the bar in a street in Paris.'

'I do not know,' said Frant.

'Stop lying!' I shouted. 'I'm sorry,' I said. I had startled myself. 'And now please, if you don't mind, I'm very tired and I'm extremely confused and I would just like you to tell me what the hell is happening.'

'I will tell you one thing and one thing only,' said Frant.

'Like fun you will,' I said.

'This is the only thing you need to know,' Frant said. 'I assure you, everything else will fall into place afterwards.'

'It better,' I said. I sat back, waiting for Frant to speak.

'I draw your attention to the title page of the *Alice*,' he said.

'Oh great,' I said. 'That again.'

'As you correctly surmised, under the title it reads "New translation by Jeremy Andrews and Anna Ferber".'

'I got that,' I said. 'No offence, but so what?'

Frant put the book down. 'I,' he said, 'am Jeremy Andrews.'

CHAPTER NINE

I looked at him. 'Pardon?' I said. 'I don't understand.'

'I am Jeremy Andrews,' said Frant. 'I'm Jeremy Andrews. I really can't put it more simply than that. *Yo soy Jeremy Andrews. Je m'appelle Jeremy Andrews. Ich heiße—*'

'Yes, all right, I get it,' I said. 'But you're not Jeremy Andrews. You're Euros Frant.'

'I write as Euros Frant,' said Frant, or Andrews. 'Do you suppose my readers, steeped as they are in fantasy and myth, would accept a book from the hand of a mere Jeremy Andrews? No, I am Euros Frant to them, a name that combines both the Celtic twilight and a good honest English village.'

'All right,' I said. 'So now I know that you and Madame Ferber translated the *Alice* into your made-up language. That doesn't help me at all.'

'Really?' said Frant. 'Think about it.'

Another expression I really dislike. Like there's something really obvious that everyone else has realised straight away without even having to work it out, but stupid here has got to think about it. That's me all over, I guess. The Mule, as they say. Nevertheless, I thought about it.

'You and Madame Ferber worked up this *Alice* yourselves,'

214

I said slowly. 'So you made up this whole language. Which is the same language as the—'

I stared at Frant.

'Now you're getting it,' said Frant.

'Which means you two wrote the Von Fremdenplatz documents,' I said.

'Strictly speaking, I did most of the actual writing,' said Frant. 'Anna was involved in ... other ways. Editing, researching and perhaps to some extent the actual initial conceptualisation.'

'You mean it was her idea and she did all the work?' I said.

'That is how she might put it,' Frant said. 'But without me it would just be a catalogue, a random collection of images.'

'Whereas with your input it's a random collection of images in a made-up language,' I said, but I knew I was wrong.

Frant could see it too, because he nodded and said, 'The Von Fremdenplatz wouldn't have worked if I ... if we hadn't rendered it into its own language. Where's the mystery in a document written in English, or German? Where's the enigma? It's the fact that nobody knows what the Von Fremdenplatz is, or what it was for, that makes it interesting. And valuable.'

'Let me get this straight,' I said. 'You knew all along what language the documents were written in because you invented it. You and Madame Ferber.'

'She really just did the grammar,' said Frant, 'which, being based on Nordic and Romance influences, wasn't particularly hard. The vocabulary, on the other hand—'

'Is mostly a mishmash of several well-known languages with a few weird words thrown in to make it a bit harder,' I said. 'Given a bit more time and a lot less running around, I could probably have translated the Von Fremdenplatz myself.

But I didn't get to see it until ten seconds before you clouted a guy with a bust.'

'Such vanity,' said Frant. 'The Von Fremdenplatz documents are one of the great achievements of the modern age, and I won't have them dismissed so easily.'

'Whatever,' I said. 'You didn't mind lying through your teeth about them to get here. They're just a bargaining tool to you.'

'A bargaining tool I spent ten years of my life creating,' said Frant. 'When I say achievement, I mean achievement. The planning, the sourcing, the writing ... the sheer expense of the project. While others of our generation were going out into the world and making their noisy mark, Anna and I worked ceaselessly and in secret on our project.'

'Why?' I said. 'Why do all this work and not tell anyone? Leave all these books in different places and just watch when some rich guy buys them and locks them away in a museum?'

'We had a plan,' said Frant. 'Anna's idea, really. She wanted to create something that existed purely for itself. It would have no roots in anything modern or contemporary and it wouldn't be part of any movement or trend or fashion.' He almost spat the words. 'It wasn't there ironically or as a reference to someone else's work or a tribute. It didn't exist for profit or fame, or to further anybody's career. And it was mysterious because that would make it more beautiful, and because then nobody could file it or label it.' He looked almost dreamy.

'It sounds like it was really important to you,' I said.

'It was the best thing I ever did,' Frant replied. 'It was marvellous. Nothing I ever write will come close to it. Even Anna, with all her books and her success, has never done anything as good. She herself would admit that.'

'Were you and she ...' I found it hard to say the words. 'Were you and she an item?'

'An item?' said Frant angrily. 'You mean were we dating? Were we romantically involved? Of course we were. You don't spend ten years of your life on something like that and not become involved. Consider, man. When we began, we were two students working on, essentially, an academic prank. We did it because we loved language and we loved ideas and Anna had the idea of rendering *Alice* into a language that had never existed. We printed up two copies for our own entertainment. They looked astonishing, like messages from another, stranger place. Then we thought, what might that other place be like? What would its encyclopedia be? Its gazetteer? And from that small idea came the Von Fremdenplatz.'

'Like Borges,' I said, remembering the article I'd read.

'Borges!' shouted Frant. 'Borges was a librarian! He never did anything. Bash down a thousand words and look at me, I've written a masterpiece. Borges wrote a little story about an encyclopedia from a different world. We *made* it.'

'But the Von Fremdenplatz documents look amazing,' I said. 'They're very professional. You must have spent a fortune.'

'Are you listening to me?' said Frant. 'We spent our youth making them. When other people were out buying houses and cars and holidays, we were making friends with printers and bookbinders, we were getting the copyrights to images and buying expensive cameras to take decent pictures with. You haven't seen the first Von Fremdenplatz document. It was meant to be a fakery of a travel document, typed on a real 1950s typewriter using a sheet of unwatermarked foolscap paper. We spent three weeks sourcing the paper, an afternoon making sure the typewriter ribbon was accurately faded, and then we had to find a printer who could scan it correctly. And that was for two pages.'

'A real labour of love,' I said, almost impressed. 'I must

admit, I find it hard to picture you and Madame Ferber sitting there at home, working on your great forgery together on a Sunday evening.'

'You're mocking me,' said Frant. 'But then, you've done nothing in your life. I've invented a world.'

'With Madame Ferber,' I said. 'That was more the part I find hard to believe.'

Frant shrugged and I almost expected him to say that they had been young and they had been in love. But he said, 'She was a different person then. Not the *grande dame* of letters she is now. I sometimes wonder which is the greatest of Anna Ferber's creations, the Von Fremdenplatz or Anna herself.'

'So what happened?' I said. 'Ten years working cheek by jowl with your girlfriend took its toll?'

'That,' said Frant, 'and a divergence of ambitions. She had always wanted to be a novelist. No, more important than that. She wanted to be a great writer. An absurd dream, of course, but by then Anna was quite an accomplished forger. She had spent a decade helping me to create an entire universe. It was no great leap, then, to write a mere novel.'

I could smell the sour grapes coming off him. I almost didn't blame him. He reminded me of one of those stand-up comics who'd been half of a double act – the half that never made it while the other guy became a big star. I didn't know if Madame Ferber was a fraud or not, but she'd put the hours in, written the big heavy books and now she was reaping the reward. Meanwhile Frant, or Stevens, was selling his unwanted books on the internet. It would be a bitter enough pill at the best of times but it was worse for Frant because he had one great achievement under his belt – the Von Fremdenplatz – and nobody knew about it.

On the other hand, he was a crook, a thief and a liar. He could have written all the big heavy books, but he had been too busy sitting at home and – well, I didn't know what Frant had been doing all this time. Plotting the theft of the documents, probably. I didn't know and I didn't really care. For me, the upshot of all this – the Von Fremdenplatz, the trip to Paris, the flight from the law, the meeting with Madame Ferber – was a simple one. I was off the hook. This was nothing to do with me any more. I could just wave goodbye to Frant, turn myself in and get down to a lot of explaining. It would be painful and dull, but once I told the police what had been going on, eventually they'd see sense and concentrate on Frant, the real villain of the piece.

There was just one thing niggling at me, though. Frant and Ferber weren't the only people involved in this. The girl must have had something to do with it. She had found, or been given, the copy of the *Alice*, and I had seen her just today, in Paris. I couldn't believe any longer that these two things were coincidence and I said as much to Frant. He just shrugged.

'I don't know,' he said.

'You must know,' I said. 'I can't believe that she just accidentally picked up a copy of your book. You said there were only a couple of copies printed.'

'That's correct,' said Frant. 'We had one *Alice* made, but then we decided to see what would happen if we printed a second and just floated it into the university library system. It was like a test run for the Von Fremdenplatz. We wanted to know if we could seed our plans subtly. Let the book go and see if it hooked in any suckers. It didn't. It just vanished.'

'So years later it turns up again and this girl finds it while working at the CCLF?'

'I suppose so. It did reappear in the library's office, after all.'

'But what about the photographs?'

'What photographs?'

'The images of the murdered girl.'

Frant gave me a look that managed to be both curious and bored at the same time. 'I don't know what you're talking about.'

Of course. I remembered then I had deliberately not mentioned the photographs. 'Never mind,' I said. 'I believe you. One more thing, though. I saw her here, in Paris. You saw her.'

'I saw a girl,' said Frant. 'A girl staring at us. I didn't know it was the girl you knew until you said so.'

I didn't know what to say. So I said nothing.

'What's this about photographs, anyway?' Frant said.

'It doesn't matter,' I said. 'I guess she must have put them there herself.'

'This is wasting time,' Frant said. He looked at his watch. 'Anna must have reached whatever her destination is by now.'

He sat down at the desk and reached for an old Rolodex. From it he took a single card.

'Nobody really changes,' he said, and picked up Madame Ferber's telephone. Looking down at the card, he dialled a short number.

'Madame Ferber please,' said Frant. 'You know who is calling.'

There was some noise at the other end.

'Well, get her then,' said Frant.

I had nothing to do while Frant waited. I could go to the police any time, I supposed. I took off my coat. As I did so, I felt the small bump of the girl's notebook in my pocket. I went into the kitchen and removed the notebook from my pocket. I flicked through the pages once more. There were the reviews, and the interviews, and the press advert with the Murdered Girl photograph. After that there was nothing else. I knew so little about this girl, I realised, and I had clung onto this notebook in the hope that it would tell me something –

anything – about her. Instead, I'd found nothing but a guide to her musical interests. I didn't even know if Carrie and the Legions were her band or just some pop group that she had liked when she was a teenager. In the end, the notebook had been no use to me whatsoever.

I was angry, I admit, and I took my anger out on the notebook. I slammed it on the counter, I shook it like a dog, perhaps hoping that some tiny piece of evidence would come fluttering out and all would be made clear. Nothing. I felt defeated. I would take one more look and, if nothing new appeared, I promised myself I would toss it into a bin. I opened the notebook. This time, to my surprise, it was blank. For a moment I panicked, then realised I was simply holding it the wrong way round, which was why the writings at the front had disappeared and all the pages were white and empty. All except one page, I suddenly noticed. Written in faint pencil on the penultimate page of the notebook was what looked to be a short message, like a reminder.

'CALL HENRY J,' it said. 'SAY NO. GET OUT OF THIS. NOW.'

Henry J. The mysterious producer who had first helped and then hindered the career of Carrie and the Legions. It was, I thought, an odd name. I knew very little about popular music, as I may have said, but I did know that it was a culture obsessed with cool and trendiness and so rock stars and rappers and, I supposed, producers all went under names that were themselves cool and trendy. Unless I was very much mistaken, no music business entrepreneur worth his salt would go under the name of 'Henry'. It was an old-fashioned, dated name, better suited to some fusty pedant.

And then it came to me. The scales fell from my eyes. I saw it all, for the first time. The meaning of the notebook. I had broken, almost literally, the code. Nothing contradicted my theory. Every line could be interpreted as a comment on the girl's life, every action could be tied in to her involvement in recent events. I had once heard my ex-girlfriend and her circle talk in awed terms about a strange musical discovery that a friend of a friend of a friend had made, that if you showed one particular 1930s movie musical with the mute button on, and played over it one of their favourite 1970s 'stoner' albums, the sound of the record and the plot of the movie tied up almost exactly. I had never understood this, as the movie was surely about an hour longer than the record, and I doubted that anybody would spend months in the studio making a soundtrack to a forty-year-old film and not tell anybody, but now I could understand the thrill that my ex and her pals must have felt. When you took the events of the last few days or weeks and laid them next to the episodes in the notebook, you had an almost exact chronology.

First of all there was the 'review' of Carrie and the Legions' first single. It was a total rave. The writer (whose identity I now had a fairly good idea about) approvingly quoted a lyric about the future and then expressed the sentiment that things would be great for Carrie. Surely this could only refer to Carrie's determination to launch herself upon the world in some unspecified way? Clearly she was a fantasist, as there was, to my certain belief, no band or musical career, but as a coded diary, this struck me as an excellent way to convey one's hopes and dreams without attracting, for example, the mockery of work colleagues.

I had myself had some experience of this a few years back when, as a teenager, I had kept a diary. It had, perhaps coincidentally, been around the time that my father had left my mother and myself, and this had almost certainly imbued the diary with a more emotional content than usual. I'm sure everyone is the same: as children, we keep diaries that endlessly repeat variations on 'Got up. Had breakfast. Went to school.' But when we are older, we find an inner life, we find new feelings, particularly for other people, and if we are lucky, we lead interesting lives. I never understood why the diaries of famous politicians are always so dull; here they are, these national leaders and moulders of destiny, and all they write about is how what's-his-name disagreed with thingummyjig over some small point in a ministerial meeting. Now, thinking about it, I suspect that politicians, more than people in other walks of life, have cause to be more discreet than the rest of us. They have state secrets, they have personal secrets, and they cannot own up to having fun or experiencing any emotions other than the most conventional. If, for example, a minister fell in love with a rabbit, they would never be able to mention it in the pages of their diary.

In retrospect, I wish I had shown more discretion in the pages of my diary. Not that I fell in love with a rabbit, or indeed anyone at that point in my life. It was just that I was so full of teenage feeling and confusion about my father's departure that I poured it all out over my journal. I can only remember one or two lines from the diary, probably because I heard them shouted over the noise of a school dinner time by an older boy, who had removed the diary from my bag. As I jumped up, trying to get it from him, his friends restrained me, and the older boy shouted lines from the diary. 'I wonder if I drove my father away!' he bellowed. 'I think my mother loved him more than me!' I finally got the diary back, but it was torn and dirty. For the rest of the term, a few boys would stop me and casually ask if my mother loved my father more than me, but I left school at the end of that year to go to college, where I took the precaution of not keeping a diary.

All of which goes some way to explaining how I was so sure that 'Carrie' had used the language and form of rock reviews to disguise her own feelings, and protect herself from scrutiny. It was even more obvious in the second piece, which was written as an unfavourable review of Carrie and the Legions' first album. Suddenly – and rather abruptly – all the promise of the future as mentioned in the first review has disappeared, and optimism and hope are replaced by disappointment and confusion. The lyric quoted is particularly distressing with lines like '*But still the dark is growing*' and '*I'm scared of where I'm going*.' Worst of all is the sign-off, where the reviewer (i.e. Carrie, i.e. the girl in the bar) concludes, 'It's almost like she knew what was coming.'

The review also seems to blame all this darkness and chaos on the mysterious 'Henry J', as does the interview with Carrie, in which she damns Mr J with faint praise. She also refers to him as a 'perfectionist', a term with which Euros Frant would be pedantically delighted. It all seemed clear to me: Carrie, or whatever the girl's name was, was feeling optimistic about a new project. She was working in the office of Frant's absurd inter-collegiate administration project (hence the notebook) and there she had met Frant aka Henry J, who had lured her into his plan, with promises of what I don't know. And the plan? That was obvious, too. To lure me, a qualified translator with a normal human heart, into Frant's web. Using the *Alice* as a hook, with the bait being the girl, I would be tricked into accompanying Frant to Paris on his apparently absurd quest. The Von Fremdenplatz wasn't exactly a red herring, as Frant wanted it badly, but it was merely a stepping stone on the route to Frant's ultimate goal.

I had been a fool. I had consistently undervalued the one thing I had that nobody else could deliver. Arguably, my isolation from the wider world caused this but it also meant that I was able to become close to what Frant desired most. Which was access to Madame Ferber. I had, to some extent, befriended a recluse. Even her publisher wasn't as trusted as I was by Madame Ferber, who had only recently consented to sign up for a second time because, it appeared, of some fondness for me. And Frant, who had been a Walker-Hebborn author, however briefly, had known this. He used the girl, he used the *Alice*, he used me, all for one purpose: so that I, the only person who could do so, would lead him to the Paris apartment of Anna Ferber, a woman who clearly had spent the last few years avoiding him as strenuously as possible.

I didn't know which I felt worse about: my involvement as a patsy in this whole scheme, or the distress I had caused Madame Ferber. Then there was the girl; obviously she had used me as she had been used herself. I had wasted my time tracking down a chimera, and what is more, a chimera who had no interest in me at all. I had been a fool, and I had been used. I could turn myself in, I was in fact longing to, but the more I examined the facts of the case, the less I imagined any policeman would understand what I was talking about, let alone sympathise with me.

I could hear Frant talking. He sounded frustrated. I marched into the next room where he was apparently arguing with someone on the other end of the phone line. I took the telephone receiver from him and set it down on the desk.

'What are you doing?' he all but hissed.

I looked at him. 'You're fond of your pseudonyms, aren't you?' I said.

Frant reached for the telephone. I picked it up.

'You're not just Euros Frant,' I said. 'You're not just Jeremy Andrews.'

'Give me the telephone,' said Frant. 'This is the most important call of my life.'

I put the receiver back in the cradle.

'You're Henry J,' I said.

Frant looked, I have to admit, taken aback. He was wearing the expression of a wrongly accused man with a decent overlay of confusion.

'I'm Henry James?' he said.

'Henry J', I said. 'Although that's how I worked it out.'

'Worked what out?' Frant said. 'Please give me the telephone.'

'How you got the name. You don't know anything about record producers or rappers, so naturally you came up with a name that didn't even sound right to me, and I don't know anything about popular music.'

Frant was looking admirably distressed now. His eyes darted to the phone and I wondered if he was thinking of wresting it from me. I gripped it more tightly.

'So when you had to think of a name for your character, when you had to invent another pseudonym to trick the girl, you took your inspiration from somewhere you knew a little about. Literature.'

'I know a lot about literature, you blithering idiot,' said Frant. 'But I have no idea what you are talking about. No idea.'

I ignored him. 'Henry J. The name confused me for a while, because as I say it was so peculiar. And then when I heard you talking about Madame Ferber, you said his name. You mentioned Henry James. Because you are him. You named yourself Henry J after Henry James, the author. It's so obvious to me now.'

'It's not at all obvious to me,' said Frant. 'I didn't call myself Henry J and I didn't invent any pseudonym to trick some girl. I've never met this girl. You met the girl. You're the only one who did. Nobody else has seen her. If it wasn't for the newspaper article, I'd think she was a figment of your imagination. That, and you haven't really got an imagination.'

I stared at him, my mind racing pointlessly like a car spinning its wheels in mud. I was so sure he was Henry J. It all fitted. He – using the pseudonym of a famous author – had lured the girl into his plan, given her the *Alice* with the photos in, and arranged for her to meet me in the bar, and the rest was history. I had been used, she had been used, and surely Henry J was the man behind it all.

'It's in her notebook,' I said.

'You mean that incoherent collection of pop music reviews?' said Frant. 'Some rock group called Carrie and the Nations?'

'Carrie and the Legions,' I said. 'I should have paid more attention. It's a code.'

'I think you've lost your mind,' Frant said. 'And I've just realised there's probably an extension to this telephone in the bedroom.'

He walked away from the desk. I put the other phone down and followed him.

'The notebook was a way of talking about what she was doing without making it obvious. The reviews, they're not about a band, they're her life. The things she's doing, where she's going wrong, where she hopes to do well, it's the story of you and her. When she says she's made a good album, she means her life is on the right lines. When she says she's lost her fans, well, that's where she knows she's messed up. And when she meets Henry J, who she thinks will turn her career around, that's you. You're Henry J. You're the Svengali who she hoped would change her life for the better, but instead you wrecked it.'

Frant stopped at the bedroom door. 'I was wrong about your imagination,' he said. 'You're a fruitcake.'

'There's only one thing that puzzles me,' I said.

'Only one?' Frant said. 'You amaze me. I would have

thought you'd have this bag of nonsense tied up with a pretty pink ribbon by now.'

'The photographs,' I said. 'The images of Carrie as a murdered girl. She seemed genuinely frightened by them. And they don't really fit into the diary. I know she called one of her songs "The Murdered Girl", but actually having pictures taken of her as a dead body is different.'

'Oh well,' said Frant, 'She sounds as barmy as you are.'

I stepped in front of him. 'You're the key to all this. You are Henry J.'

'I am not,' said Frant. 'And I have no idea what you're talking about.'

He opened the bedroom door and went in. I had to admit he was good. At no point had he let his guard slip. I made to follow him into the bedroom but as I did so, I heard the click of a key. I rattled the door handle, but I was locked out. I banged on the door.

'Be quiet!' Frant shouted. 'I'm on the phone!'

There was no point banging any further, I realised. I would just have to wait until Frant completed his call. I sat there, trying to correlate all the information, true or false, that I had been bombarded with. I knew I was right about Frant. Nobody else would have wanted to trick me into going to Paris. Everything he had done, from revealing the *Alice* to me, to attacking the curator of the institute, had been designed to speed our progress to the apartment where we now found ourselves. It was an intricate plan that only someone who combined extreme pedantry with maniacal self-obsession could have thought up. There was no doubt in my mind: Frant was behind the whole thing.

I heard shouting from the other room, and the dull clank of a phone being slammed down. Frant strode in, red-faced. Obviously his call had not gone well.

'Brewing up more ridiculous conspiracies?' he said.

'Actually,' I said, 'another odd thing has occurred to me.'

'Oh, good,' said Frant. 'You want to know if I shot President Kennedy.'

'No,' I said. 'It's this. Here I am, on the run from the police at home. Here you are, a man who assaulted a museum official. We are both responsible for the theft of valuable documents, and now we have entered the home of a prominent author and committed I don't know how many crimes.'

'Our offences are many,' said Frant. 'What is your point?'

'Only this,' I said. 'Where are the police? We've been going around breaking the law for days now.'

At that moment, a siren screamed outside, followed by another, and another.

'I think that answers your question,' said Frant, cramming the *Alice* in his man-bag. 'Run,' he added almost as an afterthought.

There was a slamming of car doors. There were raised voices, and voices coming from megaphones. I think I heard a helicopter. It was hard to tell what was happening but the sounds outside made everything clear. We were surrounded.

It's funny how the instinctive will always overrule the logical. I had spent the last couple of days going on about how I wanted to hand myself in to the police, just offload the guilt onto some station clerk and allow myself to be hauled off in irons to the cells. But now that it came to the crunch, the heart of the matter, I found myself wanting no such thing. And to be fair, I could hardly be blamed. I was in a siege. My heart was pounding. Adrenalin was in every vein in my body.

I took Frant's advice and ran. First of all, I ran blindly into several rooms whose windows were either sealed or tiny. Then inspiration struck and for once I ignored the voice of intuition and ran out of the apartment. Sure enough, an unlocked fire door swung back with my first shove and I ran up the stairs leading to the roof, hoping perhaps for a fire escape that somehow the police had left unguarded.

Presumably the architect's plan in the event of a major conflagration was to let the occupants of Madame Ferber's building burn to death, cursing him in their fiery death agonies. I all but spun around, looking for stairs leading downwards but there was none. The roof was blank and flat, leading only to a seventy-metre drop between this building and the ones surrounding it. The only way out that I could see was to take an enormously long run up towards the drop and jump over the gap, and this was clearly impossible for someone not a trained athlete.

I took a deep breath and began running towards the gap. They say not to look down when you're climbing, which I know is not the same thing as when you're jumping over a seventy-metre drop, but it's good advice all the same. As my legs windmilled in the empty air and my arms flailed helplessly, I somehow managed to throw a glance downwards and what I saw I can't say I enjoyed. The ground, while not being very, very far below, was certainly far enough below to kill me or at the very least smash me up like a rag doll full of blood and organs when I hit it. My plan had been reckless and deeply flawed.

I felt an awful crunch in my hip and a battery of thumps and bruises as I rolled across the roof of the next building. My jacket was ripped and something odd had happened to my ankle. I hobbled to my feet in disbelief. Somehow I had judged the distance correctly and reached the other side alive. There was, however, no time for self-congratulation. Even now, my escape was probably being shown live on every French news channel. I had to keep moving. I stumbled across this fresh roof and was rewarded with the sight of a rickety iron fire escape. I hopped over a railing and descended as fast as I could.

There was nobody at the bottom of the fire escape. Instead, as I walked down the road, trying to limp in a nonchalant fashion, I could see that police vehicles were still clustered around Madame Ferber's block and everyone was concentrating their attention on the entrance, perhaps in case Frant and I were about to saunter out and be taken by surprise. A moment later it was me who was taken by surprise when one of the doors opened and a man and a woman got out. They were Quigley and Chick, the cops who had questioned me at home in what seemed like another era. I stepped into a side road.

A hand thudded into my chest, palm outward. 'Stop!' said a voice. I stopped. It was Frant.

'I'm impressed,' he said. 'Obviously you were unable to find the service lift, but even so, the fact that you are here implies some hidden depths of self-sufficiency.'

'Oh, shut up,' I said.

Frant ignored my rudeness. He took out a mobile phone and dialled.

'We got out,' he said. 'Yes, that's right. I am the relentless pursuer. Now please meet with me and accede to my demands. Full rights, full apology, full monies.'

I assumed he was talking to Madame Ferber, but from his strident tone Frant might just as easily have been bargaining with a publisher.

'Excuse me?' he said. 'That's got nothing to do with me. For goodness' sake, how many people do I have to say this to? I don't care what – no, I won't put him on.'

I stared at Frant. Negotiations seemed to have taken an unexpected turn, and now I was involved.

'No,' said Frant loudly. 'No, you're just muddying the waters.'

There was a pause. Frant sighed deeply and passed the phone to me.

'She wants to talk to you,' he said.

'Hello?' I said.

It wasn't Madame Ferber who spoke, but her assistant, Camilla. 'We have been trying to convey to Mr Frant that we are not interested in negotiating with him,' she said.

'I don't see how this concerns me,' I said. 'I am not in the least interested in these negotiations, and I want to go home.'

'We are aware of this,' said Camilla. 'But Mr Frant persists. Therefore we have been compelled to introduce an extra factor into the situation, one that we are sure you will agree does concern you.'

I waited. These people were awfully fond of their pauses.

'The girl is here,' said Camilla.

'What girl?' I said, even though I knew.

'The girl you met in a bar, and did not have sex with,' said Camilla. 'The girl you perhaps know as Carrie. She is here, albeit not willingly.'

'I don't see how that concerns me,' I said. 'Any concern for whoever she is has been cancelled out by the treatment I have received from her and from Mr Frant.'

Frant rolled his eyes at this.

'Mr Frant has nothing to do with it,' said Camilla. 'Mr Frant is a clumsy planner, incapable of seeing more than a few moves ahead. We, however, are more prescient. That is why we have the girl. We are aware that you would not wish her to come to any harm. Nevertheless, if Mr Frant does not cease his harassment of Madame Ferber, the girl will come to harm.'

'I don't really know what you're talking about,' I said. 'I don't wish anyone to get hurt, but this isn't my problem. It—'

Camilla interrupted me. 'Last time, we merely staged her death,' she said. 'It was a wake-up call. On this occasion, if you fail to persuade Mr Frant to leave us alone, we will kill her.'

The phone went dead. Frant took it from me.

'I told you,' he said, 'I really don't know this girl.'

'Oh for God's sake, Frant, or Alan, or whatever your name is. Henry J, I don't know,' I said. 'Please stop lying. Everything points to you. Who else would be obsessed enough to trick me into coming here? And who else would be weird enough to plot all this instead of, I don't know, just paying someone to give them Madame Ferber's address?'

'I'm not weird,' said Frant. 'And now I think we should make good our escape.'

'I don't,' I said. 'I think we should do as they say.'

'Why?' said Frant. 'I hold all the chips. This girl means nothing to me. And she means even less to you. Look at the way she treated you.'

Frant's sudden paternal concern was both absurd and irritating. It also came a bit late in the day.

'How dangerous is she? Madame Ferber?' I said.

'Oh, you mean the popular author Anna Ferber?' said Frant, with a touch of irony. 'Why, she's the most dangerous popular author I know. Positively vicious. She's a writer,' he spat. 'She's not a Mafia killer.'

'Her secretary didn't sound so nice,' I pointed out. 'She sounded capable of anything. And what did she mean when she said that last time they staged—'

'Personal loyalty counts for a lot,' Frant interrupted. 'Not that you'd know anything about that. But I somehow doubt that looking after Madame Ferber's correspondence and declining interviews on her behalf is the same thing as having her enemies rubbed out.'

I had to agree with him. If there was anyone around who

was capable of hurting people, all the evidence pointed to that person being Frant. Ferber and Camilla had all the talk but they were unlikely to be violent killers. Besides, the girl had betrayed me. And as a third consideration, the police would now be extending their search to the nearby streets.

'Let's go,' I said.

'This way,' said Frant, and headed off up a slanting alleyway in the opposite direction.

'So who were you telephoning earlier?' I said, as Frant began to slow down and walk at a less manic pace. For a fugitive, he really hadn't thought enough about his own physical fitness. 'Back at the apartment?'

'It doesn't matter,' said Frant, clutching his chest for what I imagined were dramatic rather than medical reasons. 'Nobody.'

'You seemed rather angry with nobody,' I said. 'Were you trying your mysterious friend who could get us to America? Were you attempting to get safe passage out of here?'

'None of your business,' said Frant, and leaned against a wall to catch his breath.

I saw my moment. I leaned in and slid my hand into the pocket where I knew he kept his mobile phone. Frant made a grab for it but I slapped his hand down. I scrolled up his calls list until I found the most recent. Next to a long number was the single word AGNT.

It took me a moment, I must say.

'You called your literary agent?' I said. 'In the middle of all this you called your agent? I didn't even think you had an agent. You surely don't need one.'

'We may not have kept in touch of late,' said Frant. 'But I thought this would be an excellent occasion to re-establish our professional relationship.'

'Which occasion?' I said. 'The occasion when you hit a man over the head with a bust and robbed a respected French museum, or the occasion when you broke into a famous author's apartment and threatened her at gunpoint?'

'The occasion,' said Frant, oblivious as ever to anything I said, 'of my being able to prove my co-authorship of the Von Fremdenplatz documents. With this knowledge out in the open, I will be able to publish the documents under my own name, and their notoriety and high quality will ensure that they are worldwide bestsellers. Obviously she will receive a credit,' he added thoughtfully.

'Don't you think you might have picked your moment better?' I said. 'The burning in your lungs surely suggests to you that you might have timed this badly.'

'Not at all,' said Frant. 'As I pointed out to my agent, the oaf, a week ago I was an undeservedly obscure academic with a small reputation as a writer of the fantastic. And now I am a wanted criminal, a desperado on the run. I am a romantic figure.'

Right up there with Quasimodo, I thought. 'And how did your agent take this news?' I said. I couldn't believe we were in a dark alley, in the middle of our escape from the police, talking about Frant's agent, but we were.

'She was disinclined to discuss the matter,' Frant said. 'Apparently the last time I called her, some ten months ago, I was quite offensive. Justifiably so, I expect.'

'You don't remember?' I said.

Frant didn't reply.

'Let me guess,' I continued, 'you don't remember because you were drunk when you called her. You got hammered and decided to give her a piece of your mind.'

'That is neither here nor there,' Frant said. 'The fact is, my plan is an excellent one and she refused to listen to me.'

He looked utterly downcast. Even I could see that the events of the past few hours had taken their toll. Frant slumped against the wall, drained of all energy.

'If I get out of this alive,' he said, 'I am definitely getting a new agent.'

At that moment, something in my hand buzzed. It was Frant's phone. I moved to one side before Frant could snatch it from me.

'Hello?' I said.

'Good,' said Camilla. 'We are addressing the monkey, not the organ-grinder.'

I said nothing. Sticks and stones.

'We presume that Mr Frant has no useful reply to our proposal concerning the girl,' Camilla said.

I didn't reply.

'We thought not. In that case, please can you set your mobile to speakerphone.'

I fumbled with the keypad for a moment.

'It's on speaker,' I said.

'One moment, please,' said Camilla's distorted voice. There was silence.

'Now what?' said Frant, and I motioned for him to be quiet. As I did so, a sudden sharp noise came from the phone.

'That was a gunshot,' said Frant. He looked shaken for once.

'What did you just do?' I shouted.

After a few seconds, Camilla spoke. 'There is a girl here in some considerable pain,' she said. 'She would not be in that state if you had acceded to our demands. We will call again in exactly two minutes. If by then you have not acceded to our demands, we will cause the girl even more—'

'Wait,' I said. There was the hiss of static at the other end. 'Tell me where you are.'

Frant tried again to get the phone from me.

'What about Mr Frant?' said Camilla.

'Screw Mr Frant,' I said. 'I've had enough of this. We're coming in and we're going to end this. Just don't hurt the girl any more.'

'Very well,' said Camilla. She gave me an address.

I returned Frant's phone to him.

'What did you do that for?' he said. 'You know you should never negotiate with kidnappers.'

'I wasn't negotiating,' I said. 'I was giving in. I was agreeing. This has gone far enough, Frant. Let's go and see Madame Ferber and let's get the girl.'

'You sound like a silent movie hero,' said Frant.

'And you sound like a silent movie villain,' I said. 'I keep expecting you to twirl your eyebrows and sneer.'

Frant wasn't listening. He was trying to flag down a taxi.

'What I don't understand,' I said as we hurtled around several corners, 'and please believe me, I know that what I don't understand is merely the tip of the iceberg, what I don't understand is how you could have underestimated Madame Ferber so badly.'

'I didn't,' said Frant. 'I've always known she was a dangerous maniac. I just didn't feel it was something you needed to know.'

I didn't know what to say to that. Instead I asked, 'Where exactly are we going?'

'Gare du Nord,' said Frant. 'Which is good news for me. I should be just in time for the next train home.'

'What?' I said. 'I thought we were meeting Madame Ferber.'

'We are,' said Frant. 'I suspect, however, that she has travel plans of her own. Doubtless the police will want to know why she called them and then vanished into thin air.'

I took Frant's point. It was time for all of us to get away, although I couldn't see how we would manage this.

'You can't just get on the Eurostar,' I said. 'Your passport will give you away at once.'

'Which one?' said Frant.

'Oh God,' I said. 'Don't tell me you've got two passports.'

'The one in my real name is authentic and blameless,' said Frant. 'I only ever use it for social occasions. The one in the name of Euros Frant is not perhaps entirely legal, but suffices for the more cursory kind of check. Railway stations mostly. Of course, now I shall have to retire both it and the name of Frant. Which is a shame. I've never liked my real name.'

'What am I going to do?' I said. 'I don't have a false name or a fake passport. And I'm wanted—'

'By the police of two continents, yes, you never get tired of reminding me,' said Frant. 'Equally, you never weary of insisting on your innocence. I should imagine that a few hours in custody with a half-decent lawyer should be enough for you to demonstrate your much-vaunted lack of guilt to any number of law enforcement officers, no matter how many continents they have come from.'

I took the grenade from my pocket and forced him to swallow it. I would have too, if I'd had a grenade. Instead I looked out of the window of the taxi. It was raining now, turning into streaks of silver on the roads. The driver slowed down with the traffic. I recognised some bars and restaurants.

'I think we're nearly there,' I said.

Frant began to fuss with his coat like an old woman looking for pennies to give to a beggar. For a moment I thought he was searching for his wallet so he could pay the cab driver, but he was only checking that he had all the Von Fremdenplatz volumes with him. The evidence that would make him, in his mind at least, a respected and wealthy figure on the world stage, which was also the reason Madame Ferber was apparently prepared to kill the girl.

I found this hard to believe, although the evidence of the gunshot was compelling enough. While Anna Ferber's books often featured extreme statements and actions, at no point did any of her characters kidnap anyone and hold them to ransom at gunpoint. Purely from a reader's perspective, this was a shame; a thousand pages into one of her convoluted narratives and you really did long for a lone assassin to come in and blast away at her pompous philosophising mouthpieces.

I did once find in her file at Walker-Hebborn a long academic piece entitled *The Psychosis of Art: A.J.L. Ferber and the Killer Inside* by some professor or other, which attempted to argue, not without some force, that Madame Ferber's books were not closely argued attempts to put over a cogent worldview, but rather the grand fantasies of a megalomaniac. One paragraph stuck in my mind: 'Ferber's outlook despises the ordinary man and woman just for their ordinariness. Not for her the terraced house in a grubby street; in Ferber's world, the boulevards are wide and the buildings grand. Her mind is as if designed by Albert Speer.' As soon as I remembered those words, I thought of the clean world of the Von Fremdenplatz documents and for the first time I could picture the division of labour between the two of them, Ferber and Frant, the one designing those wide boulevards lined with plane trees and abstract sculptures, the other inventing an imperious and wordy language to express perfectly the grand design of this new, hollow world. The Von Fremdenplatz documents might be a masterpiece of detail and a hymn to human effort at its most obsessive, but they were also a tribute to emptiness on an epic scale. They had removed humanity and replaced it with nothing. That said, I still wasn't sure if Madame Ferber was nuts enough to shoot someone. Making up books is one kind of craziness, killing people is another.

The taxi came to a halt. Frant did up his coat as if to further emphasise that his purse was going nowhere. I paid and got out onto the pavement, uncertain as to what to do next. Frant seemed to feel the same way, as his eyebrows darted this way and that, never quite resting. Or maybe he was just wondering where to check in for the Eurostar.

'Are you coming with me, then?' I said. 'Or are you just going to run? Because I really don't care. Just give me the *Alice* and the Von Fremdenplatz and I'll hand them over to Madame Ferber and we can stop all this foolishness.'

'Oh no you won't,' said Frant, finally confirming my belief that one day a career in pantomime awaited him. 'The only person who can stop all this foolishness, as for once you correctly put it, is me. I intend to persuade Anna to see reason and accept the truth, for I am the only voice of reason in this monstrous regiment of women's brouhaha.'

'Yeah, say that,' I said. 'That should win her over.'

Frant's phone buzzed. On the screen was a tiny photograph. A table in a bar, and underneath it an address.

'Not far now,' said Frant. I followed him as he set off down the street and around the corner.

The bar was a sliver among other buildings, a narrow entrance with barely enough room above the door for the name. The barman looked up as we walked in and tilted his chin towards a thin staircase at the back. We clattered up the carpetless stairs to a small landing and Frant pushed open a door.

'Hello,' said Madame Ferber. She sat at the only table in the room. Against the wall were two other people. One was Camilla and the other was the girl, who looked at me imploringly. She was still beautiful, and on a different day I would have knocked anybody and everybody down to be with her, but not now. Camilla didn't look at me at all. She just took Frant's pistol from his pocket with a deft gesture and sat down to reload it.

'Sit down,' said Madame Ferber.

Frant sat opposite Madame Ferber at the small table. I was clearly not one of the great powers at this gathering. Unwilling to stand with Camilla and the girl as if we were Ferber and Frant's seconds, I took up a position by the door.

'Very well,' said Frant. 'We are here. I have what you want and you have nothing I want.'

Madame Ferber was about to speak when I found myself interrupting. 'I thought you shot her,' I said to Camilla. 'I heard a gunshot.'

Camilla shrugged.

'A moment of artifice and melodrama,' said Madame Ferber. 'Camilla fired into the skirting board. Nobody has been harmed as yet.' She turned to Frant, as if tired by her explanation. 'We've spent too much time on this,' she said. 'Please return to me what is mine and we can all return to our lives.'

'Yours?' said Frant. 'What's yours is mine. Your work is my work. I'm not referring, of course, to your otiose works of fiction.'

'My little successes?' said Ferber, a small smile at the corners of her mouth. 'I find it entertaining that you claim to want no part of my triumphs, but instead are desperate to garland yourself with obscurities from our youth.'

'It's because of you that this great work is obscure,' said Frant. 'We created an extraordinary project! We made a universe! And you would keep it under tarpaulin in a garage like an old automobile.'

'The past is the past,' said Ferber. 'It would do neither of us any good to have our student pranks revealed to the world. We have positions now, and reputations. At least, I have.'

Frant was silent and I almost felt sorry for him. Madame Ferber had success and fame. She lived in a grand apartment and won prizes for her work. Frant, on the other hand, lived in a tiny flat and people thought he was a fool. And yet they had begun in the same place, on a project that anyone could see was a remarkable achievement. I couldn't stand the man but even I understood why he felt he was entitled to get something out of the Von Fremdenplatz.

Madame Ferber clearly disagreed. She obviously believed that letting the world know that she was partly responsible for one of the great literary pranks of the last fifty years would do serious harm to her standing as an important literary figure. Me, if I'd thought of something so crazy and impressive, I'd be trumpeting it from every tall building, but I wasn't Anna Ferber. And I wasn't sitting at a small table in a Parisian bar holding a beautiful girl hostage.

'Aren't you even going to look at her?' said Madame Ferber. 'Aren't you going to say hello?'

Frant reluctantly twisted his head round to look at the girl. He seemed peculiarly sullen. I wasn't sure that sulking was an apt response to his situation, but then with Frant nothing negative was a surprise.

'Hello,' he said to the girl, absurdly.

The girl returned his sulky stare. 'Hello, Dad,' she said.

CHAPTER TEN

Frant started. So did I.

'I'm not—' he began. 'Did she tell you that I was? You can't believe what she tells you.'

'She didn't have to,' said the girl. 'I did the research. I went online, ordered up the birth certificate. You're my father. I wish you weren't.'

'She's your daughter,' said Madame Ferber, looking more amused than I felt was right. 'Just think, and you don't even know her name.'

'She's called Carrie,' I said without thinking. 'She's called Carrie and she's the only decent person here.'

The girl looked at me in surprise. 'The notebook,' she said. 'You found it.'

'Yes,' I said. I fished it out of my pocket and stepped towards her. Camilla lifted her gun.

'It's a notebook,' I said, 'it's not loaded.'

The girl took the notebook. 'Thank you,' she said. 'It's the only thing I have of me.'

It was a strange thing to say but I didn't exactly have time to analyse it. Right now my brain was filled with chaos and static.

'Carrie,' said Frant. 'What an awful name. I would never have chosen it.'

'I chose it,' said Carrie. 'She called me Isolde. Like she wanted me to get beaten up every day at school.'

I looked at Madame Ferber. 'Why would you choose her—' I stopped. 'Oh,' I said.

'Yes, oh,' said Madame Ferber. She looked hard at me, as if I were a puppy in a shop window. 'You really are no detective, are you? You're a plodder. I suppose that's why I liked you. Nobody else stood up to me about my prose, but you just plodded in and asked questions. And you were right.'

'Is that why I'm here?' I said. 'Because I stood up to you?'

'Goodness, no,' said Madame Ferber. 'You're here because he needed you. Surely you've worked that out?'

'Yes,' I said. 'I was the only person Frant could get to who knew where you lived. I wouldn't have brought him here just for a social call, so he had to find a lure.'

'Allure,' said Madame Ferber. 'I like to imagine that word being made of two other words. Allure. A lure.'

'The notebook was the clue,' I said. 'Once I realised that Carrie's entries weren't reviews and interviews but a sort of coded diary, it all became clear. She had met a man called Henry J who had offered her a way to change her life. All she had to do was find this patsy in a bar, some clown who could be reeled in using an intriguing book. And sex.'

The girl said nothing.

Frant said, 'I told you, I'm not Henry—' but a wave of Camilla's pistol silenced him.

'The girl – Carrie – vanished, making sure I'd seen enough of the book,' I continued. 'And someone reported her missing, making sure I was implicated, which put the pressure on. I had to find her and the only clue were the pages from the translated *Alice*. And who was the only person I knew who could tell me what those pages were? Frant. The rest was simple. We go to Paris, Frant hits a man, we're on the run and the only place we can hide is the apartment of the one person in Paris I happen to know slightly. As Frant well knew from his time with Walker-Hebborn.'

I leaned against the wall.

'All this so Frant could track down Madame Ferber and make her admit in public that she helped him make the Von Fremdenplatz documents.'

The room seemed very small. I could almost hear everyone in it, thinking, processing what I'd just said. It was, I knew, a lot to absorb. The girl Carrie, taken in by her own father. Madame Ferber, holed up in Paris and unaware that the one man who could unravel her reputation was hotfoot on her trail. And Frant himself, the spider at the centre of the web, plotting it all.

'Just one small thing,' said Frant. 'I do apologise for repeating myself, but I cannot emphasise this enough. I am not Henry J.'

I gave him one of my mother's old-fashioned looks. I was tired of all the lies and deceit but most of all I was tired of Frant's dogged insistence on this small thing. I must have said so because Carrie suddenly looked pained and said, 'Oh, for God's sake, he's telling the truth.'

'Be quiet,' said Madame Ferber.

'Why, what are you going to do, shoot me?' said Carrie, and once again Camilla's finger twitched. 'I mean, that's how much you care about me. Get me involved in all this, send me off to meet a complete stranger. All this and for what? She's Henry J,' she added casually.

'I said it wasn't me,' said Frant, smugly.

'How can she be Henry J?' I said.

Carrie didn't answer. Instead she was looking at her mother.

'It was the photos that did it,' said Carrie. 'One day I went into the CCLF and I opened the *Alice* and there were these pictures of me, dead. I just freaked. I was probably still freaking when I met you in the bar. I still don't know what they are or where they came from.'

'That was the easiest part,' said Madame Ferber.

'It was you?' said Carrie. 'You did that to me?'

'You did it to yourself,' said Madame Ferber. 'Believe me, I wasn't the one passed out on drink and dope every night. I had Camilla take them when you were, as usual, comatose in your room on one of your visits to Paris to borrow money from me. I was reserving them to use as a warning next time you overdosed on my premises. After she'd developed them, Camilla pointed out, with her usual acumen, how much you appeared to be a corpse in them. All it would take was a little graphic manipulation.'

'I despise you,' said Carrie. 'I despise you both.' Her voice was tremulous.

'Excellent, we all despise each other,' said Frant. 'Now can we get on with what we came here for?'

'Certainly,' said Madame Ferber. 'Just give me the books and you won't get shot.'

'You wouldn't shoot me,' said Frant.

'Camilla would,' said Madame Ferber. 'You've already assaulted her, and she has a history of violence as it is.'

Camilla clicked the safety off on her gun. 'Finally,' she said.

'You can't shoot him,' said Carrie. 'He's the father of your child.'

'And I couldn't think of a better reason to shoot him than that,' said Madame Ferber.

Carrie looked sullen, as if she had heard this before, often.

'All the years I had to waste rearing you,' said Madame Ferber. 'All the expense and the time and the effort, when I should have been writing, and thinking. The perambulator in the hall is nothing. I have suffered the vodka bottle in the cistern, the bandages in the hospital, the police in the sitting room. I do not know what sentiment failed me when I allowed you to be born, I really don't.'

Carrie began to cry.

'Oh, tears,' said Madame Ferber. 'Please. Enough is enough.' She held her hands out to Frant. 'Return to me what is mine.'

'I won't,' said Frant.

'Then Camilla will shoot you,' said Madame Ferber.

'You can't kill him,' said Carrie.

'Then Camilla will shoot you. I really don't care. Shoot him or shoot her, or both of them. I don't care. I just want to go home now and draw a line under this.' She looked at me, as if for understanding. 'I have work to do,' she said.

I looked back at her. Her eyes were the deepest brown I had ever seen. They were also as empty of compassion and love as they were full of distant intelligence. I looked at Frant, who was nervously studying his fingernails as if waiting for the results of an exam. Carrie was sitting now, still crying silently.

'You are the worst people I have ever met,' I said. 'You're so obsessed with books and literature and fame and esteem that you don't care about anything else.'

'Perhaps that's true,' said Madame Ferber. 'But I don't see how it's any of your business.'

'It isn't,' I said. 'You're right. On the other hand, I do have a man-bag.' I held up Frant's bag.

Frant started. 'Give me back my bag,' he said.

'No,' I said as Madame Ferber stared at me blankly.

'The one with the books you wanted in it,' I told her. 'Let me and the girl walk away now and then you can have it.'

Carrie looked at me with, I thought, actual compassion.

'Don't die for a book,' she said. 'Especially not this one.'

'I know what I'm doing,' I said. 'Although I agree this book isn't worth dying for.'

'Nothing will be gained by you doing this,' said Madame Ferber. 'Please give it to me.'

'Or me,' suggested Frant, as if casually.

'I'm not giving it to anyone,' I said. 'Except the police. When all this is done, I've no doubt you can all argue your case in court. Or settle between yourselves. I really don't mind.'

'Put it back!' said Frant, lunging ineffectually at me. I stepped back nearer to the door.

'Why are you doing this?' said Madame Ferber.

'He wants the money,' Frant said.

'I don't want the money,' I said.

'Then you have nothing to gain from this,' said Madame Ferber. 'Your action makes no sense. You fail to benefit financially. You certainly fail to benefit romantically as I doubt that my daughter is in love with you.'

'You can't know that,' I said, and wished I hadn't.

'Trust me,' said Madame Ferber. 'Unless you are a drug dealer or a very rich man, she might sleep with you but she cannot love you. I feel partly responsible for that, I suppose.'

I tried not to look at Carrie, but failed. I was almost relieved to see that she was trying just as hard not to look at me.

'And you fail to benefit the majority,' said Madame Ferber. 'In fact, you harm the majority. Whatever my dispute with him, it will be resolved in my favour—'

Frant snorted like a pony.

'And when it is resolved, I think I might publish the Von Fremdenplatz documents under my own name, creating not just wealth for myself but also pleasure for hundreds of thousands of people.'

'You bitch!' shouted Frant.

Camilla waved the gun at him and he subsided.

'By taking the books with you now,' Madame Ferber said to

me, 'you at best delay that moment. Your action is therefore meaningless as both a selfish act and as a humanitarian one.'

"I thought the books were a student prank you wanted to suppress," I said.

'I've changed my mind,' she said. 'Besides, all my children matter to me, no matter how weak their father is.'

'Not all of them,' I said and motioned for Carrie to get to her feet. 'Please don't try to follow us,' I said, taking her hand.

'No!' said Carrie sharply. 'What are you doing?'

I pulled her towards the door, holding the bag in front of me.

'Give me my bag!' shouted Frant. Before anyone could move, he grabbed the gun from Camilla. Carrie was standing right in front of me. I pushed her away, and he fired. There was a sudden dull thump in my chest. I looked down at it as I fell. The bag in front of my chest had a hole in it. The hole was smoking. I slipped my hand into the bag as I hit the ground and two books spun out, the *Alice* and a Von Fremdenplatz.

'How about that,' I grunted. 'Saved by books.'

'Not quite,' said Frant.

I looked down. The books hadn't been touched by the bullet, which had gone straight into me.

'You could have avoided all this,' said a woman's voice. 'You didn't have to do this. Now you're dead, like most idiots.'

'I don't care,' I said. 'I'm the Mule, I don't give up.'

I thought I heard sirens. Then I heard nothing.

PART THREE

Translation is a form of close reading, an act of criticism, not creation, and the need for new interpretation becomes apparent when new ideas arise with the passage of time.

Jay Rubin, *Haruki Murakami and the Music of Words*

CHAPTER ELEVEN

I don't know if you've ever been in a coma, but it's very odd and not at all as I would have imagined. For a start, you are at once in the world and out of the world. I would say that sometimes you are in one and sometimes the other, but that would mean that time was something you experience in that state. At various junctures I found myself listening to the conversation of doctors and nurses and hearing snatches of news stories about arrests and shootings, but also being in different places entirely.

One minute – although there were no 'minutes', just events overlaid on each other – I was completely present in the room, eavesdropping on a somehow familiar voice talking to a nurse and it was real in every way except I couldn't see or move, and the next, or rather the same, or possibly the preceding, moment, I would be back in the room above the bar in Paris, unable to move as Frant fired, not at me but at the girl. Then I would feel a thermometer's thinness in my mouth, or a hand on my skin, but at the same time I would be in another bar with a martini, watching a girl cry as she looked at photographs of herself.

And once I was drifting into sleep in a small overheated room when suddenly I was in a city.

*

The city was full of sunlight. But it was cool despite the sunshine, and a breeze ran through its wide streets. I was in a large square, surrounded by tall, evenly spaced buildings. There were people about, but I could only see them out of the corner of my eye, and they seemed vague and stretched, like the figures in an architect's drawings. A fountain played nearby, and in front of me there was an abstract sculpture on a small area of grass.

I had never been in this city before, but I thought I knew it. Perhaps I had seen photographs and drawings. I felt thirsty, and got off the bench where I had been sitting to walk over to a small kiosk selling hot drinks and cans of soda. I was about to buy a cup of tea when I realised there was another customer there already.

'Excuse me,' I said. 'I didn't see you there. Please finish your order.'

'Nonsense,' said the other man. 'Let's order together. Two teas, please,' he said to the vendor.

He turned to me and smiled. It was my father.

We sat down on a bench. My father looked exactly as he had done the last time I had seen him. He was even wearing the same aftershave.

'The weather was like this on your birthday,' he said.

I knew which birthday he meant. I was quite small then.

'Yes,' I said. 'There wasn't a cloud in the sky.'

'You were crazy about the Wild West. You wanted to be a cowboy,' said my father, smiling. 'You were always playing with little plastic cowboys. I kept finding tiny guns everywhere.'

'I had a cap pistol,' I said, remembering. 'But I never had any caps.'

'That birthday we gave you the cowboy outfit,' said my father.

'I don't remember that,' I said. I was puzzled. A cowboy outfit would have been a big deal to me when I was a small boy. I would have been very excited. I would have worn it every day and there would be photographs of me in my cowboy outfit, waving my cap gun.

'You didn't want it,' my father said. 'We were so surprised. There was a hat, and a waistcoat, and a pair of cowboy trousers.'

'I can't believe I didn't want it,' I said.

'It was because of the trousers,' said my father.

'What?' I said. 'Were they too big?'

'Not that,' said my father, smiling again. 'They fitted fine. It was the pictures.'

I was very confused now. 'What pictures?' I said.

'The trousers had pictures on them. Like drawings,' said my father. 'Pictures of cowboys. And that's what you didn't like.'

I understood now. 'I wanted to be a proper cowboy,' I said. 'And a proper cowboy wouldn't have pictures on his trousers. Especially not pictures of cowboys. It wouldn't make any sense. It was just wrong.'

'That's what it was?' said my father. 'We never could figure out why you didn't like the pictures. We thought maybe you were frightened of them.'

'I'm sorry I made you go,' I said.

He got up from the bench. 'Finished your tea?' he said, and took my cardboard cup from me. He dropped both cups in a bin.

'You didn't make me go,' said my father. 'I did.'

I woke up. I was in the hospital. There was a woman sitting beside my bed, reading a magazine.

'Hello, Mother,' I said.

'Oh, hello, dear,' she said.

I tried to sit up.

'Be careful,' she said. 'You've been lying down for several days, let the nurse help you up.'

'I had a very odd dream,' I said.

'Please don't tell me about it,' she said. 'I can't stand other people's dreams. Would you like some water? There were apples but I think they've gone off.'

'I'm fine,' I said, and was surprised to discover that I was fine. I felt my chest. There was a bandage.

'Don't play with your dressing,' my mother said. 'You were very lucky, they said. The bullet hit a bone and went off sideways.'

'I see,' I said. 'Where am I, anyway? Is this a prison hospital?'

'No. What a silly question,' said my mother. 'This is the same hospital you came to see me in. Isn't it funny? You came to see me and now I've come to see you. I can't stay long, I've left Duke at home and he's not at all continent.'

'Well,' I said, 'it's good of you to come.'

'Every day for a month,' said my mother.

I tried again to sit up.

'Don't do that,' my mother said. 'There are stitches and I'm not going to put them back in.'

She stood up. 'I've got to be going,' she said, and leaned over to kiss me. 'Anyway, you're only allowed one visitor at a time.'

She left, and I wondered what she meant. Then the door opened and Carrie came in.

I have read that in these circumstances it's common either to be struck dumb or to act in completely the opposite manner and just allow a stream of queries to fall from your lips. I seemed to have opted for the latter, if the word 'query' means a lot of single words beginning with 'wh'. 'What?' I said. 'When

– why – how?' ('How' doesn't begin with 'wh' but what the hell, this isn't a test.)

'I don't understand,' I said. 'We were in that room, and I was – I left you. With them. I don't—'

'Shut up,' said Carrie. 'I'm going to do something my mother and father could never do. I'm going to tell you a story.'

And this is the story she told.

A long time ago in a not very good university (she began) there were two bright kids. One of them was called Anna and one of them was called Alan. They didn't have a lot in common other than the fact that nobody liked them. Anna would sit in the library reading books on her own and Alan would take his dinner in the refectory alone and nobody bothered them or asked them how they were doing.

One day, so I'm guessing, they bumped trays in the refectory or she dropped her library book and he picked it up or they were stuck together in a hot study period and one of them asked the other if they'd like an ice cream. One of those things, or maybe not, I don't know. But somehow Alan and Anna met and they started – not dating, because they weren't the dating kind. But they had stuff in common. Alan liked reading all kinds of weird books, fantasy novels and fairy tales and anything set in a made-up place. If it had its own language and its own swirly alphabet, then so much the better. If he'd had any friends, Alan would have been fighting war games with armies of elves and whatnot, but he didn't, so he just read these books.

Anna liked reading too, but she was more high-faluting. She favoured the great writers – Goethe, Schiller, Henry James, Joseph Conrad – she had her own list of authors to be admired. She liked anyone with a heavy touch and a dour outlook, so much so that she would scribble down not just their own words of wisdom but a few of her own, which were terribly derivative but that didn't bother her. Anna was looking for the tone, for the voice.

One night as they were sitting in Alan's awful student bedroom, Alan called Anna's attention to a short story he was reading. It was about an encyclopedia from another world that somehow took over our own world. Alan was all fired up about this, because the encyclopedia was not just made up, but it was in a different language and it was an enigma. Normally Anna got annoyed when Alan read stuff out to her, because it was all about gnomes and pixies, but something about this story got to her. Maybe it was because it was an encyclopedia and that made it more serious.

Over the next few weeks, Alan and Anna just couldn't let go of this idea, and one day as they sat over herbal tea looking at their fellow students – some of them smoking dope, some of them horsing around and quite a few just looking dim – Alan, or maybe Anna, proposed their idea for a great hoax. A real encyclopedia from another world. Or maybe this world. There would be no way of telling. It would be in a new language, and it would describe, in words and pictures, a place nobody had seen. Only, because it was in this new language, it would be a mystery. A complete enigma.

Alan worked on the language, and Anna used her time in the library to source the most obscure photographs and images. Their first efforts were feeble; the new language looked like mushy Esperanto, while the pages of the 'encyclopedia' resembled a cheap punk fanzine. But – and this is what made them different to other pranksters – they didn't give up. Anna found printers and typesetters and spent her inheritance (she had a pretty nice inheritance) on better quality paper. Alan worked hard too, and as a test of his skills translated *Alice Through the Looking-Glass* into his invented language. Anna had two copies of this book printed to see if her printers were up to the job.

After that, there was no stopping them. They began to leave copies of their mysterious book in university libraries all over the place. They produced perfect forgeries and they made academics into fools as the 'experts' fought over interpretations of their work. They had succeeded in their great task.

Unfortunately, the stresses of producing this epic, for which there never could be any financial reward, were too much for Alan and Anna's relationship, and they fell out. Alan saw the documents as his way to wealth and fame while Anna, who had nearly completed her first novel, had different plans. They quarrelled bitterly, and Alan left. Anna completed her first novel, and discovered that she was pregnant.

It was getting dark outside. Carrie turned on the bedside light and sat down.

'So my mother raised me, and never spoke about my father,' Carrie said. 'I used to ask all the time of course, but she just told me to shut up and got on with writing another damn book. Then one day she called me in and showed me a picture of a monkey in a hat. It turns out the monkey was my dad. Then she told me the whole story about the Von Fremdenplatz and I said they were both crazy and I didn't want to hear any more. She said fine and so we never talked about it again. Case closed.'

Carrie paused. 'Except I tracked the old monkey down, and I found he was working in some college facility,' she said. 'I wanted to see him so I got a job there, right under his nose. And then guess what I found?'

'The translated *Alice*,' I said.

'Right,' said Carry. 'The second Alice, that they put into a library.'

'I thought it vanished,' I said.

'My mother took it,' she replied. 'As insurance against the future. She loved him then but she didn't trust him.'

'Your family...' I began.

'I know,' she said. 'I stamped it so it looked like it was from the facility and then I was all, oh, Mr Frant, look what I found. He went crazy trying to look bored but I could tell it had got him going.'

'He had no idea there were any copies of the *Alice* at large,' I said. 'So I'm guessing that gave him an idea. If he could use the *Alice* to get some gullible sucker interested in the Von Fremdenplatz, he could get the same sucker to take him to Paris ...'

I could feel my eyes widening with realisation. 'And if that sucker happened to be one of the few people who knew Madame Ferber's address, Frant could engineer it so they'd be on the run from the police and just have to hook up with the one person who never wanted to see Frant again.'

'Almost,' said Carrie. 'You see, when my father revealed his grand plan to me, I could see the holes in it from space. What if you didn't fall for it? What if you refused to take him to Paris? It was a stupid plan. It lacked the human element. Me.'

'I don't understand,' I said. 'Why would you go along with Frant? You didn't even—' I stopped. 'You told her,' I said. 'You went back to Madame Ferber and you told her what had happened between you and Frant.'

'I was hoping she would be pleased,' said Carrie. 'I thought if she knew I'd been talking to my father, maybe, I don't know, we could be the three of us again.'

I couldn't imagine a worse family unit but I said nothing about that. Or the fact that I had been used. In fact, 'used' wasn't a strong enough word for it. The entire family had taken turns at pulling my strings. First Frant, inventing the whole horrible plan. Then Carrie, adding herself as a human lure. And finally, making sure it all worked and nobody went off the agreed track ...

My head was reeling. 'And that's why your mother is Henry J.'

'I used to call her Henry James when I was a kid,' said Carrie. 'Because she wrote like she was constipated and she wanted so badly to be a great author. It used to drive her crazy.'

'All that stuff in the notebook about Henry J offering you a bright new future,' I said. 'Because you thought she was encouraging you to make friends with your father. Then you realised she wasn't all she was cracked up to be.'

'She wanted to get Frant to come to her, play his dumb hand, and make sure he didn't bother her again. She used me,' said Carrie.

I may not have looked very sympathetic at this point, because Carrie turned to me with a look that was, to say the least, uncharacteristic of a member of her family. I'm not always very good at reading faces, but this one was unmistakable. It was regret. Or pity. Probably both. As I say, I'm not very good at reading faces. But I was almost mollified. Then again, here I was in a hospital bed with a bullet wound and presumably half of the Continent's police sitting outside with a variety of arrest warrants.

'After that, the rest you know. We were in a bar and my father shot you,' said Carrie, as if reading my mind, 'and then we were pretty much left to fend for ourselves.'

'I'm sorry I let you down,' I said, a bit sniffily.

'You know I don't mean it like that,' said Carrie. 'You nearly died trying to save my life.'

I didn't know if I was being mocked or not, but as this was a normal state of mind for me, I said nothing yet again. It seemed to me that saying nothing was a good thing to do. If

I'd said nothing more often, maybe I wouldn't have ended up going to Paris and meeting a lot of psychopaths, one of whom shot me.

'In fact, it looks like you did save my life,' Carrie said. 'The police were outside and they heard the gunshot. Broke in, disarmed my father, handcuffs all round.'

'They were outside before the gun went off?'

'Yes, they'd been on your ... they'd been after you for a few hours but you were always one step ahead of them. It was like you knew what you were doing.'

'I was trying to be caught,' I said. 'I just couldn't quite get it right.'

'I'll say,' said Carrie. 'The police said they'd missed you at the hotel, at the institute and even at the apartment. They only found you and Frant at the bar when they heard the gun.'

'So why aren't I in jail?' I said.

'One moment please,' said Carrie, exactly as if she were a telephone receptionist. She took her shoes off and a moment later was under my hospital duvet. This time I very much said nothing.

'The police,' Carrie said, 'weren't after you. They were after Frant. They had footage on the institute's CCTV of Frant attacking that man, but there was only the one security camera and you weren't in shot. So they didn't know who you were. And when they broke down the door and found you on the floor, shot, they kind of eliminated you from the list of suspects. Excuse me.'

This last she said as she suddenly got out of the bed and with a single movement placed a chair under the door handle. She got back into bed. I remained still, for a while.

'What,' I said, when I could speak. 'What about the other police? Quigley and Chick? They were after me for your murder.'

'Them,' said Carrie, sounding more amused about the police than expected. 'They were there, yes. They'd apparently been trying to get the French police to take them seriously about a murder without a body apparently committed by a man with no criminal record, but all that pretty much collapsed when they found the murder victim, as in me, alive and the murderer, as in you, on the floor, with a bullet in him.'

'I see,' I said after a while in which some other things happened. 'But what about you? What about your ... what about Madame Ferber and Euros Frant?'

'Attempted murder, accessory to murder, assault with a bust, conspiracy to this and that,' Carrie said airily. 'I'm going to visit them, I'm not completely unfilial. But – you know ...'

She stopped talking and gave me a look that, for once, I found hard to misinterpret. I don't know if you've ever been in bed in a private ward with someone whose life you have saved, but I'm assuming you haven't, and that you can work out the details for yourself. I've got things to do.

In fact, from now on I've got a lot of things to do. I've still got to go home and explain to my publisher how his most respected and bestselling author is now in jail. In recompense for that, I've been asked by that author's daughter to see if he'd be interested in publishing a book that is about to be somewhat notorious. And suddenly I've got a personal life to deal with. Carrie says we probably won't meet again, but we'll see about that.

There is, as I say, a lot to do. But that's fine. I'm the Mule. And I don't give up.

THANKS

Special thanks to Tamsin Shelton for her brilliant editing, Susan Woods for her detailed and invaluable notes, and to everyone at Unbound for everything else.

Unbound is a new kind of publishing house. Our books are funded directly by readers. This was a very popular idea during the late eighteenth and early nineteenth centuries. Now we have revived it for the internet age. It allows authors to write the books they really want to write and readers to support the writing they would most like to see published.

The names listed below are of readers who have pledged their support and made this book happen. If you'd like to join them, visit: www.unbound.co.uk.

For Esther Richards - she knows why

Geoff Adams
John Aizlewood
Moose Allain
Anthony Allen
Jonathan Mark Allsop
Gus Alvarez
Emma Anderson
Dan Antopolski
Steven Appleby
Paul Arman
Lucy Armitage
Jesse Armstrong
Angela Arora
George Ashe
Carl Ashworth
Michael Atkinson
Shaun Atkinson
Suzanne Azzopardi
Julian Bacon
Cam Baddeley
Liz Bailey
Stuart Bailie
Jason Ballinger
Matthew Bate
Christopher Beanland
Bob Beaupré

Pete Beck
Mark Bentley
Miki Berenyi
Terry Bergin
Heidi Berry
Steve Berry
Mark Billingham
Wendy May Billingsley
Meat Bingo
Will Birch
David Blair
Marc Blakewill
Nickie Bonn
Michael Bonner
Richard Boon
Charlotte Bracegirdle
Thomas Brasdefer
Richard W H Bray
Sue and Duke Brealey
Sue Brearley
Kimberly Bright
Phil Bruce-Moore
Gareth Buchaillard-
    Davies
Johnny Bull
Victoria Burch

Adrian Burns
Alison Burns
Nick Burrow
Helen Burt
Jane Bussmann
Peter Campbell
Phillipa Candy
Sheila Cannon
Xander Cansell
Philip Caren
Paul Carlyle
Martin Carr
Cath Carroll
Steven Cassidy
David Catley
Richard Chalu
David Lars Chamberlain
Caroline Chignell
Lisa Clark
Emma Clarke
Ian Clarkson
Mathew Clayton
Sarah Clegg
Vanessa Cobb
Jonathan Coe
Dave Cohen

Brian Cole
Stevyn Colgan
Ian Collings
James Collingwood
Lorraine Colvin
Chris Constantinou
Richard Cook
Diane Cooke
Jason Cooper
Darren Corcoran
Peter Counsell
Fiona Cox
Sarah Cox
Martin Coyle
John Crawford
Martin Creed
Anthony Critchlow
Sarah Crowden
Brian Crowe
Paul Cummins
Peter Curran
Catherine Daly
Stewart Darkin
Johnny Daukes
Stuart Davidson
Laura Lee Davies
Mark Davies
Mat Davies
Stephen Davies
Andrew Dawson
Ben Dawson
Celia Deakin
Alison Deane
Royston Deitch
Stephen Delaney
Fred Dellar
John Dexter
Mark Diacono
Miranda Dickinson
Laurie Dix
Mark Dixon
Mark Doggart

Steve Doherty
Chris Douch
Robert D'Ovidio
Pat Downes
Carolyn Drake
Roger Drew
Paul Du Noyer
Aneta Dubow
Simon Dunn
Jemima Dury
Julian Dutton
Robert Eardley
Chris Eastwood
Greg Ehrbar
Charlotte Ellis
Soulla Tantouri Eriksen
Zack Evans
Simon Everett
Margaret Farthing
Peter Faulkner
Joe Fawcett
Saul Fearnley
Peter Fellows
Jem Finer
Damian Finn
Mike Finney
Helen FitzGerald
Patrick Fitzgerald
Olivier Fleurot
Dave Formula
Joe Fowler
Graham Francis
Isobel Frankish
Mal Franks
Peter Fraser
Bill Freedman
Lu Frazer
Mark Frearson
Lauren Fulbright
Andy Fyfe
Fiona, Andy, Junior
    and Nell Fyfe

Wayne Garvie
Annabel Gaskell
Rita Gayford
James Gent
Iestyn George
Duncan Gibbons
Kate Gielgud
Mark Gillies
Giulia Giordano
Chris Godsick
Lilian Goldberg
Astrid Goldsmith
Mark Goodier
Paul J Goodison
Charlie Gould
Keith Grady
David Graham
Viv Groskop
Laura Gustine
John Guthrie
Sophie H
Daniel Hahn
Simon Halfon
Chris Hallam
Nic Hamilton
Tony Hannan
Kate Hargreaves
Simon Harper
James Harris
Simon Harris
Anna Harrison
Caitlin Harvey
Jennifer Harvey
Jer Hayes
Daniel Haythorn
Tim Healiss
Andrew Hearse
Paula Hearsum
Alex Heffron
Linda Hepburn
Tim Hewett
Adrian Hickford

E O Higgins
Mary Anne Hobbs
Antonia Hodgson
Sharon Homan-
  James (TheMule247)
Mark Hooper
Barney Hoskyns
Hector Houston
Clare Howdle
Lexy Howe
Lesley Hoyles
Matt Huggins
Konnie Huq
Cait Hurley
Sally Jackson
Maxim Jakubowski
Paul Jaunzems
Gary Jones
Lesley-Ann Jones
Marc Jones
Ralph Jones
Julia Jordan
Tim Lund Jørgensen
Jane Kane
Maria Kane
Fiona Kelso
Gary Kemp
Scott Kennedy
Hugh Keogh
Lee Kern
Rachael Kerr
Olivia Key
Dan Kieran
Darren King
Ed King
Stephen Kinsella
Michael Knowles
Mit Lahiri
Jane Lamacraft
Jenny Landreth
Tom Latchem
Archie Lauchlan

Gavin Lavelle
Adam Lawrence
Iszi Lawrence
Dawne Le Good
Jimmy Leach
Jackie Lees
Dean Leggett
Stephen Lennon
Phil Lenthall
Justin Lewis
Lucy Lincoln
Vicki Lines
Deborah Lloyd
Geoff Lloyd
Michael Lloyd-Jones
Simon London
Jeremy Lovitt-Danks
Peter Lucas
Brian Lunn
Jon Lyus
Joseph MacColl
Simon MacDonald
Siobhan MacGowan
Russell Mackintosh
Ian R MacLeod
Stuart Maconie
Nick Madge
Daniel Maier
Howard Male
Rory Manchee
Linda Marric
Chris Marsh
Jeremy Marshall
Becky Martin
Ian Martin
Patrick Martin
Abbie Mason
Tim Masters
Julian Mayers
Ruth McAvinia
Polly Fiona McDonald
Chris McLaren

Shirley-Anne McMillan
Ryan McRostie
Vivienne McRostie
Vanella Mead
Phil Meadley
Alec Meadows
Sarah Merchant
John Merrigan
Roger Miles
Chris Miller
Peter Miller
Margo Milne
Paul Mitchell
John Mitchinson
Gordon Moar
J Moe
Duncan Moir
Ben Moor
Diane Moore
David Morley
Elisabeth Murdoch
Jon Naismith
Carlo Navato
Andrew Newman
Al Nicholson
Annie Nightingale
Deborah Norton
Lorraine Nutt
Matt Oakley
Occultation Recordings
Georgia Odd
Lisa O'Malley
Mark O'Neill
Andi Osho
Kate O'Sullivan
Phil Ox
Michael Paley
Pants Boys
Andrew Paresi
Demian Parker
Nigel Parkinson
Nicola Paterson

Liz Peet
Bobby Pegg
Nigel Pennington
Gary Percival
Steve Perrin
Neil Perryman
Dan Peters
Debbie Phillips
Gary Phillips
Jay Phillips
Grant Philpott
John Pidgeon
Marco Pirroni
Lynne Pointer
Justin Pollard
Matt Poole
Jacob Power
Georgia Pritchett
Donald Proud
Jenna, Alexander and
    Laurence Quantick
Del Querns
Chris Quigley
Carrie Quinlan
Leslie Ramage
Lucian Randall
Mark Randall
Amy Raphael
Michele Howarth
    Rashman
Julie Raven
Dan Rebellato
Karen Reed
Catriona Reeves
Stuart Reid
Val Reid
Sally Renhard
Emma Reynolds
Gillian Reynolds
Ian Rhodes
Christopher Richardson
Fran Rickard

Dave Ripp
Wyn Roberts
James Robertson
Swazi Rodgers
Geraint Rogers
James Rowe
Tom Ryan
Stef S
Charly Salvesen-Ford
John Sandom
Michael Sands
Abigail Sawyer
Miranda Sawyer
Tim Saxton
Adam Seeley
Gary Sharp
Dale Shaw
John Sheehan
Tamsin Shelton
Chris Shepherd
Stav Sherez
Linda Shoare
Adam Signy
Julian Simpson
Eric Sinclair
Abby Singer
Annetta Slade
Richard Smith
Simon Smith
Will Smith
Varsha Sood
Martin Spiers
Robin Squire
Richard Stephens
Tristan Stephens
Lisa and Jason Stevens
Nick Stewart
Bill Stone
Philip Stone
Phil Sutcliffe
Ingrid Sutherland
Howard Teece

Charlie Thomas
Richard Thomas
Mike Scott Thomson
Tracey Thorn
Andrea Thrift
Sue & Steve Tibbits
Matt Tiller
James Tobin
Rob Townsend
Rob Uttley
Mari Varila
Liz Vater
Tyrone W-h
Martyn Waites
Clare Wallace
Danny Wallace
Nick Walpole
Darren Walsh
Christian Ward
Ben Wardle
Matthew Wasley
Steve Watts
Paul Webster
Donald Whitaker
Andrew Whitby
Dale White
David Whittam
Ruth Whittam
Jimjam Wigwam
Jon Wilde
Derek Wilson
Jay Wilson
Sarah Wilson
Andrea Wiskin
Matthew Wood
Andrea Wright
Jonathan Wright
Paul Wyatt
Cromerty York
Peter Young
Asif Zubairy